FIRST DO NO HARM

What Reviewers Say About Emily Smith's Work

All of Me

"A good fun romance and good medical drama. Plenty of sexual tension and great main characters."—Kat Adams, Bookseller (QBD Books, Australia)

After the Fire

"I really liked both of the main characters. They are brave and tough and wore uniforms, what's not to adore?"—*Prism Book Alliance*

Same Time Next Week

"[A] story about love and making peace with your reality, and how to keep true to yourself even in ways you didn't imagine you'd have to face."—*Collector of Book Boyfriends*

Visit us at www.boldstrokesbooks.com

By the Author

Searching for Forever

Same Time Next Week

After the Fire

All of Me

First Do No Harm

First Do No Harm

by

Emily Smith

2020

FIRST DO NO HARM

ISBN 13: 978-1-63555-699-5

THIS TRADE PAPERBACK ORIGINAL IS PUBLISHED BY
BOLD STROKES BOOKS, INC.
P.O. BOX 249
VALLEY FALLS, NY 12185

FIRST EDITION: JULY 2020

CREDITS
EDITOR: SHELLEY THRASHER
PRODUCTION DESIGN: SUSAN RAMUNDO
COVER DESIGN BY TAMMY SEIDICK

Acknowledgments

This has been my favorite story to write so far. I always joke about how the second I start a new manuscript, all my past work suddenly becomes absolute garbage not worthy of lining the cat box. And while that's not entirely true, I, like I imagine most writers, tend to become increasingly attached to each of my newer works. I believe that's a sign of growth as an artist. We should be continually pushing ourselves to evolve, to be better. But *First Do No Harm* will probably always have a special place in my heart's archives. And that's mostly thanks to the woman who inspired it.

On my second date with this woman, I nervously handed her a copy of this book's parent-story, *All of Me* (she asked me to, I swear). Over the course of the next month, I read it out loud to her every night (she asked for that too, really). I even scribbled my first "I love you" in the inside cover. She became almost as attached as I was to Galen and Rowan's love story, because it so paralleled our own. Needless to say, it was her insistence that landed Galen and Rowan a reprisal in this book. And the subsequent love story of Pierce and Cassidy was born from this.

Nearly the entirety of *First Do No Harm* was written in front of the giant picture window at Café Nero on Boylston Street in Boston, just down the street from our apartment, where we'd spend hours together, her with a book and me with my laptop, drinking almond milk lattes. From the sheer perspective of memories alone, our "coffee shop dates" I associate with this story have become some of my favorite times in our relationship.

This book is also deeply personal. Sometimes it's easier than others to keep yourself out of your own stories. For example, one of my first books, *After the Fire*, was manifested out of pure imagination. Other times, at least in my experience, you get so close to your characters, to your story, that a sort of osmosis occurs. No doubt Galen and Pierce are both offspring of me, at various stages in my life. Or maybe, I'm an offspring of them? To those who know me, much of *First Do No Harm* was inspired by life—my life in the ER, my life in Boston, and most of all, my life with this amazing woman who offers me continual inspiration to *just keep writing*. A dedication doesn't feel like enough this time. So, these acknowledgments serve as a thank you to Ro (a nickname that became oddly fitting over time), for countless coffee shop dates, endless support and inspiration, and a love to rival any I could ever write.

Dedication

For Ro. For always.

PROLOGUE

I don't know, Pierce. Something just feels...off." Katie Browning, Pierce Parker's girlfriend of nearly a year, sat next to Pierce on her coffee-stained sofa, her eyes gleaming just enough to convince any onlooker that she wasn't a complete sociopath.

"Tell me we aren't doing this again." Pierce let her head collapse into her hands, actual tears contrasting to Katie's manufactured waterworks building behind her eyelids. Only a few months earlier, they'd sat in this same living room, on this same sofa, having this same conversation. The doubt in Katie's voice was so palpable it wrapped around Pierce's heart and squeezed. In an instant, Pierce's world had imploded under the hand of the one girl she'd really fallen for. And now, it was happening again.

"I'm sorry. I just...I'm not sure about us. I'm not sure this is working." Katie did her best to avoid looking at Pierce. And, considering Pierce never made a habit of letting anyone see her cry, that suited her just fine. During the first breakup, Pierce had been blindsided. Her life since she'd met Katie had been filled with cozy nights talking about their future together, how many cats they'd eventually adopt, and every other lesbian cliché they could find. For the first time, Pierce was happy, content with the day-to-day, no longer looking over her shoulder for the next best thing. Then, with a few vague statements, Katie had taken all of that from her.

"Are you breaking up with me?" Pierce knew the answer because she'd heard this speech before. She knew because of the twitch in Katie's left eyebrow and the pinch of her mouth. Pierce couldn't believe she was about to get hurt again. But a new feeling came with this second ending—shame. Pierce was humiliated. Without a second thought, she'd allowed Katie back into her life and let her toss her heart out all over again. She should have respected herself enough to let Katie go. She shouldn't have let someone in who wasn't sure about her. And Katie had never been really sure about Pierce.

"It kills me to say it, because I know you'll never take me back again. But, yes."

Pierce let out a blistering laugh. "You're damn right I'll never take you back again. Jesus, how many times do you think I can get tossed in the trash anyway?"

"I'm sorry." Katie placed a cautious hand on top of Pierce's, offering Pierce a sympathetic pout that made her even angrier. Pierce didn't want Katie's sympathy. She didn't want her pity. Pierce hated being pitied more than anything.

"You always did have one foot out the door, didn't you?" Pierce shook her head.

Katie glanced around awkwardly and stood up. "I should go."

This time, Pierce refused to protest. She refused to drop to her knees and beg for someone who didn't really love her to stay and hold the pieces of her shattered heart together. She refused to show weakness. After Katie walked out the door, Pierce could cry. She could punch the wall and dance to loud music and write bad poetry. But God help her, she would never let Katie see one more tear.

CHAPTER ONE

Six months later

It wasn't unusual for Galen Burgess's mother to call on a Sunday afternoon. In fact, it seemed that for the last couple of years, they'd taken to talking regularly, Galen even finding herself enjoying the telephone for once. As she noted her mother's name light up the screen on her cell phone, Galen smiled to herself. So much had changed since she met Rowan.

"Mom. How are you?"

Rowan Duncan, Galen's partner and fellow surgeon at Boston City Hospital, rounded the corner into the kitchen of their massive one-bedroom high-rise in Fenway. Rowan's face brightened the minute Galen laid eyes on her, and Galen wondered, as always, if that look would ever lose its ability to make her knees go soft.

"I'm doing well. Your father and I just finished watching this documentary on those three girls who were locked in a basement for years. What a horrible, tragic thing to have happen. I can't stop thinking about it!"

"And Dad? How's he handling the solitude of retirement?" Galen always hesitated to ask about her father. The cold, battle-ax chief of surgery at Boston City had finally retired two years ago, after Galen's mother had nearly died from an aneurysm. Since then, he'd managed to become even more insufferable. When he wasn't whining about not being able to operate anymore, he was playing golf at all hours of the morning with his group of cigar-toting, bourbon-soaked surgeon friends who were also searching for meaning in a life that no longer made any sense to them. Still, he seemed pleased enough with Galen's new role as attending surgeon, accepting that maybe if his time was up, he could prime his youngest child to carry on his legacy.

"You know your father. Lucky if I can get him to sit still for two hours to watch a movie with me. But he's home. And you're happy. And you have Rowan. How is she, by the way?"

Rowan, who had been listening to the entire exchange over Galen's speaker phone, smiled. "Hi, Mrs. Burgess," she shouted.

"Hello, dear. How is everything? Is my daughter treating you well? Are you eating enough?"

Galen shook her head. She loved the way her mother had taken Rowan in as her own since they'd gotten together two years earlier. It must have been hard for Rowan, being so far away from home. Especially with her parents being less than accepting of her new love. Rowan made her way behind Galen and wrapped her arms around her waist. She let her face nestle in the skin of Galen's neck, and Galen picked up the faint scent of Rowan's hair that always sent ripples of want through her entire body. After two years, Rowan's touch still felt completely brand-new.

"Yes, ma'am, I'm eating plenty. Galen's learned to be quite the chef. Did you know that?"

"My child? Impossible." Mrs. Burgess scoffed.

"Really!" Rowan answered. "Last night she grilled steak tips with some kind of fancy potatoes and green beans. And it was incredible. She really is good at everything. It's kind of annoying."

"She gets that from her mother."

Galen shrugged. "Is everything okay, Mom? You sound like you have something on your mind."

"I don't know how you do that. Rowan, did you know that ever since she was a toddler, Galen was incredibly sensitive? She could always tell when something was bothering someone."

"Galen? Sensitive? Never." Rowan winked at Galen and turned to face her, wrapping her arms around her neck and kissing all over her face until Galen couldn't help but try to suppress a laugh.

"But there is something I wanted to ask you about," Mrs. Burgess said.

"Is anything wrong? Was it your appointment with Dr. Heins? Is the aneurysm repair okay?" Galen, always calm and confident, was the first to go into a tailspin when a crisis involved her mother or Rowan.

"Everything's fine. But I just got off the phone with your Aunt Linda in Tulsa. You know your cousin, Pierce?"

"Pierce? God, I haven't heard anything from her in ages. Isn't she in school to be a physician assistant somewhere or something?" Galen's interest was piquing.

"She graduated years ago. She's working in the emergency department now, at a hospital in Atlanta. Anyway, I'm calling because Linda asked if you could help her out. Apparently, Pierce is desperately looking to move and needs a new job. She's interested in Boston, and since you have your connections in the ER still, I thought you could, you know, pull some strings for her? Get her a job?"

"I mean, Mom, I haven't seen Pierce since she was, like, eight." Galen was at least seven or eight years older than her cousin, and her last memory of Pierce consisted of an obnoxious little overall-clad girl with bowl-cut hair throwing crab apples at her at their grandparents' farm. It was hardly much to go on for a recommendation.

"I know. I'm just asking for you to meet with her. She's flying into town this Wednesday and really wants to talk." Mrs. Burgess wasn't asking, and Galen knew this full well.

"Okay, sure. Why not? Give her my cell number. I'll set up coffee or something and see what I can do for her."

"There's one more thing. Pierce is a lesbian."

"Can you not say it like that, Mom?" Galen shuddered.

"Like what?"

"You know, like it's some foreign country off the coast of France you saw a travel special on once."

"Oh, stop. You know I'm the most accepting person in this city of your sexuality. And Pierce's." Mrs. Burgess laughed.

"I know. It just sounds…weird. So, what does Pierce being gay have to do with this?"

"Linda wasn't supposed to say anything to me, but apparently she's leaving Atlanta because of a bad breakup with her girlfriend. She's been pretty crushed. Maybe you could, you know, take her under your wing. Professionally, and personally?" Once again, Mrs. Burgess was not asking.

"Yes, Mom. Now, will you please go find Dad and make him take you out to dinner or something? Ro and I are going to run some errands. I love you."

"You're my favorite, you know that?" Mrs. Burgess was clearly teasing.

"Of course I do. Bye, Mom."

Galen hit the red button on her phone and immediately noticed Rowan grinning at her.

"What?" Galen asked.

"You. You're very sweet for doing that."

"Ugh. Like I had a choice. Now I have to play big, gay mentor to my punk-ass little cousin, and I may have to work with her?" Galen sighed.

"You know what I think?" Rowan moved closer to her again and put her hands on Galen's hips. "I think it's sexy."

Some of Galen's irritation began to dissipate, and she couldn't resist a small smile. She brushed a stray piece of Rowan's hair away from her face. "Is that right?"

"Incredibly." Rowan moved her hand to Galen's cheek and kissed her, slowly, softly at first. Then, just as Galen's breath caught, Rowan kissed her harder. It was the kind of kiss that said Rowan never wanted to kiss anyone else for as long as she lived. It was the kind of kiss that still knocked the great, sturdy, headstrong Dr. Galen Burgess to the ground in one perfect second.

It was entirely Pierce's mother's idea to reach out to her cousin, Galen. From what little Pierce knew, which consisted of information gathered from casual social-media browsing, Galen was some hotshot surgeon at Boston City Hospital. It looked like she had some hotshot surgeon girlfriend too, who Pierce couldn't help but notice was a total fucking smoke show. The Burgesses had money, and lots of it. Pierce had seen pictures of Christmas parties at Galen's million-dollar apartment, and their cute fucking dog, and perfect fucking life. Pierce had always been the black sheep of the family. Even when they were little, their grandparents always preferred Galen and her sisters to Pierce and the Parkers. When Pierce decided to become a PA and Galen had followed in the other Burgesses' paths and become a doctor, that just seemed to solidify Pierce's status. She groaned as she put her coat on and tied her boots. *What kind of family is so elitist and overachieving that the outcast grandchild is a goddamn PA?* She hadn't even left the hotel yet, and Pierce was already regretting her decision to meet with Galen.

Although they hadn't laid eyes on each other since they were kids, Pierce recognized her cousin immediately. Facebook has an eerie way of keeping people connected at the most superficial level. Pierce knew Galen's job, her girlfriend, even what she'd had for dinner last week. But they were total strangers. Galen sat in the corner of the Starbucks, scrolling intently through her phone. She wore an expensive-looking, tailored wool jacket and had a fresh haircut and a face that belonged in ad campaigns for cologne or maybe even some really fancy clothing brand like Versace or YSL that Pierce knew next to nothing about. Pierce sighed to herself as she walked over. Who was she kidding? She didn't dislike Galen. She hardly knew her. But, from what she did know, Galen was everything Pierce wished she could be. Everything a girl like Katie would probably want. Pierce internally kicked herself for thinking of Katie. For Christ's sake, it had been six months already. Was she ever going to stop thinking about her?

"Let me guess. Reading up on robotic surgeries? Necrotizing fasciitis? Lap choles?" Pierce managed a cordial smile at Galen, who looked up from her phone.

"Readitt, actually…Have you seen the latest season of *Stranger Things*? There's some crazy theories out there."

Pierce relaxed, and she pulled out the chair to sit across from Galen. "Is there anyone who hasn't seen it? That shit is brilliant."

"Right?"

"Honestly, I'm surprised you have time to watch TV, being a surgeon and all." Pierce tried to control the disdain in her voice. She wasn't being fair to Galen. This was her family. This was blood. Pierce needed to put aside whatever preconceived notions she'd come to. Galen was offering to help her. She was doing her a favor.

"I didn't when I was a resident. My life was the hospital and, if I got lucky, maybe a little eating and sleeping mixed in there. But you know what that's like."

Pierce's cheeks warmed with surprise at Galen's camaraderie. She knew forgoing medical school to become a PA meant giving up the prestige of calling yourself doctor. Often, that meant Pierce just assumed everyone with an MD after their name looked down on her. But that usually wasn't the case. They'd been sitting here for only five minutes, and Pierce had already been entirely wrong about Galen.

"I do. And hey, thank you for meeting with me. I know this is kind of awkward, and it's been like, a million years. But I really appreciate it. Sorry my mom put you in this position."

"I get it." Galen laughed. "Moms, right?"

"Totally." Pierce found herself sinking into a comfort with Galen she wasn't expecting, one that felt far more familiar than she'd anticipated. Maybe this wouldn't be all bad?

"So how do you like being a PA?"

"I like it. I mean, it doesn't give me the same autonomy as a doctor, but I do most of the same things they do in the ED—chest tubes, intubations, running codes. It's not a bad gig."

"Yeah, and you didn't have to go through a million years of residency like I did." Galen took a sip of her espresso.

"It has its perks, that's true. But my skin still crawls every time a patient calls me nurse." Pierce burned a little inside at the thought of the mislabeling. Just when she thought she'd gotten over the lack of status that came with being a PA, she realized she was still entirely too hung up on it.

"I know what you guys do. I know your skills and how smart you are. You're as good as any of us. And if it helps, most of my colleagues know that too. The general public just has to catch up."

Pierce smiled. Galen was proving to be much humbler than Pierce had ever imagined. "Thank you. That means a lot."

"I hear you're looking for work?"

"Actually, yes. I've been in Atlanta a few years now, and I think it's time for a change. Boston seems like a good place to look."

Pierce had to wonder how much her mother had actually disclosed to Galen about her reasons for leaving Georgia.

"You know it's cold as hell here, right?"

Pierce laughed. "I remember. I grew up in Fitchburg."

"That's right. You used to come over for Thanksgiving when you were little."

Pierce hardly recalled visiting Galen's family. She must have been only five or six years old. But Galen was old enough to. She hoped for a minute that her childhood angst hadn't left any kind of lasting mark on Galen. Pierce wanted Galen to like her, and she found that longing very unsettling.

"I guess I did. Besides, I like to ski. I know it's asking a lot, but your mom figured with your connections in the ED at Boston City, you might be able to put a word in for me."

"I'll be honest. I haven't worked down there since I was a first-year resident. But I do know some of the attendings still, and I'm happy to do my best to talk to them about any openings. And hey, if not, I always need good PAs on my service!" Galen winked.

"I appreciate that, but surgery isn't my thing. Too sterile and slow. No offense."

Galen chuckled. "None taken. Listen. I'll ask around this week and see what I can do, okay?"

"Thanks. Anything to get the hell out of Atlanta is good by me."

Chapter Two

The lonely one-bedroom apartment in downtown Atlanta was even lonelier with Pierce's things parceled out into boxes and trash bags. She couldn't wait to get the fuck out of that place. Katie's ghost hung like the bad curtains she'd left up, and Pierce figured the only way to cleanse herself of her past was a fresh start. She'd certainly considered all the clichés about not being able to run from your problems. But she chose to ignore them anyway. A new life in Boston felt like exactly what she needed. Her flight was scheduled to leave at six a.m. the next morning. All of her things were packed, which was impressive considering how much Pierce actually owned. For one person, she had enough T-shirts for an entire Little League team. She didn't have anything left to do except order a pizza and reflect on everything she was leaving behind. Pierce had a job she enjoyed but didn't love. She had friends who were more like acquaintances. And she had an ex who haunted her even after so many months. Leaving was the right thing. Pierce's family was in Massachusetts. She had a new job at one of the best teaching hospitals in the country. Now, she might even have a cousin to befriend her. The future wasn't looking as bleak as she'd thought. Pierce smiled to herself, ready to put her old life behind her. A new start, a new Pierce Parker.

❖

Pierce hated absolutely nothing more than a first day. From kindergarten through PA school, she'd dreaded the beginning of the year, tormented with anxiety about who she was going to talk to, whether anyone would like her, if she'd screw everything up. That fear only got worse the older she got. Her first day at Atlanta General she nearly threw up she was so nervous. It would take only a couple of hours to settle down and begin a new routine, but those few hours were always excruciating. Starting at Boston City was no different. Pierce was awake at three a.m., in her new apartment that was cold and unfamiliar. Nothing decorated the walls, and the small space still felt incredibly empty with just her bed in it. The walls were a dingy white, and the windows leaked the frigid January air. A clunky radiator occasionally roared to life, but Pierce wasn't convinced it was giving off any heat. This place was squalor compared to her apartment in Atlanta. But she'd known to expect that before she moved to Boston.

After an hour of tossing from side to side, followed by a podcast she'd hoped would lull her back to sleep, Pierce eventually gave up, made a cup of coffee, and turned on the TV. She'd been binging the original *Twin Peaks* for the second time. At least the show would be weird enough to distract her from the terror of her upcoming day.

Finally, at five a.m., Pierce got in the shower, made a second cup of coffee, and put on a pair of clean scrubs. Not wanting to risk being late, she took the T to the hospital, arriving no less than ninety minutes early.

The Boston City emergency department was similar in size and structure to the one where Pierce had worked in Atlanta. When her shift started that day, she'd been briefly tutored in the electronic medical-record system, which, thankfully, she was vaguely familiar with, and then was left with Margot, one of the senior PAs.

Margot was warm and energetic, like she'd always just had a little bit too much coffee. She let her tight ringlets with highlights of a bright purple loose in spite of what seemed inconsistent with the rigidity of the job. She had a couple of tattoos on her arms and a small stud in her nose. Pierce liked her immediately. Margot showed her around the department, the tour taking all of thirty seconds due to Margot's lightning feet, then told her to start seeing patients. Pierce expected this. It was how medicine worked. "Orientation" consisted of "here's the cafeteria and the bathroom" and a whiff of good luck.

Her first patient was an older woman with leg swelling. Pierce walked into her room, legs shaking like she'd just graduated. She only hoped the panic would dissipate soon.

"Mrs. Green, I'm Pierce, one of the PAs. Nice to meet you." She greeted every single patient, every single time, this way. It felt comfortable, and practiced, and the words seemed to bring back some of her missing confidence.

"You're the what?" The obese, gray-haired woman lying in the bed scowled at her.

"The physician assistant. I'll be taking care of you."

Mrs. Green's doughy face continued to look unimpressed. "You're the assistant? When am I going to see a doctor? I've already been waiting here for three hours."

Pierce fought the urge to groan. She'd run into constant misunderstanding about her position back in Atlanta. But she'd forgotten just how rude Northerners could be. "I'm sorry to hear that. And you will see a doctor eventually. But right now, tell me what brings you in today."

Mrs. Green sighed and seemed to relax a little. Pierce had a way of instilling confidence in her patients. She could declare herself the PA a dozen times and still often get called "doctor." She walked with her head high and her shoulders up, and she spoke with clarity and decisiveness. By the end of her time in a room, nearly all her patients seemed to be persuaded that whatever her title, Pierce could handle their issue.

Emergency medicine doesn't provide any breaks. It's not the kind of office job or private practice where you can take thirty minutes to sit down and enjoy a sandwich. In fact, most of the time you're lucky if you can pee every six hours. Pierce even had a rotation in PA school where not only did the clinicians have no designated break, but they had to eat whatever they could directly over a designated sink. It became known to Pierce and her classmates as "the eating sink." Boston City wasn't quite that extreme. But she still didn't have time to sit and have a meal. At any given point, she was juggling seven or eight patients. That meant she was in charge of ordering their tests and medications, and following their lab results and imaging studies. When one of them was in pain and needed more morphine, Pierce would be called. She had no "break." This routine left her exhausted by the end of the day, and she usually had to inhale a peanut-butter sandwich at her computer in between notes. But she didn't mind. This fast-paced work was the only kind Pierce could see herself doing.

"Thought I might find you down here." Pierce was rocked out of her state of intense focus while charting on a patient with suspected sepsis. She recognized her cousin's voice right away. Without thinking, she jumped from her chair and hugged Galen, an immense sense of relief washing over her. She hadn't realized how tense and lonely she'd been since she arrived in Boston several days earlier.

"Whoa." Galen laughed but didn't turn away from the embrace. "Rough day?"

"It's been good, actually. What are you doing down here?"

"Came to check on you. And I figured you probably needed another coffee. Come on. I'll show you where they keep the good stuff."

"I have, like, six patients right now. I don't think I can—"

"Sure you can." Galen nudged Pierce's shoulder. "Trust me. Those patients aren't going anywhere. I bet five of them are waiting for CT scans, am I right?"

Pierce grinned. "Four. One's waiting for an ultrasound."

"Listen, Pierce. If there's one thing I've learned in my old age, it's that you have to take a minute to yourself every now and then. Otherwise, this place will kill you."

"Your old age, huh? You're, like, the same age as me."

"I'm thirty-six now. And you're, what, twenty-six?"

"Twenty-eight," Pierce said boastfully.

"Still, I've got almost a decade on you, kid. Stick with me. You might learn a couple of things."

Pierce rolled her eyes. "Okay, Dad."

"Come on." Galen laughed. "I'll buy you a coffee."

It was Rowan's idea for Galen to go check on Pierce down in the emergency department. Of course it was. Rowan was like this perpetual saint, always giving money to the homeless guys holding signs on the parkway. It was so bad, actually, that she couldn't walk past one of those Save the Children volunteers, or whatever they were, without making eye contact. And then, she was in. Rowan would be stuck talking to them for an hour, listening to their speech on why they needed her donation. Galen would rib her impatiently, but she also found Rowan's empathetic, kind soul one of her best features. She was always going to be a Southern girl at heart, even once she'd left the ranches of Texas for the cold steel of Boston. Galen loved that about her.

"Oh, there is no question you two are related." Rowan had been waiting at one of the small tables inside the hospital Starbucks as Galen and Pierce walked in. Galen hadn't noticed it before, but Pierce did bear a little resemblance to her. They both had the same strong, angular face and thick brow line. Pierce was a little taller but had the same stalky build as Galen. And it didn't hurt that they wore their hair in the same short, swept-back cut.

"Well, hello Dr. Duncan." On seeing Rowan, Galen briefly forgot anyone else was in the room and moved closer to her, putting her hands on her hips.

"Hello yourself, Dr. Burgess." Rowan kissed her softly and gazed at Galen with the same flare in her eyes she'd had since they first kissed years earlier.

The energy between them was rattled slightly by the sound of Pierce loudly clearing her throat.

"Sorry. Ro, this is my cousin, Pierce." Galen flushed just a little, but then decided she was still unapologetic about her often-disgusting display of love and devotion to Rowan.

Rowan shook Pierce's hand. "It's so nice to finally meet you. Galen's very excited you're here."

Galen hadn't exactly said that, but Rowan's words seemed to put Pierce at ease nonetheless.

"I'm excited to be here. I feel like I already know you. Instagram has a way of doing that." Pierce laughed awkwardly. "That sounded stalkerish. Sorry."

"Hey, you better back off, Parker. She's spoken for." Galen punched Pierce playfully on the shoulder.

"But I'm always looking for a newer model," Rowan said, winking at Galen.

"She doesn't mean that. I just get better with age." Galen grabbed Rowan around the waist and pulled her close.

Rowan sighed. "She's not wrong about that."

"You two are pretty gross, you know that?" Pierce said.

"I know." Rowan laughed. "Sorry about that. We've tried to tone it back a little, so you can imagine what we used to be like."

"Ro couldn't keep her hands off me. It was really embarrassing." Galen kissed Rowan's cheek.

"Sure. Let's go with that, then," Rowan said.

"No, I think it's really sweet, actually. I just went through a nasty breakup myself, and it's nice to see that happily-ever-after is still a thing." Pierce smiled and her gaze grew far away.

Galen knew she'd have to address Pierce's breakup sooner or later. After all, she had promised her mother she would mentor her professionally and personally. Besides, she was beginning to really like Pierce. Maybe it was DNA or something primal, or just two kindred spirits who were crossing paths, but Galen found herself wanting to help Pierce in whatever way she could.

Pierce hadn't dated since her breakup with Katie. The prospect paralyzed her with fear of being hurt again, fear of being rejected, fear of having no goddamn clue how to date. For the entirety of her gay life, Pierce had been a serial monogamist. She rarely left one relationship without making sure she had another to fall back on. The habit had felt harmless enough at the time, but after Katie, she realized she needed a change. Pierce's entire sense of self-worth seemed to have become tied up in whatever her current partner thought of her. Katie had only confirmed that fear by telling Pierce she was "exhausting" and "needed too much." As emotionally unavailable as Katie was, maybe she had a point. Pierce was dependent on being part of a couple, and she was never going to fix that flaw without learning how to be alone.

Several weeks had passed since she moved to Boston and started working in the Boston City ER. Her apartment was organized, she was beginning to feel settled in her job, and she even saw Galen and Rowan at work for coffee or lunch every now and then. Her only real friend so far was her fellow PA, Margot. They occasionally went out for pizza after a late shift, and Pierce would text her about whatever patient of the day stuck some foreign object in an orifice they shouldn't have. Pierce was grateful for Margot—and that her cousin was taking the time to show her the intricacies of the hospital system. All in all, things were going well. So well, in fact, that as Pierce lay on her bed, staring up at the ceiling fan, she thought it might be time to try her hand at love again, or something resembling it.

Before she could think of a trillion reasons not to, she scooped her laptop up from under the bed and opened it. It had been nearly two years since she'd had to do this, and for the life of her she couldn't even remember what dating sites people were using these days. They seemed to change so quickly. Pierce had met Katie on GayDate, but was that still a thing? Navigating the waters of online dating, between hookups and straight sites and Christian Mingle, felt daunting. But one by one, she went through each site she could think of—Tinder, Plenty of Fish, Her—crafting a profile she hoped would make her look not only desirable, but datable.

28, gay, female. I'm an emergency medicine PA so I have tons of cool stories. Let's go to yoga and eat tacos together.

Yoga? Tacos? She couldn't have sounded more basic if she tried.

28, gay, female. I'm an emergency medicine PA. My workdays are spent suturing toddlers and trying to rein in the chaos of the ER. I like a good Netflix binge, particularly Making a Murderer *or the likes, and in my spare time I play a little guitar. Looking for someone to take to Fenway Park this spring.*

Pierce sighed. She wouldn't exactly say she played the guitar, but she could strum a few chords and knew how to sing well enough to fake it in order to impress a girl.

"Nobody reads this shit anyway," she mumbled to herself.

After uploading a few carefully selected photos, Pierce closed her laptop and waited.

"Call her up and invite her for dinner." Rowan stood in the bedroom, hands on her hips, looking at Galen with eyes that said this wasn't a suggestion.

"Do I have to, Ro?"

"Yes. You do."

Galen pouted defiantly, then took a couple of steps toward Rowan, securing her hands around Rowan's wrists and gently moving them from her hips to Galen's. "But why? Don't you want a nice, romantic dinner in with just the two of us? I was going to make chicken piccata. It's your favorite."

"Actually, your steak tips are still my favorite." Rowan smiled, remembering the days when Galen couldn't so much as boil macaroni. She'd fallen in love with Galen's charm and rebellious spirit and painfully good looks. But over the last couple of years, she'd fallen in love with her all over again. This time, with the woman who wore a buffalo-plaid apron and danced around the kitchen whisking and sautéing, just to make Rowan something that would impress her. This time, with the woman who made sure the apartment was clean when Rowan was at work for long days on end. This time, with the woman who would do anything to see her happy for the rest of their lives.

"You know, you eat far too much red meat."

"We all have our vices. Now, stop avoiding it, and call Pierce. She's lonely! She's only been here a few weeks, and she hardly knows anyone. I bet she's sitting at home right now ordering takeout for the eighth time this week, watching garbage TV." Rowan's protest remained fierce. Galen was so strong headed and stubborn, it was often hard to be more outspoken than her. But Rowan had learned when necessary.

"You mean like you were doing before you met me?" Galen smirked, and Rowan pushed her away gently.

She had to change her tactics.

"Baby. Please. For me?" Rowan pulled Galen in again, puffed her lips, and ran her fingers through the back of Galen's short, soft hair. Galen closed her eyes and sighed dreamily. Sometimes, when defiance didn't work, Rowan had to use the still-magic spell she had over Galen.

"Okay. Fine. But only because she's lonely. Not because you're being all cute and whatever. I don't want this to become a habit to get your way. It won't work."

Rowan traced her index finger over Galen's lower lip, sucking her own into her mouth and biting until it was red and surely inviting. After years with her, Rowan knew exactly how to turn Galen into a Jell-Oy mess. And it was entirely mutual. "Thank you. I'll go to the store and pick up some extra chicken. You call your cousin."

"Oh, Dr. Duncan. You sure do know how to work me."

Rowan smiled. "Right back at you, Dr. Burgess. Right back at you."

❖

Pierce was surprised to receive a text from Galen that night asking her to come over. It sure as hell beat leftover Chinese and watching the latest crime documentary that was streaming. The minute she'd gotten home from her shift, she'd stripped off her scrubs, showered, and put on sweatpants. It was rare she had to wear anything else. For the first time in a while, she pulled on a pair of jeans, spritzed down her short, wild hair with a spray bottle, and headed out the door.

Idling in front of her apartment building stood a shiny, deep-navy BMW, its halogen headlights blinding her as she crossed its path. The car was a far cry from the mid-2010s Toyotas and Hyundais parked on the street, and Pierce knew immediately it had to be Galen.

"Nice ride," she said, gliding across the pristine leather of the passenger seat.

It was dark, but she was pretty sure she could see Galen beaming a little.

"Thanks."

"Five series, x-drive? Very nice. What year?" Pierce watched Galen's expression brighten further.

"2019. Just bought it at the beginning of the model year. I'm kind of obsessed with her…"

"I can see why. Thanks for picking me up. I haven't had a chance to register my car in Boston yet, and my Georgia plates are no good here. Oh, and uh, thanks for having me over for dinner." Pierce's cheeks warmed, and she looked out the window, grateful for the guise of darkness.

"No problem. We're happy to have you. Figured you could use a little change from whatever takeout you'd been eating lately."

"You aren't kidding. I must have gained seven pounds since I got here. So, what's Rowan making?"

Galen laughed. "And why do you assume Ro is the cook here?"

Pierce flushed again. "I just…You're so…"

"Butch?" Galen reached over and whacked Pierce in the shoulder.

"I was going to say busy, but yes, that too." They both broke out in a fury of laughter that lasted the entire way back to Galen and Rowan's apartment.

"Hey, baby, we're home." Galen shut the door to the apartment behind her and turned the latch.

Pierce couldn't help but gawk at the stunning surroundings. Boston was notoriously ranked one of the most expensive cities in the country. Even someone on Pierce's salary, which was nothing to scoff at, couldn't afford more than a one-bedroom with zero amenities in a moderate part of town for under $1800 a month. Galen and Rowan's apartment was enormous. The ceilings seemed to reach all the way into the sky, and the floors were a gorgeous hardwood. Stainless steel and granite spanned the entire kitchen that was immediately to the left of the entryway. Everything was meticulously decorated, with furniture that had most definitely not come from Craigslist (like most of Pierce's) and Simon Pearce light fixtures. And, to complete the dream, the place sat on the 19th floor of one of the handful of high-rises in the Fenway neighborhood, their picture window in the living room overlooking Fenway Park.

"Well. Holy fuck." Pierce moved absently to the window and took in the scene below her. Although it was winter, and baseball season was long since over, the field lights from the park blazed like the world's biggest Christmas tree. She could see all the way down the third-base line. The horizon expanded out toward what must be Charlestown or somewhere equally as far, and little dots of white lit up the night sky to a hazy gray.

"Pretty great, huh?" Galen said.

"Great? I've never seen anything like it. I'm a huge Sox fan, you know." Pierce had left Massachusetts when she was just a kid, moving around several times to follow her father who was in the army reserves. But Boston always felt like home.

"Is that right? So are we. The three of us will have to get to some games this spring." Rowan had joined them by the window.

"I've always wanted to live in a place like this. You know, right in the heart of things," Pierce said.

"You know, when I met Galen I lived in this slummy little place in Brighton. It was absolutely awful." Rowan put her hand on Galen's shoulder.

"I can't imagine trying to live in Boston on a resident's salary," Pierce added. "I can barely make ends meet with what I make, and I get paid well."

"You'll get there, Pierce." Rowan was reassuring her.

"So, what you're saying is 'marry up'?" Pierce immediately regretted her words. She often had trouble thinking before speaking, and sometimes things came out entirely wrong. Fortunately, both Galen and Rowan erupted in laughter, and Pierce eventually joined in.

"If anyone's marrying up here, it's me," Galen said, leaning toward Rowan and kissing her quickly.

"Is she always this smooth?" Pierce asked.

Rowan rolled her eyes. "Always."

Learning to cook had really come out of necessity for Galen. For her first four years of residency, she'd survived off saltine crackers, peanut butter and jelly, and espresso. Of course she hadn't learned to fend for herself growing up. Her family had a chef and a housekeeper, Gwen, and even when she moved out on her own, Gwen would come to Galen's apartment to do her laundry for her. The system had always worked well enough for her. Until she met Rowan. Rowan also tried to sustain herself on a diet consisting mostly of white carbohydrates and things that could be microwaved. Then, on the first Thanksgiving they'd spent together, Galen had attempted to cook an entire dinner for her to surprise Rowan at the hospital. The meal was a disaster. The turkey was charbroiled, and the vegetables were ice. Rowan was eternally grateful and charmed. But as they began to spend more and more time together, and Galen's schedule graduated from that of a resident to an attending, she tried again. This time, she started gradually, with easy chicken recipes she'd found online, sprinkled with a few helpful tips from Gwen. Everything Galen made seemed to impress Rowan immensely, probably because Rowan, who once had to find capers at the grocery store and didn't even know what they were, couldn't make pancakes from a mix.

Galen had really grown to love cooking for Rowan. On the evenings they were both home, she'd find some new recipe to make and skirt around the kitchen in her plaid apron Rowan had bought her for Christmas, listening to Taylor Swift as she sliced potatoes with the precision of the surgeon she was.

Every so often, Rowan, who'd be hanging around the kitchen fiddling with this or that, or reading her latest book, would come up behind her and wrap her arms around her waist, and they'd sway for a minute to the music and smile. This was really the reason Galen liked cooking for Rowan.

"I hope you like chicken piccata, Pierce," Rowan said.

"I like just about anything that doesn't come in a take-out container or Tupperware."

They sat at the aptly sized dining-room table, and Galen brought out a glass dish with perfectly portioned chicken cutlets sauced in lemon and white wine and capers. As delicately as she did anything, Galen took each cutlet one by one out of the dish and gently placed it on the plates. After this, she took a sprig of parsley, pulling off each individual leaf and sprinkling it on the chicken.

"What's she doing?" Pierce leaned over and whispered to Rowan.

"She's gotten very into her plating lately," Rowan said, smiling sweetly at Galen in a way that reminded Galen just how lucky she was to have found someone who found her quirks endearing.

"Presentation is key," Galen said. "There. Done."

"It looks amazing," Pierce said. She picked up her fork and knife, but before she could cut into the food, Galen jumped.

"Wait!"

"What?" Pierce asked, surprised.

"We have to get a picture first," Rowan said.

Galen didn't need any further direction. She knew to go to the same spot in the corner of the kitchen she'd been going for the last year, where she'd hold the plates up proudly and wait for Rowan to snap a picture for her archives.

"Sorry," Galen said, heading back to the table to sit down. "You can eat now. Ro and I have been chronicling my cooking forever now, and it's kind of become a thing. Initially, she was taking shots to make a book or an Instagram account or whatever, but now it's just become this tradition. I'm kind of superstitious about it now."

Pierce laughed. "You surgeons are all a bunch of weirdos."

"Careful. I'm pretty sure it's genetic." Galen winked at her.

She liked how comfortable Pierce seemed with them already. Galen had been the youngest of all her sisters, and it was nice to feel like she could take someone under her wing for once. Being the older and wiser one wasn't something she was used to. But it felt good.

CHAPTER THREE

Once, Pierce had thought dating would be fun. It didn't take long for her to realize that assumption was, in fact, completely false. She'd been out with three or four different girls since venturing into the online world, and they'd all come with their own brand of disappointment. It wasn't that they weren't kind, or funny, or successful, or didn't each have her own something to offer someone, but something was always missing. Sometimes it was obvious, other times, not. And Pierce was beginning to realize just how rare it was to find someone you hit it off with and also happened to want to sleep with, and how lucky she'd been to have found that combination several times in the past. And, maybe, how stupid she'd been to dismiss it.

Now that her training period at the hospital was over, and her schedule had freed up, Pierce decided to throw herself into meeting new people—particularly new girls. As the perpetual serial monogamist, she was under the extreme misconception that it was easy to find love or, at the very least, lust. Over the last few weeks, she'd realized just how wrong she'd been.

Tonight's date was Amy. They'd met online, on a dating app, of course, and had chatted for several days over text. Amy seemed smart and well-read and worked as a writing professor at one of the local universities. From her profile, Pierce thought she was probably cute, with fiery red, curly hair and a sweet smile. As much as Pierce hated first dates, Amy had potential.

And Pierce fucking hated first dates. Add this to the list of things Pierce was learning about herself over the months. As outgoing and extroverted as she appeared to the world, she despised meeting new people, especially in a high-pressure setting like a date. She feared the inevitable awkward silences and, of course, the always unanswered "will they like me?" Her first date with Katie had been so easy. They'd instantly connected. The conversation flowed, and she'd never enjoyed talking to a stranger so much. Around that same time, she'd had only one other date with someone else, which was mediocre at worst. Her relationship addiction had left her with the impression that it was easy to find people you wanted to sit with for five hours straight, and they, of course, always wanted to go home with you. As she was learning, this was not the case. Katie was the hard exception and in no way a rule. Pierce was finding that the disgustingly vast majority of first dates are lackluster, even painful. And as much as she hated to admit it, Pierce supposed she'd been lucky in the past.

For the first three first dates Pierce had gone on since moving to Boston, she'd spent hours picking out what to wear and getting ready. Now, it was impressive if she showered before she went. She figured the odds were about a million to one that her date was going to amount to anything anyway, so why put in all the effort? Pierce realized she sounded jaded already, but she couldn't help it. Besides, there was always that quiet part of her that said, "This could be it." She would forever be the hopeless romantic.

Fifteen minutes before she was supposed to arrive at the bar, Pierce changed her T-shirt, put on a denim jacket, spritzed a substantial amount of cologne on, and headed out the door. She had yet to decide whether it was best to be the one to get there first, forced to wait awkwardly, alone, until the other person got there, or to show up late and figure out how to approach them with some degree of confidence and coolness she seemed to lose on those initial encounters. Basically, both options were dreadful. This time, she was the first one there. She waited outside for Amy, not entirely certain who she was looking for. Pictures online have a tendency to mislead. Everyone wants to post their best version of themselves on their dating apps, so what you often find in real life is someone with minimal resemblance to the cyber version.

A taller, much curvier version of the girl in Amy's photos came around the corner. Pierce assumed her photos were probably from several years ago and found herself wondering, as she often did, how many times girls had been disappointed by the real-life version of her. Amy was fine looking, with nothing inherently unattractive about her. But immediately, Pierce felt what she feared most—nothing. No initial buzz of electricity, no "wow," just "oh. Okay then." This had been an ongoing theme for her since she and Katie broke up and, she assumed, was almost always something that was reciprocated on her dates.

Amy was friendly and a good conversationalist. She chatted about feminism and sex-positivity and her writing, and asked all the right questions. Pierce enjoyed her company. They were both old souls in many ways. But no matter how much Pierce wanted there to be, they just had no spark.

By the end of the first drink, Pierce was ready for the date to be over. She moved to close the tab, using her usual line about having to work in the morning, even when she usually didn't have to. They walked down to the corner wordlessly.

"So, I'm going this way," Pierce said awkwardly.

"I'm going that way."

They chuckled and looked at their feet. Then, Pierce quickly hugged the much-taller girl, said "thanks," and rushed off.

Pierce usually didn't end dates quite so abruptly. But she was feeling off and, for whatever reason, just wanted to be home in her sweatpants watching *The Twilight Zone*, eating a giant cheeseburger. She'd been thinking about Katie a lot that day. And that left her in no mood to pretend to be interested in someone she wasn't. Besides, Amy hardly seemed upset about the finality of it all. Pierce was pretty certain it had been entirely mutual, as usual.

It was an exceptionally busy afternoon in the ER. Stretchers containing groaning patients lined the hallways, some holding emesis basins and others wrapped up dramatically in blankets. A psychotic man screamed continuously from around the corner that he was being held against his will and wanted to leave. Pierce smiled to herself as she sat at her computer, documenting her last three patients, all of whom had some version of the gastrointestinal illness spreading through the city. This place was disgusting and chaotic and strange. But Pierce couldn't think of anything else she'd rather be doing.

"You aren't, by any chance, the one looking for a surgical consult, are you?" Pierce turned at the familiar voice. Rowan stood just behind her, her contagious, sunny smile temporarily lightening the thick air around them.

"Jackson? With the strangulated hernia? That's me."

"You know, I try to avoid the Pit as much as possible, but for mini-Galen, anything." Rowan winked at her.

"Oh, come on now. I'm nothing like Galen." But Pierce secretly warmed at what was a tremendous compliment.

"That's a joke, right?"

"Tell me. How am I like her?"

"For starters, you look alike."

Pierce chuckled and rolled her eyes. "Please. That's just because people think all of us butches look alike."

"Honey. Trust me. You do not all look alike." Rowan laughed. "Besides, you clearly have her same annoying stubbornness, her intensity, and her charm. Considering you two hardly knew each other most of your lives, it's absolutely fascinating."

"Well, I suppose there are worse things than being compared to the great Dr. Galen Burgess." Pierce's cheeks flushed.

"Much, much worse."

"I wish I had her luck with girls though…" Pierce mumbled the words before she had time to wish she hadn't.

"What do you mean?" Rowan put a friendly hand on her shoulder.

"Nothing. Just, this online-dating thing is kicking my ass."

Rowan sighed. "Ah, dating. I'd actually dare say it's the worst thing in the entire world. Not getting far, huh?"

"Not exactly, no. A lot of duds. Jesus, when did I get so picky?"

"Picky is good. Picky is discerning. Listen. I don't have a lot of dating experience myself. But you know who does?"

Pierce laughed and nodded her head. "My cousin?"

"You have no idea the number of women she went through before I came around. I bet she'd have some words of wisdom for you. Why don't you come over tonight after your shift? I'll pick up some takeout on the way home, and you two can chat."

"I…I don't know, Rowan. I don't want to be a burden. I feel like I'm over there a lot. And I know you and Galen don't have a lot of time to yourselves with your schedules." But Pierce wanted the company of her family more than anything.

"Stop that. You are never a burden. You're coming over. End of discussion. Now, tell me about this patient you have for me."

Pierce realized Rowan wouldn't take "no" for an answer, and she liked that. Rowan seemed to care about her. Because she cared about Galen. Pierce only wished she could find anything close to that kind of love.

"Jackson. He's in room 5. He'd had this ventral hernia for years, but today it started causing him pain for the first time, and I couldn't reduce it. His lactate is up, so I'm a little worried. Do you mind taking a look at him for me?"

"Of course not."

Pierce knew Rowan was a third-year resident now and probably unlikely to be doing much in the way of simple ER consults. She had a feeling Galen had sent her down to check on Pierce. And suddenly, all the bad dates in the world seemed bearable when she had people like Galen and Rowan in her life.

Pierce left for Galen and Rowan's immediately after her shift ended. She'd been in Boston only a few months, but she already had a key to their apartment and felt comfortable enough to let herself in. Galen had assured her that she could come over any time, day or night. It didn't matter if they were home or not. Somehow, that gave Pierce a sense of security she hadn't realized she needed.

"Hey," Pierce said, pushing open the heavy door.

"Hey. Ro told me you'd be coming by." Galen appeared from down the hall in a pair of basketball shorts and a worn Yale sweatshirt.

"I hope it's okay."

"You know it's always okay. Besides, I got the impression she sort of didn't give you much of a choice in the matter."

Pierce laughed. "Does she do that a lot?"

"All the time." Galen smiled and took her coat. "Come in. She'll be home with dinner any minute now."

They moved into the living room and sat on parallel chairs.

"Drink?" Galen asked.

"What do you have?"

"What are you into?"

"Mostly whiskey. Bourbon in particular. But I like an occasional scotch. And beer is fine too."

Galen grinned. "You're a bourbon drinker, huh?"

"Definitely."

"Wait right there."

Galen returned two minutes later with two clear tumblers, filled about an inch with an amber liquid, no ice.

"What's that?" Pierce asked.

"This, my friend, is fucking bourbon. Pappy Old Van Winkle. 1989." Galen brought the glass to her nose and inhaled, closing her eyes.

"Jesus. Doesn't this stuff cost, like, two hundred dollars an ounce or something?"

"Three hundred and fifteen." Galen took a long, slow sip. "It was a gift from my Dad when I became an attending."

"Don't you want to save it? For a special occasion or something?"

"Whatever." Galen waved her hand dismissively. "You can't take it with you, right?"

Pierce nodded thoughtfully.

"I mean that, though. All this shit?" Galen gestured to the representations of overwhelming wealth and success that adorned the apartment. "This is just shit."

"Yeah, well, it's nice fucking shit."

"Sure, it is. The cars, the house, the expensive suits, the rare whiskey—I'm grateful for it all. But that's not what matters."

Pierce felt a lecture coming on. "Is this where you tell me how what matters is love and friendship and family and memories and all that?"

"Yes!" Galen rubbed her temple thoughtfully. "Seriously though, Pierce. Before Ro, I had money. I had all this stuff. But it was just stuff. My life was my work. I didn't realize how unfulfilling that was until I finally fell in love."

"You know, we can't all be so lucky to find what you and Rowan have."

"I get that. And I understand what you're feeling, because I felt the same way. I honestly believed I was going to be stuck with meaningless flings and one-night stands for the rest of my life."

"Yeah, well, I can't even find one of those," Pierce shot back. She hadn't meant for the words to come out so snarled.

"Rowan told me the online-dating thing isn't going well."

"It's awful. I'm telling you. Do you know what I'd give to have someone like Rowan to come home to every night? Someone to laugh at my jokes and take care of me when I'm sick. Someone I want to learn to cook for and spend my holidays with." Pierce was bringing herself further and further down the more she spoke.

"That's the dream, isn't it? And you will find it. You will. You just have to be patient."

"I am being patient!"

Galen laughed. "You have the patience of a Burgess, my friend."

Pierce continued pouting for a moment, and then her mouth gradually rose into a small smile, until she was laughing too. "You're right. Patience isn't my thing."

"Mine either. But I'm telling you, it will happen for you. You'll meet her."

"I hope you're right." But Pierce found herself trusting Galen in a way she wasn't expecting.

"Tell me about what happened with this other girl then. The one who forced you out of Atlanta."

"Katie." Pierce felt the familiar grip around her heart whenever she said her name still. "She crushed me. Twice, actually. And I let it happen."

"Don't blame yourself. We've all been there."

Pierce raised a skeptical eyebrow. "I bet you never have."

"I've been hurt like that before." Galen's blue eyes grew slightly darker, until they were the color of cold ocean water.

"Really? By whom?" Pierce found it impossible to believe anyone had ever dared break the heart of her impenetrable cousin.

"Rowan, actually…"

"I…" Pierce was suddenly struck silent, not wanting to push what could have been a tremendously touchy subject.

"It's okay. It was a long time ago. But when we first started dating, Rowan actually broke up with me to get back with her boyfriend."

"No way."

"Really. In fact, they were even engaged for all of five minutes."

"I'd never believe that now. You two are like, all the relationship goals. Seriously."

Galen laughed. "She quickly realized the error of her ways, and we got back together. And the rest is all happily-ever-after. But my point is, Pierce, don't let your past define you. What this girl did to you was horrible, and it hurt like hell, I'm sure, but it doesn't predict your future."

Pierce hadn't fully realized how much of her ability to trust Katie had taken with her when she left. And she immediately cursed her again for continuing to do damage in the life she'd so easily discarded.

Chapter Four

A s she fixed her hair in the mirror for the third time, Pierce thought she should probably stop trying so hard. In spite of Galen's advice to "just be patient," so many of her first dates lately had ended at just that—a first date. And, to be honest, Pierce hadn't had sex in so long she thought she'd probably combust if she didn't touch another human being soon. Maybe it was purely the prospect of sex, or intimacy, or at the very least, a decent first kiss, that led Pierce to continue to make the effort. Especially tonight. She'd been talking to Victoria for over a week now. In fact, they'd been talking nearly all day, from the time Pierce's alarm went off until she finally passed out at night. Given, it were only text messages, but it resembled a connection. They seemed to have a lot in common. And Victoria had a sense of self and individuality that Pierce found attractive. She dared even think this was the first time since Katie she'd been truly excited about a first date.

Pierce arrived at the bar early, fluctuating between usual first-date jitters (which usually meant the strong desire to turn around and leave) and the buzz of possibility. Victoria arrived exactly on time. She looked like her photos—a strong but pretty face set behind strong cheek bones and eyes as intense as Pierce's. Victoria wasn't the archetype of the "hot" girl Pierce usually found herself drawn to, but she was attractive in her own unique way, and Pierce was intrigued.

"Hi!" Victoria smiled, and Pierce noted a hint of trouble behind her expression that she liked.

"Hi there." They hugged, and immediately Pierce felt a sense of ease she didn't usually experience so early on.

"I'm really glad we're finally getting to do this." Victoria sat down beside her and took off her coat.

"Me too. We've been talking so much I feel like I already know you, which is great, considering how much I hate the awkwardness of first dates."

"They are the worst! Seriously. I just want to skip ahead to the part where we watch Netflix and hang out with our cats."

Pierce laughed, her shoulders relaxing out of her ears, reminding her how nervous she'd actually been. "Same."

The conversation flowed instantly and easily, which was a tremendous relief to Pierce, considering the uncomfortable silences were always her least favorite part of getting to know someone. Something about silence made Pierce squirm and desperately search for something to fill it with. But Victoria was a talker. And so was Pierce. It worked. For two hours they discussed their families and their hometowns, Pierce sipping a Makers on the rocks while Victoria giggled from the buzz of a couple of glasses of wine. They had chemistry, no doubt. Not the life-changing, blow-you-clear-out-of-your-sneakers chemistry, but it was there nonetheless. And Pierce hadn't experienced much chemistry lately.

"Want to get out of here?" Victoria had inched closer to Pierce as the night went on, her knee now pressed against Pierce's thigh.

"Absolutely."

Although the winter was more or less behind them, the biting New England cold still hung in the air, even in early April. Victoria wore a long down coat with a fur hood that Pierce found adorable, and as they walked through the nearby park, Pierce pretended not to be freezing in only her thin, canvas jacket. Pierce found little reasons to touch Victoria, putting a hand on her back when she laughed or brushing her arm. It had been so long since she'd had anything even resembling affection, and it felt good. Really good. On her first date with Katie, Pierce had known nearly instantly that she wanted her. Maybe it was her impulsive nature, or just her intuition, but when Pierce knew, she knew. And it was very clear that night that she did not know about Victoria.

Still, she was enjoying herself. The nearby city lights flushed the night sky with yellow hues, and a mild wind occasionally breezed past. A hint of spring in the air promised something good to come. Seasons weren't the same in Georgia, and Pierce had forgotten how much she'd missed them. They strolled through a deserted playground, Victoria laughing as she sat on a nearby swing. Pierce sat next to her and pumped her legs back and forth like a child. As they fought to get as high and as fast as they could, they laughed louder, until a feeling Pierce hadn't had in a long time engulfed her—joy.

Victoria waited until she built up as much momentum as possible and gracefully shot off the swing, landing effortlessly on her feet in a way that made Pierce think she must have been a dancer at some point. Pierce, never known for her grace or coordination, attempted the same. Her timing a millisecond off, she flew through the air, catching her toes on the grass and tumbling in some drunken version of a somersault.

"Oh my God! Are you alright?" Victoria rushed to Pierce's side, where she sat, momentarily stunned, holding her right ankle.

"I...I think I sprained my ankle." They were silent for a moment, and then Pierce began to laugh, Victoria joining her until they were rolling on the ground in hysterics, holding their bellies and crying.

"That was the most ridiculous thing I've ever seen. Really." Victoria could hardly contain herself. "Are you sure you're okay? Can you walk on it?"

"Hey, I'm the PA here, remember?" Pierce was teasing but realized she wasn't sure she could actually walk.

"Should we go to the hospital?"

"No! Really, it's nothing." Pierce stood slowly. The subtle pain that had been idling around the outer aspect of her ankle built into a crescendo, and she fought off the grimace she knew her face was making. The last thing she wanted was for Victoria to have to spend their first date in the ER because Pierce couldn't stick the landing off a stupid kids' swing.

"It doesn't look like nothing."

"Look. I can walk." Pierce gently put her foot down.

"You think you're pretty tough, don't you?" Victoria stepped closer to Pierce until Pierce could feel the heat coming from Victoria's full mouth. It had been a while, but Pierce still remembered exactly what this was.

"I know I'm pretty tough." She grinned, allowing her lips to part slightly. Pierce felt out the tempo of the moment, allowing just enough silence to pass before leaning closer, slowly but with conviction, and brushing her lips against Victoria's. Their mouths fumbled against the other, each one's rhythm slightly off, as Pierce ran a hand through Victoria's hair. In a few seconds, it was over. The hint of chemistry was still there. And it was a nice kiss. Pierce didn't feel like she would spontaneously combust, but still, she was ready for it to happen again.

As they pulled apart, Pierce smiled, and Victoria giggled. There is a moment, and Pierce couldn't help but remember this, after every great first kiss. That moment your lips finally separate, but it's like a magnet is still trying to pull them back together. You stay just inches apart, your eyes closed, barely breathing. Every muscle in your body seems to let go at once, and you actually feel your knees shake a little. Your heart beating in your ears is the only thing reminding you this is real. Neither of you can speak. Then, you finally open your eyes, and you see it on their face too. And you know. You just know.

This was not that kiss. But Pierce realized that kind of kiss was exceedingly rare. And "nice" was hard enough to find these days. She kissed Victoria again, as if to see if that elusive moment was just late to show. But it wasn't.

"Come on. Let's call a cab and get you home." Victoria wrapped an arm around Pierce's waist as Pierce limped toward the street, feeling like her luck might have finally changed.

Dr. Cassidy Sullivan hated firsts. She hated first days of school, first days of work, first dates, first everything. A true introvert with a tendency for routine, Cassidy ate breakfast at the same café every morning (alone), sat on the same bike in spin class, called her mom at the same time every week, and woke up at the same time nearly every day. Being an emergency-medicine resident, she'd found this level of routine particularly difficult lately. But she'd managed, at least until her residency program at a small teaching hospital in Rhode Island went up in smoke and her entire life had scattered like Boston street trash.

Now, she was forced to start over, before even the end of her first year, at a new hospital, in a new city, where she knew absolutely no one. It wasn't even July yet. It wasn't like she could start with the other second years and at least pretend some degree of normalcy. When her program director was caught laundering money from major donors, her residency program had been shut down. And that was that.

It was her first shift at Boston City Hospital, and Cassidy was fully prepared to hate it. She had spent her morning with one of the senior residents, whose name she believed was Bryce or Brent or Brad, who asked her what she "wanted to work on today."

What I want to work on, Cassidy told herself, is surviving this fucking place.

The next patient she had to see was a twenty-eight-year-old with an ankle injury. Without bothering to check in with anyone, Cassidy picked up the chart and ventured down the hall to find the patient. This task was always much more daunting than it should be, considering the hallways were usually lined with at least ten patients, and none of them were physically where their charts had them listed. After scanning the many beds, she decided that it probably wasn't the older woman with gray hair gripping her flank or the man with no teeth singing to himself. Somewhere in the middle of the line was a woman with short, dark hair and eyes that were both stubborn and inviting. She wore scrubs and fidgeted on the stretcher. Truth be told, if Cassidy hadn't been forced to search for Pierce Parker in the sea of patients, she still would have inevitably noticed her. Pierce was attractive. Very attractive. And Cassidy would have picked her out in nearly any crowd.

"Pierce? I'm Dr. Sullivan. You can call me Cassidy." After several months, Cassidy still wasn't used to referring to herself as doctor.

The girl on the stretcher in front of her showed the smallest hint of a smirk, and Cassidy instantly felt as if she was missing something. "You're a new resident."

"How did you..." Cassidy suddenly felt warmth cascading over her entire body as realization struck. The scrubs. Of course. "You work here, don't you?"

Pierce let out a charming laugh and nodded. "I'm a PA down here. I guess no one briefed you before you picked up my chart?"

"You know how ER nurses are...brutal. Anyway, can we try this again?" Cassidy looked down at her clogged feet, took a deep breath, and looked back up at Pierce, whose sharp, green eyes had turned a hazy blue. Her heart caught in her chest for just a moment, and words were nowhere to be found.

"Pierce Parker. I'm a PA here."

"Cassidy. I'm an emergency-medicine resident. A very, very new resident, obviously."

Pierce reached out a hand and shook Cassidy's with a firm, confident grasp. She smiled again, and Cassidy's belly tightened in a way that was both unnerving and unfamiliar.

"Did you just start here?"

"First day." Cassidy wondered if it was that obvious.

"Ugh. Hate first days." Pierce shook her head, and something about her made Cassidy simultaneously nervous and at ease. To be fair, it had been a long time since Cassidy had been with anyone. When her last relationship ended during medical school, she'd thrown herself into matching in a decent residency. Before she knew it, residency had started, and that was all she'd had room for. She'd been on sporadic dates since then. But they were usually with men, and almost always accidental. No way would Pierce know she was gay. No one ever did. Goddamn femme invisibility, she cursed silently.

"They're the worst. But so far, this place seems okay."

"It's only April. Aren't you guys supposed to start in July?"

"I did start in July." Cassidy knew she'd have to offer this explanation several more times over the upcoming weeks, given how unusual her circumstances were. "My residency program shut down mid-year. We all got split up, and I ended up here."

"I'm sorry to hear that." Pierce smiled kindly. "But we're happy to have you. Or, at least I am."

Was she flirting with her? God, it had been so long since Cassidy had been attracted to anyone, she wasn't sure she'd even recognize it. No. There was no way. With her long, blond hair, petite frame that hardly weighed over ninety pounds, and tendency for mascara and leggings, absolutely everything about her screamed straight. Maybe that was Pierce's thing—straight women. Maybe if she knew Cassidy was gay, she wouldn't be flirting at all. If she was even flirting, that was. Cassidy closed her eyes, trying to quiet the overly analytic noise that always ran at a dull roar in her brain.

"Thanks. So what about you? Have you been here long?" *Good. Deflect the conversation away from yourself. Don't give yourself a chance to embarrass yourself, Cass.*

"A few months, actually. I just moved here from Atlanta."

"Atlanta? What brings you all the way to Boston?"

Pierce rolled her eyes. "What else? Girl problems." She immediately looked as if she wished she hadn't shared so much, and Cassidy relaxed just a little for the first time since they began speaking. Maybe she wasn't the only one who was nervous without a single seemingly good reason?

"Sorry." Cassidy searched desperately for something she could say to let Pierce know she understood. But she was certain that unless she tattooed a rainbow on her forehead, she wouldn't have any subtle way to tell her. She supposed it really didn't matter anyway. Even if Pierce knew she was gay, she'd never be interested. Not when she was so cool and confident and good-looking. Not when Cassidy was the living and breathing definition of awkward. "Anyway, tell me what happened to your ankle?"

"It's nothing. I twisted it the other night jumping off a swing set like a moron, and my chief is insisting I get it checked out."

Cassidy couldn't help but laugh. "A swing set?"

"Stupid, I know. I forget I'm twenty-eight instead of eight sometimes."

"If it makes you feel any better, I broke my foot last year trying to hop a fence. Let's just say tequila was involved."

"Isn't it always?" Pierce tucked her chin a little and grinned, and Cassidy suddenly realized she'd been staring at her mouth. It was the sexiest mouth she'd ever seen, which Cassidy found strange, since she'd never really noticed anyone's mouth before. Pierce had full, pink lips and a set of straight, white teeth with the tiniest gap in the middle. Her smile was laced with a hint of trouble, and two small divots pitted her cheeks when she laughed. Cassidy thought about what it would be like to kiss that mouth—how soft those lips would be and how knowing that tongue was.

"You know, I'm sure it's just a sprain," Pierce said. And Cassidy realized she hadn't heard a word she'd said.

"Oh. Yeah. Probably." She inhaled sharply, trying to pull herself back down to earth where she could be a professional, not some teenage fool with a crush. "Let me look." With completely manufactured confidence, Cassidy began palpating around Pierce's ankle, moving it this way and that, until she was sure it at least looked like she resembled a doctor.

"X-ray?"

"Already ordered. I've gotta go see some other patients, but I'll let you know as soon as it comes back." Cassidy stood as tall as she could, wondering if Pierce could sense just how off-kilter she was, even for her.

"No rush. I'm not going anywhere."

"You better not. I know where you work now." Cassidy winked and then immediately scolded herself for letting her nerdiness show so boldly. She turned quickly, heat cascading across her cheeks. But not before she noticed Pierce smiling at her.

Chapter Five

Victoria arrived at Pierce's apartment a little after seven the next night. They'd planned to have dinner, and Pierce had been looking forward to it. But she reluctantly remembered the eagerness of waiting for her second date with Katie. The first date had been so spectacularly mind-blowing, neither Katie nor Pierce could wait to see each other again. But their schedules had kept them apart for several days, so by the time that night approached, Pierce felt like she was waiting for Christmas Day. Once again, she was reminded that this was not that. But she was looking forward to seeing Victoria, and that was nice enough.

"Hi!" Pierce stood in the doorway of her building, still in her socks, unwilling to brave the cold spring evening.

"Hey, you." Victoria approached, and they smiled at each other awkwardly, finally kissing quickly.

"Come on in. I just have to put some shoes on, and we can go get something to eat. Are you hungry?"

"Very. Where are we going?" Victoria followed Pierce down the hall and up the stairs to her apartment.

"There's a great Indian place down the street. My favorite taco place is also around here. Can't go wrong with a good street taco."

"I should probably tell you now that I have some food issues."

Pierce pulled on one of her boots and tightened the laces. "What kind of food issues?"

"I'm gluten intolerant."

Before she could stop herself, Pierce looked up at Victoria with what she was sure was a face that did nothing to hide her cynicism. After years in health care, Pierce was beyond skeptical about things like gluten sensitivity, certain chronic diseases that had no medical basis, and other hype words. Her reaction had become so engrained in her, she hadn't had a chance to hide it. "No problem. What do you usually eat?"

"Oh, I can find something just about anywhere. Don't worry about me."

"Right. Indian then?" Pierce smiled, trying to grossly overcompensate for the near eye roll she'd just offered Victoria.

"Perfect."

Victoria was a great conversationalist, well read, passionate, and, Pierce's favorite, highly versed in LGBT history and culture. Pierce loved talking with her about Stonewall and gender identity and comparing the brutal beatings in *Stone Butch Blues* to the current times. Victoria was clearly intelligent. And she was also stubborn. She blamed her Irish heritage, but Victoria didn't back down from a fight. Pierce could tell already that she could call her out on her bullshit, which was a good thing. She loved strong women. She loved when they challenged her. She loved when they taught her. And Victoria certainly seemed to fill that bill.

After dinner and several drinks, followed by Victoria nearly wrestling the check away from Pierce, they headed back to Pierce's apartment. Victoria's car was parked there, but Pierce also thought, by the way the night was going, it would probably turn into more than that.

"Do you want to come in?" Pierce was pretty sure she knew the answer by the way Victoria had touched her knee at the bar and run her fingers just under the hem of Pierce's shirt after Victoria had finished her second glass of wine.

"Yes." Victoria put her hands on Pierce's hips and kissed her, the same hurried clumsiness that had been between them earlier resurfacing. Still no fireworks, no butterflies, no clichéd tingles or light-headedness or shaking knees. But maybe Pierce was putting too much stock in chemistry.

They made small talk in Pierce's kitchen for a while, the undertones of what was about to happen painting the walls around them. Pierce assumed it would be up to her to make the move, which was one of the more annoying aspects of dating femme girls. They always expected her to fill the traditionally male roles, when it suited them—making the first move, paying for the first date, holding the door. But the second she brought it to their attention, most of them turned into raging feminists, denying any such thing. Victoria didn't seem like that type, though. She talked about her hatred for gender roles, especially in lesbian relationships, which was why Pierce wasn't surprised when Victoria grabbed her face and started kissing her again.

Pierce stumbled backward through the poorly lit kitchen, bumping into the refrigerator as Victoria pawed at her back and hair. By the time they managed to find their way into the bedroom, Victoria already had Pierce's shirt unbuttoned. They stopped their kissing to finish undressing. Victoria took off her blouse, then her bra, almost as if getting ready to shower, so matter-of-fact that Pierce felt innately uncomfortable. Sex never made her uncomfortable. Still, it had been so long. And the attention was nice. Maybe she was just out of practice.

Once they were fully naked, Pierce perched on top of Victoria, kissing down her neck and chest. She traced her fingers down her belly, which held just a hint of roundness, and watched for Victoria's reaction. Pierce was good in bed. She knew she was. More than a few girls had told her she was the best they'd had. And she humbly credited that compliment to one simple fact—her ability to pay attention. She'd learned to become completely attuned to what each girl was feeling, thinking even. She'd watch their faces, listen to their breath change, their muscles tighten and release. When she did something right, she'd mentally note it for the next time. It wasn't hard. It was simple trial and error. But she couldn't get any kind of a read on Victoria.

As Pierce continued to touch her, trying everything she could think of in her arsenal of skills, Victoria remained content, which was the only way Pierce could think to describe it. She wasn't panting or screaming Pierce's name, or even writhing on the bed. She was just...there, probably enjoying herself, but no earth was being shattered in that particular moment.

After it was over, which was difficult for Pierce to determine since Victoria hadn't cum, Pierce rolled over onto her back. She had no interest in any kind of reciprocation at this point, her ego slightly bruised and her libido dwindling. They lay under the covers, Pierce feeling vulnerable and exposed, wishing she could find a way to get Victoria to leave. Was this what sex after Katie was going to look like? Passionless, uncomfortable nakedness just begging for an excuse to be over with? Pierce finally had someone new in her bed, and she'd never felt more alone.

"So? How's the ankle?" Cassidy approached Pierce in the physician work area early the next day with a shyness that made Pierce think she had almost been waiting for her.

"Totally fine, thanks to your great care."

Cassidy's pale cheeks were suddenly brushed with a faint pink, and she looked at her feet and giggled. "Glad I could help rip you from the jaws of death."

"You and me both. So how are you settling in, anyway?" Pierce liked Cassidy, her warmth and a kind of innocence that wasn't easy to find in the ER.

"Okay. Everybody seems nice enough."

"Look, I know I haven't been around much longer than you, but if you have any questions about anything or need any advice or whatever, I'm happy to help."

Pierce could swear she saw another hint of color penetrate Cassidy's skin. "Thanks. Maybe you can start by telling me where they keep the good coffee around this place."

"Now that I can definitely do. Got a second?"

"Just waiting on some scans to come back."

"Let's go."

Cassidy turned and took a couple of steps, her back to Pierce, who couldn't help but spend a fraction of a second noting what a fantastic ass she had. Of course, Cassidy was straight. Girls that hot always are. Still, Pierce looked for just a moment.

Pierce led the way up the stairs to the main lobby of the building and around the corner, where a small café sat tucked away.

"Now, don't get too excited, okay? It's nothing to write home about. But it sure beats that cafeteria swill that tastes like liquid garbage."

"I'll take it." Cassidy ordered a latte from the woman behind the counter. "What are you having?"

"Just a medium black."

"It's on me. It's the least I can do for showing me this place." Cassidy put her credit card on the counter.

"Not a chance. You saved my life yesterday, remember?" If Pierce had thought Cassidy might be gay, she'd have been nervous, fumbling her words and filling the awkward silences with petty small talk. But she was completely comfortable. Admittedly, Pierce's gaydar was pure shit. Really, a girl had to look like her, or be sitting directly between Pierce's legs, for her to know she was interested. Still, not a single thing about Cassidy Sullivan even whispered queer. And even if it did, Pierce didn't stand a second's chance with a girl like her.

"Oh yes, those life-threatening ankle sprains. Isn't that what I'm giving up seven years of my life for?" Pierce liked the sass behind Cassidy's sweetness.

"Shoulda gone to PA school. I was out in two. Then again."

"Ugh. That wouldn't be the first time I've had that thought. I tell myself all this madness will be worth it when I'm an attending with a lake house and a Porsche."

"Huh. That's funny. You don't really strike me as the Porsche type. More like a sensible hybrid." Pierce took the lid off her coffee and inhaled, letting the steam paint her face.

"You're actually very correct. I have zero interest in a fancy car. But I don't mind girls who drive them…"

Pierce's head bobbed. Had she just heard what she thought she'd heard? Had Cassidy just said "girl"? As in, "I would like to kiss a girl." As in, "Man, that girl is cute." As in, "Mom, Dad, this is my girlfriend." No. Not a chance. Pierce must have misheard her or, at the very least, misunderstood. But she could have sworn...

What if she had said it? Was Cassidy going out of her way to let Pierce know she was interested in women? Pierce shook her head, reminding herself that she was a solid six or so, but no way would a gorgeous, young, queer doctor look her way.

"Hey, where's my coffee?" Galen's voice broke the clatter in Pierce's head.

"I heard they ran out," Pierce said, teasing her. "Cassidy, this is my cousin, Galen. She's a surgeon here."

"Nice to meet you." Pierce watched Cassidy's face carefully as she shook Galen's hand. Her cheeks were once again flushed, and her eyelashes fluttered just a little. The cutest, tiniest dimples crested over the corners of her mouth, and she seemed to stick out her chest just a little, angling her body toward Galen's. Not a slam dunk, Pierce thought, but definitely a hint. Galen probably wasn't the best reference point, though, since women of just about every sexuality seemed to throw themselves at her. An obnoxious wave of jealousy swept over Pierce, and she tried to brush it off. Of course Cassidy would want Galen. Galen was exactly the kind of woman someone like Cassidy belonged with.

"Cassidy just started her EM residency here," Pierce said, deciding to once again ignore the familiar envy that struck when it came to her cousin.

"Just started?" Galen asked, perplexed.

"It's a long story," Cassidy said, brushing back a piece of stray hair that had fallen and smiling again.

"Maybe I can hear it sometime. You and Pierce should come over for dinner. I'm sure you don't know many people in the hospital yet."

Pierce cleared her throat, wanting desperately to leave as quickly as possible. Clearly, Galen thought she was primed to play some kind of matchmaker. Pierce was mortified.

"I'm sure Cassidy's really busy, Galen."

"Actually, I'd love to." Cassidy grinned coyly, and Pierce's humiliation turned back to indignation at Cassidy's blatant interest in Galen. Until she turned that flirtatious smile in Pierce's direction. "With Pierce, I mean."

Words failed her. Breathing very nearly failed her. So Cassidy *had* said "girl" earlier. And now, it seemed, she was making some version of a pass at Pierce.

"Rowan and I would love that," Galen said.

"Rowan's her girlfriend. Her very serious girlfriend," Pierce said, immediately feeling foolish the second the words left her mouth.

Galen raised her full, perfect eyebrows at Pierce. "How about tomorrow night?"

"Tomorrow night sounds great," Cassidy said. "What can I bring?"

"Just yourself. Oh, and my cousin, I suppose." Galen laughed and rubbed Pierce's short hair. "See you later."

What on earth had Cassidy just agreed to? One minute she was ordering a latte, and the next she was scheduling a double date with Pierce and her cousin. Was it even a date? Technically, Pierce hadn't even asked her—Galen had. In fact, Pierce hadn't even really said she wanted to. *Could you be any stupider, Cass?* She walked back into the ER hoping she could avoid running into Pierce for the rest of the day.

Her shift trucked on, and Cassidy found it hard not to look for Pierce around every corner. She tried to shake off her disappointment when she didn't see her for several hours.

"Hey, Cassidy. I need some help in here." The afternoon had grown chaotic, and everyone seemed tied up with their own complex patients. Cassidy was on her way to find the bathroom for the first time since lunch when Pierce poked her head out from behind the curtain in room fourteen. Fourteen was one of the Fast-Track rooms. This was the area where most of the non-urgent patients were sent— the concussions, the lacerations, the extremity injuries. One of the PAs usually ran it, when they weren't busy on the other side of the department. Cassidy realized this was where Pierce had been all day and took immediate note of the tumbling that began in her stomach when she saw her.

"What's up?" She did her best to keep her words as cool and casual as possible. The less she said, the better.

"I think this guy's about to crump in here." Pierce's face was just a shade paler than usual, and her eyes were tinted dark with worry.

"What's going on?" Cassidy rushed to her, forgetting just how badly she'd needed to pee.

"He came in as a simple closed head injury—tripped on a stump running outside. No loss of consciousness. Just a little headache. I hadn't even gotten a chance to see him yet before he started complaining of severe pain. A second ago he was slurring his speech, and now he's totally out."

Cassidy, the nervous teenage girl, went into recess, and Dr. Sullivan, the trained emergency-room physician, appeared, rubbing the patient's sternum with her knuckles. The man groaned but didn't move. "Sir, can you hear me? Open your eyes." When the man didn't respond, Cassidy pried his eyelids open with her gloved fingers, shining her penlight into both of his pupils.

"Shit, his left pupil's blown." Pierce grabbed the nearby bag valve mask and hooked it up to oxygen, placing it over the man's mouth. "It wasn't like that five minutes ago."

"Did you CT him?"

"Of course not. It was just a minor injury."

Cassidy realized she sounded like she was scolding. "I know. We need an attending in here."

"I tried to call for one. No one's around." Pierce glanced nervously at the monitor over the patient's head, which displayed his steadily climbing blood pressure.

Cassidy pulled back the curtain again, standing in the door, looking around for anyone with a white coat who knew more than she did. Several nurses bustled around with their computers on wheels. "You. Can you help us in here?"

"Her name's Jean," Pierce whispered. "Hey, Jean, this guy's in bad shape. I think he's got a bleed."

The short, plump nurse with hair graying at the temples and a soft, pleasant face entered the room calmly. "What do you need?"

"Can you call down to CT? Let them know we're coming," Cassidy said.

"Wait." Pierce spoke slowly and confidently in a way that impressed and reassured Cassidy in a crisis. "I think we need to tube him first."

Cassidy looked down at the patient again, observing his breathing, which had quickly turned to irregular, gurgling snores. "You're right. Look at his arms. He's starting to posture. He's herniating. Jean, can you set us up for intubation?"

"Don't you want an attending first?" Jean asked, clearly having seen her share of cowboy residents in her day.

"We don't have time. Grab one hundred of succs and twenty of etomidate, and let's get ready with two hundred of propofol," Cassidy said, trying not to let the sheer terror of the moment show.

"I've got suction going. He's preoxygenating with a non-rebreather. But we need to move, fast," Pierce added.

The hands on the clock moved in double time as they waited for Jean to return from the med room with the vials.

"I've got one hundred of succs and twenty of etomidate," Jean said.

"Let's go ahead then." Cassidy took a deep breath and exhaled slowly.

"Etomidate is in. Succs is going in now."

For nearly a minute, they stood and watched, Pierce at the head of the bed, Cassidy to her left, giving time for the sedatives and paralytics to kick in. Finally, the man's breathing ceased altogether.

"You take the tube," Cassidy said to Pierce. She was never one to give up a procedure, but this was Pierce's patient. And something about seeing her work in the face of death was unnervingly sexy.

Pierce unflinchingly picked up the laryngoscope used to open the man's mouth with one hand and the endotracheal tube with the other. "I've got a good view of the cords."

"Oxygen sats are ninety-six percent and holding," Jean said.

"Tube's passed. I'm in," Pierce said confidently.

Cassidy placed her stethoscope over the man's chest. "Good lung sounds. Nice job. Let's get him down to CT. Come on, Pierce. You drive, I'll bag."

❖

Pierce sat in the back of the department, tapping her foot and repeatedly clicking the refresh button on the computer.

"Come on…" she muttered.

"Be patient. They'll be up in a minute." Cassidy stood behind her and put her hand on Pierce's shoulder for just long enough to make Pierce forget the sickening crater that had opened in her gut. This was what she loved about being in the ER. In a matter of minutes, her very stable patient had become critical, and she had the tiniest window of time to intervene. As she waited for the CT images of the man's brain to appear on her screen, she thought something must be wrong with her that allowed this sense of excitement to always accompany the horror. Pierce sighed. As much as she'd love to have a nice, cushy nine-to-five schedule, her patients' biggest problem a runny nose and occasionally a need for their blood-pressure medications to be tweaked, at least for now, she was too much of a sucker for the chaos and unpredictability.

"There." Pierce nearly jumped out of her seat. The scans finally loaded, and she pointed eagerly to a crescent-shaped patch of white stretching across the edge of the brain. "Subdural. It's big, too. Look at that midline shift."

"Holy shit," Cassidy whispered.

"That your guy in fourteen?" George Turner, one of the ER attending physicians, appeared behind them.

"Yeah. Damn. Think he'll make it? That's a huge bleed," Pierce said.

"I don't know. It's pretty impressive. But he's young and healthy. He has a chance if they get him up to surgery right away. Neurosurg knows, right?"

"They're already on the way down," Cassidy answered.

George put both of his big, paw-like hands on their heads like they were his young children who'd just gotten into some kind of trouble that he secretly found endearing. "Nice work, you two."

Pierce liked George. He was one of her favorite attendings so far. "I'll let you know when neuro gets here."

"Good." George smiled and walked away.

"That's it? We're not going to get chastised for tubing a patient without an attending? Not even a scolding?" Cassidy asked, gawking.

"Do you want to be scolded?" As soon as the words left her mouth, Pierce hated herself. What a stupid, accidental come-on. A stupid, hypersexual, gross-sounding accidental come-on.

Cassidy looked at her for a long time, her expression stoic. Pierce couldn't even find the words to explain she'd meant nothing by it. Instead, she remained silent, still, feeling like an utter idiot.

"Is that an offer, Pierce?" Cassidy's brow twitched for a second, and she smiled with her full, pink lips—first with just the corners of her mouth, and then with her entire face.

"I…It was…Shit." Pierce looked at the floor and shook her head, squeezing her eyes shut.

"Hey. I'm just teasing." Cassidy touched Pierce's shoulder again, and heat spread across Pierce's chest, her heart beating just a little bit faster and her hands tingling just enough to remind her that something was happening between them. It was probably nothing, Pierce told herself. Just a little harmless attraction. But whatever it was certainly wasn't subtle.

CHAPTER SIX

R o? I'm home." Galen opened the door to the apartment, where their Lab, Suzy, was waiting with a wagging tail and a stuffed elephant in her mouth.

"Hey, Suz. Where's Mom?"

Suzy just continued to look at Galen adoringly, finally jumping to her feet and pouncing, no longer able to control herself. As Galen wrestled with Suzy on the kitchen floor, she noticed the shower running.

"Ro?"

"I'm in here." Rowan's voice came muffled from behind the bathroom door. Galen temporarily abandoned Suzy and opened the door. "Hi," Rowan said, her head emerging from behind the shower curtain.

"Well, hello there." Galen leaned over to kiss her, the water misting onto her own face and hair.

"How about you get in here and join me?" Rowan grabbed Galen's shirt collar and pulled her in, kissing her again, this time with more need and conviction.

"I can't say no to that." Galen pulled off her shirt, then her pants, letting them fall to the floor. Finally naked, she pulled back the curtain and stepped in, the hot water caressing her back and neck. She grasped Rowan's hips, pressing their bodies together until they were so close even the water had a hard time falling between them.

"You feel so good," Rowan said, moaning. "I missed you today."

"I missed you."

"How was the day?" Rowan dribbled some shampoo into her palm and began lathering it through her long hair as Galen continued to gently rub her back. The water made her fingers glide easily down to the curve of Rowan's ass, and Galen's focus momentarily blurred.

"It was fine. But Pierce may have met someone."

Rowan's head, still soapy, bobbed up. "Really?"

"I mean, I don't know. I saw her with this new resident today. And they were pretty cozy. Pierce seemed pretty into her. I think it was mutual."

Rowan grabbed Galen's hands and pumped them up and down. "Tell me more! Who is she? What's she like?"

"Whoa. I met her for, like, a minute. Her name is Cassidy, I think. She's a new EM resident who just transferred here for some reason. That's literally all I know. Why are you all jazzed up about Pierce's love life anyway?"

"Because." Rowan put her palm sweetly on Galen's cheek. "She's your cousin. And she reminds me of you when you were that age."

"You didn't know me when I was that age." Galen smiled and kissed her hand.

"True. But it's what I imagine you were like. You know, besides all the hopeless womanizing."

"Whatever." Galen rolled her eyes.

"I think Pierce used serial monogamy in the same way you used sleeping around. She was trying to fill this void of finding the one."

"You sure you aren't thinking about a career change? Maybe psychiatry?" Galen loved teasing her and how sensitive Rowan was. She also loved that she was so invested in Pierce's happiness.

"I'm the best damn senior resident you have, Dr. Burgess. Don't make me take you into the bedroom and have my way with you."

"Oh, no. That would be horrible, Dr. Duncan. Please don't." Galen pulled Rowan into her again and kissed her earlobe, then followed with a trail down her neck and shoulder as Rowan giggled uncontrollably.

"I really hope Pierce finds someone," Rowan said, putting her arms around Galen's neck.

"I hope she finds her Rowan," Galen said, kissing her softly. After all this time, her insides still tossed and tumbled hopelessly when their lips met. And she knew that would never change.

"You're very sweet."

"No one's ever called me 'sweet' before."

"That's because you were a dick before me." Rowan grinned and kissed her forehead.

"What can I say? You bring out the best in me. But there's one more thing. I kind of invited Pierce and Cassidy over tomorrow night. I don't know. It just came out before I could think about it. I'm sorry if it's too much. I can make something easy, and it'll be super low-key. I promise!"

"It looks like I'm wearing off on you. I love that idea. And I love you."

It was dumb for Cassidy to be so worked up about a non-date date. Pierce hadn't even invited her. She was probably just being polite. God, Cassidy must have sounded like such an eager little puppy, just jumping at the chance to spend more time with her. Pierce knew she was gay, now. I mean, Cassidy had all but spelled it out for her when they were getting coffee. Hadn't she? And Pierce hadn't so much as smiled her way since then, unless they were working on a patient together or crossing paths at work. Maybe she had a girlfriend? Or maybe she just plain wasn't interested.

Cassidy's bed was littered with piles of dresses and skirts and tops. She must have tried on twelve different outfits, and everything looked blah at best. Finally, she settled on an olive-green, wool pencil skirt and a white blouse cut just low enough to show off what slight cleavage she had. She futzed with her hair, tying it up in a tight bun first, but then she decided she looked far too much like a schoolteacher out of a porno and let it down to fall wildly across her shoulders. Finally, she stepped into her favorite pair of Chelsea boots and zipped up the side. Pierce wasn't tall. Maybe she wouldn't want Cassidy towering over her like some kind of amazon? *You are being fucking ridiculous, Cass.* She kept the boots and walked out the door of her apartment, down the stairs to where her Uber was waiting.

Galen's apartment building was a dream. Cassidy hadn't even been inside yet, and she was already impressed. Still, maybe that's what you got when you were a surgeon. She inhaled for a count of four and blew her breath out in a strong gust, lifting her chest and walking into the building. The elevator stopped at the 19th floor, and she got off, searching the doors for the apartment number Pierce had given her.

One more deep breath, and Cassidy knocked confidently. The shuffle of feet and friendly voices radiated out, and then the door opened. Pierce stood in the entry way, wearing a pair of tight black jeans faded in all the right places and a leather moto jacket over a button-down shirt that fell open to show the subtle muscles of her chest and shoulders. Cassidy felt her mouth drop a little, and a faint warmth grew between her legs. What was wrong with her? She hadn't even slept with Pierce, and she already wanted her more than she thought was entirely reasonable.

"Welcome," Pierce said, smiling. Did Pierce have any idea what kind of absurd response her body was having? She should have let Pierce think she was straight.

"Thank you." She mentally pulled herself together and stepped into the apartment. "I brought some wine." She handed the bottle to Pierce.

"Very thoughtful. You look great, by the way." Pierce's cheeks pinked, and the warmth between Cassidy's legs returned stronger than ever.

"So do you." As Cassidy willed herself to keep her voice even and strong, a stunning woman in a baby-blue dress came from around the corner.

"You must be Cassidy!" The woman, who Cassidy had to assume was Galen's partner, hugged her. "Sorry. I'm from the South. We're huggers."

"That's okay. So am I." Cassidy laughed.

"I'm Rowan. I'm so glad you could make it over tonight."

Rowan was warm and kind, and Cassidy liked her instantly. "Thank you for inviting me."

"I think it was all these two," Rowan said, gesturing to Galen and Pierce, who stood side by side, leaning against the dining-room table, simultaneously sipping from glasses of bourbon on the rocks.

"The resemblance is eerie, isn't it?" Cassidy asked.

"Almost creepy." Rowan nodded. They laughed, and Cassidy felt more at home than she had since she moved to Boston.

Cassidy sat across from Pierce at dinner, and as the meal continued on and the wine flowed, she found it more and more difficult not to stare at her. It was that damn mouth again. So full, and warm, and inviting, just begging for Cassidy to kiss it. God, it had been so long since she'd kissed anyone. In fact, the last kiss she could even remember was when her senior resident forcefully bumped his mouth against hers on a work retreat. Cassidy had managed to slap him hard enough that she actually knocked the drool out of his mouth. They hadn't spoken since.

"So, Cassidy, do you have any family or anyone around the area? Parents? Siblings? Girlfriend?" Galen flicked her eyebrows at everyone around the table.

"Nice, baby. Very subtle," Rowan said, reaching over and squeezing Galen's hand. Cassidy laughed uncomfortably and once again found herself looking at Pierce, whose eyes were glassy. She wasn't sure if it was the whiskey or the topic at hand.

"Not really, no. My family is all over the place. Dad in Wisconsin and Mom in Delaware. I have a brother in Vermont, but that's about it." A brief chill ran down Cassidy's neck at the thought of her parents. It had been almost a decade since the divorce, which she still so shamefully blamed herself for. Nearly losing a child is a lot to put on a marriage. But she pushed the thoughts aside, as she always did when it came to those horrid years in the hospital. Everything was fine now. She was fine.

"And, um, girlfriend?" Rowan said, leaning over her elbows intently.

"Now whose gift is subtlety?" Galen asked, teasing her.

"What? I'm just trying to get to know our new friend better!" Pierce threw her arms dramatically up in the air. "Guys... really?"

"No." Cassidy laughed. "No girlfriend either. But how did you..."

Rowan raised a hand boastfully. "I actually have the world's best gaydar."

Pierce and Cassidy looked at each other, befuddled.

"She's right," Galen said.

"But...you've only been out for, like, five minutes! How is that even possible?" Pierce asked.

"Excuse me. I'm going to pretend that remark didn't offend me. And I don't know how. It's a gift, I guess."

"I knew you were gay too," Galen added.

"You did not," Pierce said.

"Well, I had a hunch at least." Galen glanced at Pierce, then at Cassidy, and winked. Shit. Had it been so blindingly obvious in the coffee shop that she was checking Pierce out? Did that mean everyone they worked with could see it too? Oh God. Maybe she'd have to quit and find another residency? How could she? She'd just started there! No one had ever switched residencies twice! Oh God, oh God, oh God...

"I guess that femme invisibility can't fool you two," Cassidy said, smiling coolly.

"Are you kidding?" Rowan said. "I've been the poster child for femme invisibility since I came out. Do you have any idea how many times my male colleagues hit on me? I've found myself on more—"

"—accidental dates?" Cassidy answered.

"Yes! Accidental dates! You too?" She laughed.

"Constantly." Cassidy looked across the table again at Pierce and Galen, who stared blankly at each other.

"That's a problem I've never run into," Galen said.

"Same," Pierce added.

"Thank God for Galen, or no one would have any idea I was queer. She's like my little gay calling card. I walk down the street with her and, bam, rainbows."

Galen turned to Pierce and grinned. "Guys hate it," she whispered.

"But really. No girlfriend?" Rowan grew more serious. "That's really interesting. You know, Pierce is also single."

Pierce jumped from the table. "Rowan! Jesus! And here I was thinking Galen would be the one whose mouth I'd have to suture shut!"

They all laughed, and Cassidy couldn't help but notice just how much she liked the husky pitch Pierce's voice took on when she was just a little embarrassed.

"No more. I promise." Rowan brought her index finger and thumb to her lip and mimed a zipper closing.

The conversation moved forward, but Cassidy's mind couldn't. She'd been hoping Pierce was single. But she didn't see how that would be possible. Now she was torn between the thought that Pierce was clearly available, and the thought that she'd clearly made no advances. The deduction of reason led only to the path that Pierce just wasn't interested.

Dinner had run late into the night. In spite of the fact that all four had to get up early for various callings at the hospital, they'd spent the evening laughing and drinking and talking, until Rowan finally insisted everyone disperse to get some sleep. Pierce's phone had gone off half a dozen times from her pocket. It was most likely Victoria, but she was enjoying herself far too much to pay any attention. Cassidy had fit in seamlessly with Rowan and Galen. It was as if they'd all been friends for years.

Pierce lay in her bed sometime after one a.m. She scrolled through all Victoria's unanswered texts, which sounded more and more frantic as they progressed, but she didn't respond. She couldn't think about anything but Cassidy and the ease of her laugh across the dining-room table as she looked at Pierce with something Pierce couldn't quite parse out. Was it longing? Curiosity? Fondness? She wasn't sure. But whatever it was, it was intense. And it pulled Pierce in with such a force that her eyes couldn't move—didn't want to.

Victoria was a nice girl. Pierce liked her well enough. They had potential to go somewhere. Cassidy was just a coworker, or maybe a friend at best. She saw no point in dredging up the impossible.

Cassidy walked to the locker room, nearly delirious from a ten-hour shift that had quickly become a fourteen-hour shift after two of her patients took turns for the sicker. It was after midnight, and she wished she could teleport home somehow to avoid spending one more minute awake. She was so focused on collecting her things and leaving that she almost didn't see the one other person in the room, her broad back and square shoulders turned to Cassidy, struggling to get her keys out of her coat pocket.

"Late night for you too, huh?" Cassidy asked.

Pierce turned, a smile already painting her face at the sound of Cassidy's voice. "Yeah. Let's just say Fast Track wasn't so fast today."

"Any more head bleeds?"

"Nope." Pierce shut the metal locker with a clunk and tossed her backpack over her shoulder.

"Then I'd call it a success." Cassidy pulled off her stethoscope and shook out her ponytail, trying hard to stretch the taut muscles in her shoulders.

"How about you? Why are you here so late?"

"Hmm…a septic guy who needed a central line about twenty minutes ago, and a status epilepticus I had to intubate."

"You love this shit, don't you," Pierce said, laughing sweetly.

Cassidy shrugged. "I can't help it. I really do."

"It's a sickness. Really, I get it." Pierce paused awkwardly and shifted back and forth on each foot for a minute. "So, I'll see you tomorrow?"

"I'll be here," Cassidy said, all too eagerly.

"Great. Well…bye." Pierce raised her palm in the air, then turned quickly and moved toward the door. Before she opened it, she stopped again, spinning around to face Cassidy as if she'd just changed her mind, or maybe forgotten something important. "Hey, listen. Are you hungry?"

Cassidy's heart began to vibrate in her chest, and her palms grew clammy. "Starving. I haven't had a chance to eat since breakfast."

"You, uh, want to get a burger or something?" Pierce's gaze never left the floor.

"Sure. I mean, yeah. A burger would be great. Know a place?"

"There's a sports bar down the street that's pretty good. If that's okay…"

"Sounds perfect." Cassidy pulled on her jacket and zipped it shut, trying to contain the fountain of nerves bubbling out of her.

Pierce smiled and opened the locker-room door for her. "I'll drive."

Mike O'Leary's had been a favorite of Pierce's since she got to Boston, partially for its proximity and partially for its ten flat-screen TVs always playing a different sporting event. It wasn't the ideal place to take a girl on a first non-date, but it was the only place she knew that was still open, and she hadn't exactly had much time to come up with options. Pierce was not planning to ask Cassidy out. Not by any stretch of the imagination. But as she got ready to leave the locker room that night, she looked at Cassidy's long, blond hair and green eyes that were a little bit lonely and a little bit curious, and the words just tumbled out.

It wasn't a date. Of course it wasn't. First of all, she'd never take a date to Mike's. Especially not someone as smart and sexy as Cassidy. Second of all, there was Victoria. Pierce reminded herself as they drove away from the hospital that she and Victoria had gone out only a couple of times. They'd slept together. They'd had fun. But they hadn't made any promises. Still, she found herself wracked with gratuitous guilt, even on a non-date date. Stupid. Cassidy surely didn't consider this a date anyway.

"Ugh. I'm so bummed I missed the home opener tonight," Cassidy said, glancing up at one of the massive televisions in the corner.

The corners of Pierce's mouth curled involuntarily. "You're a baseball fan?"

"Huge. All sports, really. But especially baseball and football." Pierce must have been staring, because Cassidy laughed and reached across the table, tapping her playfully on the shoulder. "What? Never seen another girl who likes sports before?"

"Not one that looks like you." The words left Pierce's mouth before she had time to rethink them, which was not an altogether uncommon problem for her, and Cassidy looked away coyly. Pierce certainly didn't want Cassidy to find herself on another accidental date, thinking she was just getting an innocent burger and then being bombarded with unreciprocated affection and flirtation.

"Thanks," Cassidy finally said, still smiling. "And I bet you didn't know I was gay either."

"Honestly? I had no clue. But in my defense, I have terrible gaydar. You essentially have to look like me or actively try to kiss me for me to have any idea you're interested. I mean, not you, you. I meant like, you in the general sense. Not you in particular…" Pierce rested her forehead on the tips of her fingers in defeat. "Never mind."

Cassidy laughed and leaned closer. "I knew what you meant."

"For the record, I don't think Rowan would have had any idea either. And Galen's spent her entire life just assuming everyone's gay, since they all end up wanting to get in her pants anyway."

"You know, I did try really hard to look less 'straight' at one point. I had an edgy haircut and everything."

"How edgy are we talking here?"

"Oh, very. The entire left side was cut short, but the right was long and choppy. I was going for a whole Portia De Rossi thing, but really, it was just awful."

"I don't believe it." Pierce laughed.

"No, really! I did!"

"I don't believe you could possibly look terrible." *Stop it, Pierce. Stop flirting. You sound like an idiot.*

Cassidy didn't answer but glanced down at the table and pushed her menu around a few times before finally looking up at Pierce over the tops of her glasses with a shy grin. Was Cassidy possibly finding this conversation endearing?

"How did you end up a Red Sox fan, anyway? You didn't grow up around here, right?" Pierce asked.

"No. I was an army brat. We moved eight times before my parents finally divorced, so I didn't settle anywhere until high school. But my dad is a huge Boston sports fan, so I grew up with an onslaught of Adam Vinatari and David Ortiz until, luckily for my dad, it stuck."

Pierce had only been half joking when she said she'd never met a sports fan who looked like Cassidy. Every girl she'd ever dated had despised sports or, at the very best, tolerated them. Stereotype or not, she was more than slightly surprised.

"Is it true?" Cassidy asked, after the conversation had slowed and a comfortable silence had fallen over the table.

"Is what true?"

"What Rowan said the other night, about you being single. I find that hard to believe."

Pierce's pulse accelerated, and she gripped her knees under the table. "Definitely true. And how about you? How are you possibly single?"

Cassidy laughed. "You're kind of charming. Did you know that? Anyway, I got out of something toward the end of med school. And when that ended, I decided to sort of throw myself into my residency. So…I've been a doctor. And that's about it."

Pierce realized that Cassidy was directly addressing a subconscious and fleeting thought Pierce had had since their dinner with Rowan and Galen; Cassidy had no time to start a relationship. She shook her head, trying to remind herself that that was so far from mattering it shouldn't have even crossed her mind.

"But…I think I'm ready to change that…" Cassidy smiled shyly, and Pierce's legs trembled a little as they brushed Cassidy's. "Are you, you know, seeing anyone?"

It took a lot for Pierce to think anyone was interested in her. But Cassidy was sending signals about as subtle as flare guns and traffic-cone orange. Maybe it was the beer, or just the epic fatigue from an endless day. It was impossible, but something seemed to be happening between them.

"I suppose I should call it a night," Cassidy finally said, once the waitress had cleared away the final nacho crumbs and empty glasses. A sinking disappointment swamped Pierce at the thought of leaving her.

"Same. What time do you work tomorrow?"

"Seven a.m."

"No, really." Pierce was certain she was joking.

"I'm serious...I have to be back at the hospital in about...five hours?"

"I'm so sorry! You should have said something. I would never have kept you out so late."

"You didn't keep me out." Cassidy reached across the table and brushed Pierce's thumb with her index finger for the briefest second. "Besides, usually when I give the seven a.m. start line, it's an excuse to get out of a date. Or, if I'm really nervous, I'll fake a page."

"I can't help but notice you haven't gotten any pages since we've been here," Pierce said, curling the corner of her mouth into a wry grin.

"Didn't even take it out of my bag."

Their eyes locked for several seconds, the energy that had been pulsating between them now thickening into a firestorm of questions and possibilities and all kinds of things Pierce hadn't felt in the longest time, until the waitress came to pick up the check, only partially breaking the spell they'd been under.

"Do you want a ride home?" Pierce asked as they approached her waiting car.

"Actually, I'm only a few blocks in the other direction..." Cassidy bit her bottom lip as if she'd just been found out, and Pierce silently noted that she'd made the walk with her just to have a few extra seconds.

"So, I'll see you tomorrow then?"

"Absolutely."

They hovered on the street corner, both of them seeming to dare the other to leave, or stay, or maybe even move closer. Pierce stood just near enough that if she took a step toward Cassidy, she would be in her arms. But Pierce wasn't thinking about kissing Cassidy. She wasn't planning to do anything more than say good night and walk away. Kissing her had never entered her mind. Yet, completely possessed by the same magic that had been engulfing them all night, she somehow found herself taking that single step, until her hands rested on Cassidy's hips and her lips lingered just in front of Cassidy's lips. Slowly, but without a hint of apprehension, Pierce brushed her mouth gently against Cassidy's. Once again, like so many other kisses before, no spark ignited. An explosion occurred—a combustion of cells and matter and energy and something that even science and God couldn't put words to. And it was nothing like so many other kisses before.

It wasn't until she finally broke away that Pierce noticed her legs had been shaking. Her whole body, actually, vibrated as if everything inside her had suddenly woken up. The cold night air had turned hot and dreamy, like the warmest week of the summer with a hint of an ocean breeze. She couldn't explain it, but the world looked different.

Chapter Seven

That kiss. Oh my God, that kiss. It was now sometime before four a.m., and Cassidy lay on her back in bed, wide awake, staring at the crack in her ceiling. She was never going to get to sleep. Not if she kept replaying that moment with Pierce in her head like a crazy person. She couldn't help it. She loved the tumbling in her stomach and the tightening in her belly whenever she remembered. She loved feeling like this.

Was Pierce thinking about it too? Or was she home fast asleep, like nothing had ever happened? Maybe it was nothing to her. Maybe she kissed a lot of girls like that. Cassidy picked up one of her pillows and pressed it over her head. A designated devil and angel were perched on either shoulder, one prompting her to wonder what kind of dress she'd wear if they ever got married, the other reminding her she was being nothing short of certifiable. Then, she would grow angry with herself for getting so many miles, states, continents ahead of where she should be. She finally picked up her phone, carefully, strategically drafting the skeleton of a text message that she didn't plan to send for several hours.

Hi you! Just wanted to say that I had such an awesome time on our date.

She quickly deleted the word date. Pierce hadn't asked her on a date. She'd asked her to share a plate of nachos at a sports bar after their mutual shifts ended. It was nothing but an impulsive outing without pretense. Then again, Pierce had kissed her...

Hi you! Just wanted to say that I had such an awesome time last night. I'd really like to see you again. You know, outside of work. PS. May or may not have spent a significant amount of time so far daydreaming about that kiss...

It was bold, for sure. And Cassidy wasn't sure if she'd ever actually send it. Still, maybe putting it out into the universe like that would help her relax a little. Once she laid her phone back down, she tossed from side to side, unable to shake the feeling of Pierce's hands on her waist. And she watched any hope of sleep vanish into the night, knowing whatever was happening was unlike anything she'd ever known, or anticipated.

Pierce wasn't expecting to hear from Cassidy. At least not for a day or so. The night had been amazing, but Cassidy was a resident—a doctor. She worked day in and day out and probably wouldn't have time to think about petty things like first kisses. That was why when her phone went off sometime after nine in the morning, she was surprised to see Cassidy's name. Surprised and, admittedly, ecstatic.

She read the text carefully, taking in each word like rays of sunshine after the winter thaw. And when she finished, she read it again. And again. Until she basically had the entire message memorized. So Cassidy had been thinking about the kiss after all. And, from the sound of it, she'd been thinking about it a lot. Pierce smiled to herself with a smile so big anyone who'd walked into her bedroom would have thought she was high. In a way, she was high. That kiss. Oh God, that kiss. The moment played on repeat in her head, each time making it harder and harder for Pierce to go another second without kissing Cassidy again. She made her way into the bathroom and splashed some cold water on her face, patting it dry with a towel and staring in the mirror.

"Get it together, Pierce. Be cool." But she was terrible at cool, especially when it came to a girl as perfect as Dr. Cassidy Sullivan. By ten that morning, Pierce could no longer contain herself. She had to tell somebody what she was feeling, and the only logical choice seemed like Galen.

"What are you doing here?" Pierce arrived at Galen's office door a couple of hours later, desperate to share the myriad of thoughts whizzing around her head.

"Got a minute?"

"Of course I do." Galen seemed to be noting Pierce's gray hooded sweatshirt and dark jeans. "Isn't today your day off?"

"Yeah. I just…I needed to talk."

"Sit." Galen gestured to the large leather armchair across from her desk. "I know that look. It's a girl, isn't it?"

"Am I that obvious?"

"Only because I've seen it before. Every time I looked in the mirror when I first met Ro. Is it Cassidy?"

Pierce's heart unexpectedly began to rumble in her chest at the mention of Cassidy's name. "Doctor McSmokeshow…" Pierce mumbled under her breath.

"Oh my God." Galen laughed heartily. "You've nicknamed her already? Pal, come on."

"Just…help! I'm in a bad way, okay? So if you could keep the teasing to a minimum I'd really appreciate it." Pierce buried her head in her hands, closing her eyes tight until the darkness began to comfort her anxiety.

"Okay. I'm sorry. So tell me what happened with…Dr. McSmokeshow." Galen laughed one more time. "I mean, Cassidy."

"We went out last night. After our shift ended, I took her to Mike O'Leary's. It started off as harmless nachos and talking about the Red Sox. I thought we were just, you know, hanging out. Like coworkers. Except when one coworker is really fucking hot—"

Galen held up her hand. "Got it."

"It was amazing. The best first date that wasn't really a date I've ever been on. And at the end of the night, I kissed her. And she seemed to like it. She seemed to like…me." Pierce still couldn't quite believe the words leaving her mouth—a sentiment that would become a theme over the upcoming months.

"That's great! I'm really glad you two are hitting it off." Galen smiled, then looked down at her laptop as if the conversation were finished. But Pierce had yet to even get to the point. She wasn't sure what the point was, but still, she knew she hadn't gotten there.

"It is great. It's really great. I mean she's…amazing. I haven't felt like this since Katie, which is also the single most terrifying thing I can possibly think of. And then there's Victoria."

Galen looked up again. "Who?"

"You know, Victoria. The other girl I've been seeing?"

"Oh, right. The mousy girl with the short hair."

"G, you've met her twice."

Galen shrugged. "What can I say? She's a nice girl. Just apparently not that memorable."

"There's still a little bit of an asshole in there just trying to climb its way out, isn't there?" Pierce shook her head and grinned.

"Sorry. I didn't mean it like that. I just meant I never saw your face light up like this when you talked about Victoria."

"That's so gay."

"You *are* so gay. And it's true. You're just this bundle of nerves and dopamine and impulsive decisions right now. I can actually see you planning the names of your future cats."

"Shut up." Pierce slugged Galen in the shoulder, then sighed, defeated. "But you aren't wrong. God, how can I like someone that I just met so much? I can't stop thinking about her. All I want to do is kiss her again."

"That, my friend, is exactly what it should feel like." Galen took a sip out of the tiny espresso cup on her desk and nodded wisely.

"Should I ask her out again? And what about Victoria? I feel so gross dating both of them at once. I mean, I like Victoria and all, but the *bam* just wasn't there."

Galen looked at her, perplexed. "The what?"

"You know, the *bam*. Fireworks? Explosions? Chemistry! The thing that keeps you up all night replaying that moment over and over."

"Oh." Galen smiled: "The *bam*. I know it well. Look, Pierce. You don't need to make any rash decisions about who to keep dating. That's what dating is, right? It's all about figuring out who you want to try to make it work with."

But Pierce knew exactly who she wanted to make it work with. She just felt foolish for thinking it so early on. "I guess you're right. Thanks."

"Just one more thing. Are you sure you want to take dating advice from a reformed playboy? Maybe next time, for your own good, you might want to consider going to Rowan."

Pierce laughed, stood from the chair, and reached over the desk to hug Galen. "You're probably right," she whispered, and left, knowing exactly what she needed to do.

It had been several hours since Cassidy sent that pathetic, needy text to Pierce, and she had yet to hear so much as a blip from her cell phone. The anxiety was starting to engulf her like a wildfire. And the feeling that followed, one of disappointment, was even more disconcerting. She realized, reluctantly, that she would be crushed if Pierce didn't want to see her again. How was it possible that she could be so invested, so connected to someone she'd shared one simple kiss with? No, that wasn't fair. That kiss was anything but simple. It was the kind of first kiss that altered paths for entire lifetimes. She couldn't downplay that fact, even if Pierce had decided she was no longer interested.

"Dr. Sullivan." Cassidy was beginning to get used to the suffix, but was caught completely off guard when she heard the words in Pierce's quiet tenor.

"Hi!" The immediate enthusiasm that consumed Cassidy quickly turned to humiliation when she remembered the unreturned message she'd sent earlier. Pierce must have thought she was such an idiot. She was probably just coming through the ER to get her paycheck, or maybe her gym bag she'd forgotten. Cassidy just so happened to be in her line of sight.

"I'm sorry I didn't get to text you back yet."

"Oh, that." Cassidy waved her hand dramatically, heat permeating her skin, and she wanted desperately to run. "Just ignore that."

Pierce closed the distance between them, standing so close Cassidy could smell Pierce's faint cologne and signature musk that was already so uniquely her. "That's too bad. Because I came down here to see what you were doing tonight."

"I..."The wind was being sucked out from her lungs, and her vision narrowed into small pinholes. "Nothing. Why?"

"Well." Pierce looked away and stuffed her hands in her pockets in what appeared to be a rare moment of uncertainty. "I was thinking maybe you wanted to watch the Sox game...with me..."

Cassidy wanted to jump six feet in the air. She wanted to run through the ER screaming "yes" until her coworkers thought she was losing her mind and needed to place her in a locked room. She wanted to kiss Pierce again, right then, right there.

"Sounds great. I'm done here at six. Why don't you come to my place? It's not much, but it's near the park, and we have a great roof deck where you can actually see into Fenway." Cassidy mentally congratulated herself on keeping her cool at what she considered at least a modest level.

"You've been holding out on me. And here I was thinking I was impressing you by taking you to Mike's."

Cassidy looked down. "You didn't need to take me anywhere special to do that."

"I'll see you tonight then." Pierce brushed Cassidy's little finger with her own until they were locked together for just the briefest instant, but long enough to leave Cassidy burning to touch her again.

The serial monogamist that still lingered inside Pierce told her to keep Victoria around, on the back page, just in case things didn't work out with Cassidy. But that urge was nothing more than a visceral reaction to the fear she might have met someone she actually liked again. Regardless of what happened with Cassidy, Pierce had to break it off with Victoria because she'd never come anywhere close to feeling with her what she was feeling as she dressed to go to Cassidy's apartment that night. She hadn't felt this sort of anticipation in over a year and had thought it might have been gone for good. She'd forgotten just how good it could be.

Pierce's lingering sense of guilt vanished as she told Victoria the truth over the telephone. She couldn't keep seeing her. Nothing was wrong, really. Enough wasn't right.

Pierce had forgotten how cold it could still be in April in New England. She eyed her warmest winter coat but decided on a thinner, more flattering, but far less practical choice. What was a little chill if it meant impressing Cassidy?

The ride over wasn't nearly long enough for Pierce to clear some of the nerves causing her body to pulsate and her mind to run at lightning speed. In fact, the closer she got to Cassidy's apartment, the harder it was to slow her racing pulse and breath that came in anxious whispers. She wiped the palms of her hands on her jeans and jumped out of the cab at the address Cassidy had given her, all at once wanting to either turn around out of fear or run as fast as she could to Cassidy's door.

Several moments later, the door to Cassidy's four-story building that sat on a side street not far from where Galen and Rowan lived opened. Pierce's previously ragged breathing stopped altogether as her gaze settled on Cassidy. She wore a pair of dark jeans that hugged her ass so closely it was a wonder she could walk. A white linen shirt fell just low enough for suggestion. And her long, blond hair flowed freely around her shoulders. Pierce was used to seeing her at work, in a pair of wrinkled scrubs with no makeup and a ponytail. It wasn't that Cassidy didn't absolutely stun like that, but this was a new level entirely.

"Hi." Pierce smiled, hoping desperately that her expression would buy her some time to remember how to speak again.

"Hey!" Cassidy took a half a step forward, and they embraced tentatively. Pierce didn't want to push. She didn't know if it was even okay to touch Cassidy again. But once their arms had locked around each other, it was clear that it was very much okay.

Cassidy led Pierce up to the third floor. The apartment was much older than Galen and Rowan's, without the amenities and embellishments. But it also held an old Boston charm like so many of the buildings around the city that had been there for decades.

"I hope you don't think I'm a total creep for taking you back to my apartment on our second date," Cassidy said once she'd unlocked the door.

Pierce laughed. "Absolutely not." If she'd had any doubt about the subtext to the evening, Pierce figured Cassidy had just cleared that up.

"Here. Let me take your coat." Cassidy held out her arm, and Pierce draped her jacket over it.

"This is a great place. And you can't beat the location."

"I mean, technically, this is Mission Hill. But if you stand on the roof in just the right spot, you can actually see into the park. The view's completely obstructed, and if you don't bring a flashlight you'll definitely fall down the stairs getting back and break your neck, but otherwise, it's stellar. Sorry. Do you feel misled now?"

"Are you kidding? That sounds amazing." Pierce stuffed her hands into her pockets, wanting to get closer to Cassidy again. She wanted to kiss her again. It was all she'd been thinking about since their last kiss, or first kiss, actually. She just couldn't tell if Cassidy was thinking the same.

"Do you want a drink? I bought some hot chocolate and schnapps earlier. Did I mention it's freezing up there on the roof? And we have to sit on this ratty blanket one of my neighbors stuck up there." Cassidy winked playfully. Pierce didn't know her well yet, but she was already getting the sense that Cassidy was the kind of girl who was up for just about anything—bar nachos, grungy-rooftop baseball games, schnapps. Not to mention the blood and guts. Every second with her was already making Pierce long for the next and dread the minute she'd have to leave.

"You know you're doing nothing to keep from selling this, right? If you tell me there's a homeless guy squatting up there, then I'm all in."

"There are two, actually. And one has a pet pigeon named James."

Pierce laughed. "Well, what are we doing down here then?"

Cassidy handed Pierce a thermos full of hot chocolate, their hands brushing just long enough to send a blistering heat up Pierce's arm even in the cold apartment. They stood frozen in the moment just long enough for Pierce to know Cassidy had felt it too, until Cassidy smiled and turned toward the door.

Cassidy had not been exaggerating about the rooftop. It was small, with a cracked foundation and overgrown vines half dead from the winter winding in and out. A tattered, plaid blanket sat oddly positioned somewhere off to the side with an empty beer can abandoned next to it. Pierce thought it was all very Boston, and she couldn't think of anywhere in the city, or the world, she'd rather be.

"Come sit right here," Cassidy said, walking to the blanket.

"You sure I won't get lice or something?"

"I can't guarantee anything. But you don't strike me as the squeamish type."

Pierce shrugged and grinned. "You're right. I'm not."

Sure enough, directly over the horizon stood the majestic lights of Fenway Park, as bright as a carnival. Several trees stood in the way, but through them you could make out the large Jumbotron and center field.

"On a really clear night, you can sometimes see Jackie Bradley Jr. out there running for a catch," Cassidy said.

"That may be the sexiest thing I've ever heard a woman say." Pierce sat close to Cassidy, their eyes fixed ahead, but their shoulders and knees touching. Without looking at her, Pierce reached behind Cassidy and gently placed her hand on Cassidy's lower back. Cassidy inched in closer to her, until her head was resting on Pierce's shoulder, Pierce's heart pounding so loudly she was sure Cassidy would hear it.

The park was too far away to hear the crowds, but Cassidy had brought a tiny radio that broadcasted one of the local sports stations.

"You know there's an app for that," Pierce said, as Cassidy fussed with the dials trying to get a better signal.

"What can I say? I'm old-fashioned."

Pierce smiled but fought a wave of disappointment as Cassidy moved briefly out of her grasp. She wasn't gone long, though. Once again, she leaned back into Pierce as Pierce secured her arms around her. The feeling of holding this girl was a high—one that even the ER couldn't compete with. Pierce looked up at the sky. Since she didn't see any stars to thank, she'd have to settle for the city lights instead.

By ten p.m. the air had grown nothing less than frigid, and Pierce began to regret her choice of fashion over function. She shivered from the inside out, trying to keep the tremors to a minimum so Cassidy wouldn't see just how uncomfortable she was. She was afraid to leave the roof. She was afraid to leave that moment. She didn't know how the next moments could possibly compare.

"Okay, I have to admit it. I'm freezing," Cassidy finally said.

Pierce laughed and rubbed her hands briskly up and down Cassidy's shoulders. "Thank God."

"We can finish the rest of the game inside?"

Pierce exhaled with a gust of relief at the realization that the night didn't have to be over yet. After all, she hadn't even gotten a chance to kiss Cassidy again, yet. Maybe it had been the cold, or the very subtle shyness that Cassidy always exuded, or maybe Pierce was just scared. But the timing had to be just right.

"Absolutely."

Once in the warmth and comfort of Cassidy's apartment, Pierce took her coat off and relaxed a little. She looked at Cassidy as she scurried around the kitchen to refill their hot chocolate, deciding she would never be anything less than terrified. For just a second, Cassidy stopped what she was doing, seemingly catching Pierce's stare, and gazed back at her. Her green-blue eyes were soft and welcoming, and the corners of her mouth turned in a coy grin. Pierce smiled back, this time stepping toward her and catching Cassidy's chin in her fingers, bringing her mouth slowly to Cassidy's and kissing her.

Pierce hadn't known what to expect of the second kiss, if there even was one. She did find it difficult to believe that it could possibly live up to the level of extraordinary that the first brought with it. And yet, there it was. All the *bam* and then some. As their lips moved, everything around them dimmed until the world outside of that particular moment in time grew blurred and irrelevant. She couldn't think. And even if she could, she had nothing to think about. Only feeling existed—a complex rainbow layered with possibility and fear and lust and risk and longing. This was the most exquisite jumble of emotions she'd ever experienced. And when it was over, and her legs shook all the way down from her knees, Pierce thought this must be what drugs felt like. She could see exactly why it would be easy to throw your life away for a high like that.

"Wow," Cassidy said, her eyes still closed and her mouth slightly ajar.

"Yeah. Wow."

"I don't know if I can stand up much longer."

Pierce laughed, shaking her head. "Jesus, me either. Can we go sit on the couch?" Pierce's legs felt ready to buckle. But she was also already thinking about kissing Cassidy again.

"Great idea."

It was after midnight as Pierce and Cassidy sat on the sofa, talking and laughing, and of course, kissing some more. The Red Sox game that provided the background noise had quickly become the post-game commentary. They laughed at David Ortiz's strange comments and debated the likelihood of a playoff berth. And then, when they looked up again from whatever piece of conversation they'd become invested in, it was after one a.m., and an episode of *Cops* was playing. Pierce knew it was late. She knew neither of them really had much interest in *Cops*, either. But still they stayed, laughing at the drunk woman who reminded Cassidy so much of one of her patients on her last shift and mocking the shortcomings of the criminal-justice system. Pierce couldn't have even recapped what they'd talked about that night, because it wasn't just talking. It was being in the other's presence. It was enjoying someone else's existence in a way that made her think of anything she could to prolong the night.

"Oh, man, it's two a.m.," Pierce said. She was waiting for Cassidy to give her a sign she was ready for her to leave. But that sign just wasn't coming.

"I'm not going to lie to you, Pierce. I kind of really don't want this date to end."

Pierce felt a smile materialize, and she placed her hand on Cassidy's knee. "Me either."

"Maybe just another half hour then. Besides, we can't miss this informercial about the Dr. Ho Belt!"

A small Chinese man now jumped eagerly around the TV spouting gospel about the magic belt he'd invented that cured lower back pain.

"I mean, how could we miss Dr. Ho?"

The perils of a cumulative sleep debt were beginning to catch up with Pierce, and her eyes began to feel dry and heavy.

"I should let you get to bed," Pierce said reluctantly, once the clock hit two thirty a.m. The last thing she wanted to do was wear out her welcome with Cassidy. She wanted to leave her wanting more. She wanted to keep Cassidy thinking about her until the next time.

"You should get some sleep too. But I really don't want you to…" Cassidy jiggled her head back and forth. "No. We can't have a sleepover on the second date."

Pierce felt a tiny surge of disappointment as she realized she'd been quietly hoping Cassidy would ask her to stay the night. So many of her recent dating endeavors had involved expedited intimacy. And Pierce had decided that hadn't worked out too well so far. Sex was the ultimate vulnerability. Doing it with someone you didn't know yet could complicate things unnecessarily. But it wasn't just sex with Cassidy Pierce was thinking about. In fact, as attracted as she was to her, Pierce felt like she could wait. She really wanted just to spend as much time as possible in Cassidy's orbit.

"Of course not." Pierce laughed. "So, when can I see you again?"

"My schedule is pretty insane."

Pierce's heart pounded as she heard the words. She knew this was part of the deal. A relationship, if that was even where this was going, with a resident wouldn't be easy. Pierce was already willing to do whatever it took to see Cassidy again. But she wasn't sure Cassidy felt the same.

"I totally get it."

"I'm off this weekend though."

"Yeah? Me too." Relief doused any of Pierce's apprehension. Cassidy was in this too. Already. They were there. Together.

"I can't wait, then." Cassidy took Pierce's face and pulled her closer, kissing her slowly until Pierce feared she might not be physically able to walk out the door any longer. But finally, she did, leaving the night behind her and an entire future of possibility ahead.

Chapter Eight

Cassidy was smart—top of her class at Harvard, high school valedictorian, National Honor Society, president of this and that—and all with the background of nearly endless sessions of chemo and radiation to contend with.

She was smart. And she was damn sure she was smart enough to know dating someone you worked with was beyond risky. If she'd been asked a month ago if she'd ever consider falling for a colleague, especially in the beginning of her residency, she would have scoffed. Then again, a month ago, she didn't know Pierce Parker. Cassidy was smart. And she was smart enough to know that all bets were now off.

Regardless, Cassidy couldn't help but think that announcing her newfound romance to the staff was a less than brilliant idea. It would be prudent to keep her relationship with Pierce a secret until it had had time to declare itself. She silently scolded herself as she walked into the ER the following afternoon. She had no relationship with Pierce. They'd shared two dates and several amazing, cell-altering, leg-quivering kisses. It was far too early to be talking about labels and commitments and exclusivity. And yet, that already seemed like the easiest place in the word for Cassidy's mind to go.

As the automatic doors to the hospital splayed open, the familiar flutter of nerves and anticipation she felt every time she came to work engulfed her. She loved this about the ER. But now, the added element of Pierce amplified those feelings a millionfold. Anything could happen. Everything could change. It already had.

Cassidy knew Pierce wasn't on the schedule for the day because, as creepy as it made her feel, she'd checked. Of course, instead of just asking Pierce, she took to stalking the master book kept in the attending's lounge when no one was looking. That was it. She'd officially reached an entirely new level of crazy, and it was still early.

Although she enjoyed putting on makeup and a nice dress, before a shift she usually threw her hair into a bun, tracked down a pair of only moderately wrinkled scrubs, and brushed her teeth. She didn't care. She had no one to impress, and her patients certainly weren't interested in how even her skin looked that day. That afternoon, she'd followed her usual routine, noting that with Pierce expected to be nowhere in sight, she still didn't have anyone to pass as more than presentable for. Cassidy's shift started like a firecracker, with a young man with bacterial meningitis fighting to keep his blood pressure to a sustainable level and a sixty-year-old whose heart had stopped while on an outing with her walking club. By six thirty p.m. Cassidy had already put in two central lines, three endotracheal tubes, and pulled three liters of fluid off an alcoholic's belly using a large needle. It was a candy store. And Cassidy was on her game like never before. She glided through the department with a confidence, a glow, that even the nurses couldn't help but notice. Several of the surliest among them had stopped her to tell her she looked unusually chipper. Cassidy would just smile slyly and glide away.

"Is Pierce here yet?" Cassidy's ears actually seemed to twitch when one of the other PAs mentioned Pierce's name.

"I haven't seen her," another PA nearby answered.

"Sorry, but is Pierce working today?" Cassidy nosed her way into the conversation happening behind her, trying to seem as nonchalant as possible for what was a very conspicuous interruption.

"Yeah. One of the others banged out sick, so she agreed to come pick up the rest of the shift."

Cassidy's legs misbehaved in a way not altogether different than they did when kissing Pierce, and she steadied herself on a nearby counter. The immediate surge of excitement and absolutely ridiculous childish giddiness quickly shifted to panic as she remembered the train wreck she looked like. In the past, Pierce had seen her without a spot of makeup, in hideous blue scrubs, with hair that said, "I just saved someone's life, so fuck you." But things were different now, after the spiked hot chocolate on rooftops, and Dr. Ho infomercials, and kisses that made her forget she'd ever kissed anyone before.

"Janie, can you cover my patients for ten minutes? I'll be right back, I promise." Cassidy frantically pulled her pager off her scrub pants and tossed it to one of her fellow residents.

"Uh, I guess so?"

"You're the best."

She took off toward the elevator and pushed the up button several times. As seconds passed, she tapped her foot quickly on the floor, drumming her fingers against her thighs.

"Come on, come on, come on," she mumbled. Several other people gathered around to wait for the same elevator to descend, and with that, Cassidy turned and jogged to the nearby stairwell, her jog turning into a sprint up the two flights of stairs to the main entrance and out onto the street. Her sprint continued for four blocks, until she reached the door of the CVS, winded and still panicked.

"Can I help you find anything, miss?" An older gentleman sat behind the register in the nearly deserted store looking desperate for something to do.

"No, thank you." Cassidy walked through the aisles as quickly as she could without drawing too much more attention to herself. Finally, she came across the one she was looking for. She scanned the products for no more than thirty seconds until she grabbed a single tube of mascara, scurrying to the man at the front.

"Anything else today?" The cashier picked up the mascara, examining it for what felt like hours, turning it over in his fingers and squinting as he tried to read the small print.

"No, that's all, thanks." Cassidy's anxiety was expanding like hot air inside her as she waited. She needed to get back to her patients. But she was also mortified that she'd been petty enough to run out to buy makeup to impress Pierce.

"Do you have a CVS card?" The man slowly, meticulously placed the mascara in a much-too-large plastic bag.

"I don't." Cassidy glanced at her watch.

"Would you like to sign up for one? It only takes a minute, and you get all kinds of coupons and such." The cashier smiled at Cassidy, and she imagined he was probably a very sweet retiree trying to bring in some supplemental change. But it still took everything in her not to grab the mascara and the mile-long receipt and run.

"Not today, thanks. I'm in kind of a hurry." She returned his kind smile, trying not to let him see her nervously tap her thumb on the counter.

"Of course. You have a wonderful day, miss."

"You too."

She walked briskly to the door and, once she was outside, broke back into a full run until she reached the ER entrance.

"What's in the bag?" Jane, her co-resident, asked once Cassidy had returned.

"Huh?" She'd been in such a rush to get back she'd forgotten to dispose of the evidence of her embarrassing midday shopping trip.

"Oh, just…tampons. Yeah. Tampons."

"Is that what you had to run off for? Dude, I have like a million in my locker."

Cassidy laughed forcefully. "Whoops. Should have just asked, I guess. Anyways, thanks again."

Without waiting for a response, Cassidy bolted for the staff bathroom and locked the door. She uncapped the makeup and painted on a quick layer of brown to her lashes, until she felt a little less like a *Gray's Anatomy/Night of the Living Dead* crossover star. When she was done, she took a second to finally get ahold of her breathing again, and left the bathroom.

Of course she didn't want to go looking for Pierce. She was already bordering on a new level of crazy and was more humiliated by the second that she'd actually cared that much about what Pierce thought of her. But then she heard Pierce's voice coming from behind the curtain in room 16. Just what Cassidy had thought. All bets were off.

❖

Never in her entire career had Pierce voluntarily come into work on her day off. But when one of her coworkers had called out that day, she'd almost jumped at the chance to. Cassidy would be there. And even if it meant seeing her in passing, as they brushed arms in the hallway or spoke quietly outside a patient room, even if she just got to watch Cassidy work for a minute or two, it was well worth it.

The ER was thumping when Pierce walked in, the pulse of the afternoon's traumas and sicknesses nearly palpable through the department. Mid-April sunshine had welcomed her on her short drive in, and the hint of spring in the air held a promise of everything good to come. Pierce was in the best kind of mood. And not even the saltiest drug seeker could break it today.

It was only Wednesday, but Pierce had known when she left Cassidy's in the early morning hours the day before that she'd never make it until the weekend without seeing her again. Torn between gratitude for Jimmy Hames for getting a late-season flu and questioning her sanity for agreeing to work only to be a little closer to a coworker, Pierce gave up on rational thought and hung her backpack on the hook in her locker out back. Her pulse quickened unexpectedly at the thought of rounding the corner and going back into the main department—at the thought of seeing Cassidy again.

"Margot, how's the day been?" Pierce exhaled some of the tension out of her shoulders when she saw Margot sitting at one of the computers in the Fast Track. The face of a friend would help ease her nerves.

"Nuts. I'm glad you're here. Everyone's sick as shit today."

"You know how much I love sick-as-shit." Pierce winked and walked off to pick up the next chart on the rack of patients to be seen.

"You're kind of messed up, Parker," Margot called after her.

A large crowd was gathered around and in room 8. This meant one thing, and one thing only—someone was critically ill. This kind of spectatorship was usually reserved for cardiac arrests and major traumas. Pierce couldn't help but gravitate toward the controlled chaos, her curiosity always winning out.

Out of the room spilled respiratory therapists and techs and nurses. The familiar hissing of high-flow oxygen and singing of the monitors echoed into the hall in spite of the surrounding noise. And if she hadn't looked closely, she might have missed the tiny blond doctor standing at the head of the bed, commanding the attention of every single person there.

"Let's get set up to intubate," Pierce heard Cassidy announce in a voice much louder and more authoritative than she'd anticipated.

"Are you sure? You know these guys are really hard to get off the vent once they're on." Ted Markey, one of the attending physicians, stood off to the side, his large, hairy arms crossed and his heavy brow raised quizzically.

Cassidy closed her eyes for the briefest of moments. It was so brief, in fact, that Pierce was sure no one but her had noticed. Because no one could possibly have been staring at Cassidy with the attention that she was as she watched from outside the open door. "Yes. I'm sure. He's been on bipap for thirty minutes now. His repeat CO2 is still 88. He's not waking up the way I'd like, and he looks terrible. I don't think we have any other choice."

Cassidy was right. Ted was testing her confidence, letting the stress of the moment pile on top of her to see if she might break. But Cassidy just stood up taller, holding an outstretched hand to the respiratory therapist and asking for the laryngoscope. Ted nodded, and Cassidy continued.

"Get ready with the intubation meds. We're going to have to go fast here, I suspect. Everyone ready?" Cassidy looked around the room at the faces of everyone on her team. Even the bitterest of the nurses seemed to trust her in that moment.

Pierce watched until the tube was in and the patient was safely on the ventilator, and the crowd began to disperse. The waiting room was full of people with sore throats and broken wrists and chest pain who needed to be seen, but she couldn't pull her eyes off Cassidy. Of course, she'd meant to escape before Cassidy actually saw she'd been watching like some kind of stalker. But she caught Cassidy's sharp, green eyes before she could. *Crap.*

"Were you watching me work?" Cassidy carried a timid grin with her as she left the resuscitation room and walked to Pierce's side. "Can't say I wasn't..." The color in her cheeks would give away any attempt at a fib. Besides, Cassidy didn't entirely seem to mind the prospect.

"And?"

She took a half step closer to Cassidy until she could feel the heat coming through her thin scrubs. "That was the sexiest thing I've ever seen."

Cassidy bit her bottom lip and glanced around her as she nervously thumbed her ID badge hanging from her neck. "You need to get your glasses checked then." She laughed.

"Just did. Last month. Trust me. I'm seeing everything better than ever." Pierce raised her eyebrows and flashed a quick smile before taking off.

"Hey, Pierce?"

"Yeah?"

"It's really good to see you..."

The day wasn't over yet for Cassidy. But Pierce would be leaving soon. The patient flow had dwindled as the evening progressed, and Cassidy was currently only waiting on the results of an MRI and a phone call back for a very non-urgent consult about a rash. Sometime after nine p.m., she noted Pierce walking toward the break room. As soon as she could, Cassidy slipped away from the main department and to the lockers. The time for worrying about being creepy or aggressive or overly eager had come and gone. And she saw no point in pretending she was thinking about anything other than being alone with Pierce again.

"All done for the night?" Pierce jumped a little. Maybe she could still turn down the awkward-factor just a bit.

"Yeah. What a day, huh?"

"Sorry. I didn't mean to sneak up on you like that." Cassidy kept her distance, standing at the end of the doorway while Pierce pulled off her stethoscope and ID and tossed them into her locker.

"You kidding? Best surprise of my night."

"So I..." Cassidy actually had nothing coherent to say. Only a want, a need that ran so deep words felt petty. In a single second, she made her way across the room, folding her arms around Pierce's neck and pressing her lips against Pierce's. It was not the slow, simmering kisses that had existed between them before. Not the smolder. It was heat. Pure, blinding white heat, with nothing gentle or probing about it. Just Pierce's hands quickly finding their way to the small of Cassidy's back and under her shirt until her fingers were gripping hard enough to leave divots. Just Cassidy's mouth opening, willingly, pleading for Pierce's tongue to find its way through and conquer it. Cassidy's nipples were so hard under her thin bra they ached, and it took every ounce of her will not to beg Pierce to take them in her teeth. She'd never needed like this. Control was everything to Cassidy, and for the first time in her life, she had absolutely none.

"Oh, shit." A stranger's voice, muffled and dreamlike, came from behind her, and Cassidy had trouble sorting reality from fantasy.

"Sorry...Margot...we were just, uh, leaving." Pierce cleared her throat and smoothed her hands down her scrubs, so much quicker to come down to earth than Cassidy seemed to be.

"No worries, you two." Margot smirked and then walked toward her locker.

"I'll see you around here tomorrow then, Cassidy?" Pierce straightened her shoulders and cleared her throat again.

"I'll see you tomorrow, Pierce."

Margot smiled at them again and left, Pierce following quickly. Cassidy was left with a staggering need that was far from being met. She ran a hand through her hair and forced out a gust of hot air. But the heat between her legs would be a persistent reminder for the rest of the night that Pierce wasn't going anywhere.

CHAPTER NINE

I want to talk about sex." Pierce had nearly exploded through Galen's office door the following afternoon.

"What do you think this is, *Game of Thrones*?"

"Gross. Not sex with you, idiot." Pierce welcomed herself in and sat without pretense in her usual chair across from Galen.

"Okay." Galen sighed. "Is this going to be another one of Pierce's exhausting, head-spinning diatribes about love? I just want to know how much espresso I'm going to need."

"I'm serious. I need your help."

Galen looked at her for a long time, tipped her chin, and loaded the nearby coffee machine. "Sounds like a double to me, then."

"At least." The espresso machine hissed one final breath of steam, and Galen plucked the tiny ceramic cup from beneath it. "You want one?"

"I'm usually more of a black-coffee kind of person," Pierce said.

"So was I, when I was your age."

"Are we really doing this 'when I was your age' bullshit again?" Pierce rolled her eyes.

"I'm thoroughly enjoying it, actually. Now," Galen closed her eyes, kicked both feet up on her desk, and took a long, dramatic sip, "you were saying something about sex?"

Pierce knew Galen well enough to be certain sex was one of her favorite topics of conversation, and usually somewhere in the forefront of her brain at most times when she wasn't in the OR.

But she also allowed Galen the guise of not being all that interested in what she had to say. Because, truth be told, she needed Galen's wisdom. Or, at the very least, her vast experience.

"My second date with Cassidy is tonight."

Galen stared at her, eyebrows raised expectantly. When Pierce didn't continue, Galen nodded thoughtfully and smiled. "And you're planning on getting lucky."

"I…No! I mean, I would never plan on that. Did you? Plan on getting lucky? With all those other girls before Rowan?"

Galen chuckled with just the smallest hint of boastfulness Pierce could tell was left over from another time, another version of her cousin. "I didn't have to plan on it. It always just sort of happened." She shrugged, and Pierce looked for the slightest hint of longing in her eyes for a life Galen had left behind. But she saw none. Galen focused on Pierce with the eyes of an addict who'd finally found sobriety and never looked back. For some reason, this gaze settled Pierce from her core all the way out to her limbs.

"Of course it did. Have you ever struggled with self-confidence for even a second, Galen?"

"All the time! But this isn't about me. This is about you. What are you so worked up about, anyway? Aren't you excited about seeing Cassidy again?"

Excited wasn't the right word. Excited was how you felt when your Little League team was up six to five in the bottom of the ninth. Excited was Christmas Eve night, in your pajamas, by the tree. Excited was a beach vacation, or a surprise party, or a visit from your best friend. Pierce didn't even have vocabulary for this. Elation, maybe. That was probably as close as she could get unless she invented a new word. This feeling was so upheaving Pierce wanted to crawl out of her skin. It was like taking Adderall with a side of cocaine, followed by a shot of heroin just for the dopamine effect. At least, that was what Pierce imagined. A "speedball," they called it in the ED. It was deadly but probably one fucking hell of a way to go.

"I'm elated," Pierce said. That was as close as she was going to get outside of her own speedballing brain. "I'm also petrified."

"Of what? Sex?" Galen was clearly trying to grasp what Pierce herself couldn't even process. What was she afraid of? Sure, sex was part of it. The idea of being naked with a girl like Cassidy Sullivan was enough to send her cowering in a corner until her days ran out. But also the simplest of things left her shaken and uncertain. She wanted to say the right things. She wanted to make Cassidy laugh. She didn't want her to catch on to the fact she was so far out of Pierce's league, Pierce was in the stands picking up hot-dog wrappers after the game. So many baseball analogies, Pierce thought. *Get your shit together.*

"Of everything. She's all I can think about. I can hardly focus on work. And when I'm not at work, I can't find enough to do to keep myself busy enough so I'm not incessantly texting her, talking to Margot about her, making playlists for her on my Spotify account." Pierce immediately regretted this last one, even before Galen had a chance to hold out her hand, accompanied by a cacophony of laughter.

"Wait a minute. You really made a playlist?"

Pierce groaned, wondering how someone with such horrendous ADD made such a great surgeon. "Focus, G."

"Right. Sorry." Galen's eyes—which so strongly resembled her own when she looked in the mirror—went soft and dreamy. "I remember those days. It's like you're on drugs."

Pierce felt her face relax. Maybe Galen understood her better than she thought. "Exactly."

"As for the drugs, I will say this much. Hang on and enjoy the ride, my friend. Because if you're asking me how to safeguard your heart, there isn't a way. I almost lost the love of my life once. And then she came back to me. And not a single minute of that was in my control."

"I had no idea doctors could be such fatalists."

"I wouldn't say that. But every time you love, you risk. No way to have one without the other."

The sentiment oddly comforted her. Galen was right. There was a chance, maybe even a damn good chance, that things with Cassidy wouldn't work out. The odds always favored the latter. "So, it's out of my hands."

"Not exactly, no. You can always choose to be lonely. But what kind of life is that?"

That wasn't even an option. Pierce guessed, then, that soul-crushing heartache was the alternative, except for that quiet voice in her ear, telling her, "Maybe not this time. Maybe this is it." And that was enough to keep her going, especially when that voice was talking about the apparent girl of Pierce's dreams.

"Great. So, that was largely unhelpful."

Galen laughed. "Sorry. They don't pay me for my bedside manner."

"Said every surgeon ever."

"Are you done ragging on surgeons yet, or did you want to talk about something I might be able to be a little helpful with?" Galen smirked.

"Sex."

"I am, as some might say, well-versed in the subject."

"Oh, believe me, I've heard how well-versed you are from just about every nurse in the ER, not to mention the few I've run into in the PACU and the cath lab."

Galen couldn't seem to help but puff her chest out just a little. "Is that a fact?"

"Don't look so pleased with yourself, Burgess."

Galen deflated a little, and her smile softened. "Just a little side note here. I'd trade every single one of those girls for one night in with Ro watching *The Great British Baking Show* and eating Thai food."

Pierce returned her smile. "I know. I'm looking for my own days of Netflix and Thai food. Meaningless sex just feels, well, meaningless now. That's what scares me."

"You're scared of how much is at stake this time."

"Yes! I know it sounds crazy, but I already feel like if this didn't work out, I'd be heartbroken." It was the first time Pierce had put words to the fear. She was already invested in Cassidy, and it was only going to get worse from here.

"And sleeping with her is going to be like putting that through a Xerox machine and blowing it up to 300 percent."

"Outdated reference, but okay, yes. I always get attached when I have sex with a girl. It's ridiculous. I've known girls I had little to no interest in, and the second we put our clothes back on, it was like I suddenly saw sunset picnics and meeting each other's families. It's biology, I know."

Galen stared at her blankly. "Huh. I never experienced that."

"Yeah, I know."

"Except with Rowan, I mean. I was already in up to my eyeballs before we had sex, but after? I was drowning in it. Obsessed. A lost cause."

Pierce took some relief knowing that even the great Galen Burgess could fall the way she seemed to be. "Let me guess. Nothing I can do about that one either, right?"

Galen made her finger into a gun and pointed it at Pierce with a wink. "Right. So just—"

"Sit back and enjoy the ride?"

"I was going to say 'buckle up.' But you know, insert any cheesy 80's movie catch phrase of your choice."

"Can you give me some tips on the mechanics, at least?" Pierce's cheeks warmed.

"The mechanics? Dude, don't call it that. It's sex, not assembling IKEA furniture."

"Again, you've been entirely unhelpful."

Galen tilted her chin and inhaled, clearly pensive. "Do you know what makes someone good in bed, Pierce?"

Pierce thought about it for a second. She really had no idea. Panic engulfed her, swelling from her feet up to her throat, until the room seemed to heat up to one hundred degrees. She had no idea! Oh God, what if she was horrible in bed and didn't even know it? She desperately scrolled through her mental black book of lovers, trying to remember anyone who might have said she held any kind of skill whatsoever under the sheets.

"Okay, first of all, stop doing that," Galen said.

"Doing what?"

"That. Overthinking everything. Sex isn't about thinking. In fact, if you're doing it right, the thinking comes before, and after.

But not during. Everything during sex is feeling, and acting. That's it."

"Feeling, and acting." Pierce parroted her.

"Good. You need to remember only two things."

Pierce pulled off a Post-it Note from Galen's desk and picked up a nearby pen.

"Two things, Pierce. You don't need to write this shit down." Galen gently pulled the Post-it away like an intervention, and Pierce took a deep breath. She was worked up, even for her. Speedball, she thought.

"Right. Go on."

"Pay attention to her. Listen to her noises, her breathing, her voice. If something makes her breath catch, do it again. If something makes her tense, do it again. Every woman's different. No one likes the same things. But if you're really tuning into her, you'll figure it out so quickly she won't be able to say your name fast enough."

Pierce liked the way all that sounded. "And what's the second thing to remember?"

"Let go," Galen said.

"What do you mean?"

"It's like what I said about not overthinking. Let your body, your mind, your heart, your…soul, or whatever, connect however it sees fit. Remember, so much of this is out of your control. At least let this be the fun part of that."

Pierce nodded. "Not so entirely unhelpful after all." She smiled, said good-bye to Galen, and left her office. She had a lot of letting go to do before that night.

Talking about the beginning of Pierce's courtship with Cassidy made Galen all kinds of sentimental. It wasn't hard to remember the kind of pure, unfiltered pining Pierce displayed. Every time Galen looked at Rowan, even years later, she still saw the same surgical intern with the glasses and high bun whose presence hardly seemed to fit in her tiny frame. And with that sight came the same longing and downright appreciation Galen knew she would never stop feeling, no matter how many decades or centuries passed between them.

"Baby?" Galen opened the door to their apartment only to be greeted by a bombardment of Walk the Moon coming through the small Bose speaker in the corner.

Rowan came dancing around the corner from the bedroom, wearing one of Galen's button-down shirts, open at the collar, over lace panties. She flashed sultry eyes at Galen as she dropped her ass to the ground and ran her hands down her thighs, then quickly shook her head to the beat of the music until her hair was flowing like cotton on a line. Galen laughed heartily and dropped her briefcase, sidling up to her and taking both of Rowan's hands. In one smooth motion they'd practiced many times in their very own living room, Galen twirled Rowan under her arm, catching her around the waist and dipping her back until her wild hair brushed the floor.

The music was still too loud for either of them to speak, but Galen didn't mind. She grabbed Rowan around the hips and swayed with her, looking into the eyes that felt like home. Pure, unfiltered home.

"Marry me," Galen shouted over the final cadence of the song.

"What?" Rowan stopped, finally hit pause on her phone, and laughed. "Sorry. I got caught up in my own dance party here. Suzy hated it. What did you just say?"

Galen smiled, keeping her gaze locked hard on Rowan's and still grasping her hips. "I said," she paused, wanting to slow the words down as much as possible, "marry me."

Rowan wound her arms around Galen's neck and kissed her. "Anytime, anywhere. You know that."

"I'm serious, Ro."

"So am I. But I want a real proposal, Dr. Burgess." Rowan moved her hand to Galen's cheek and moved with a deliberately torturous pace, finally brushing her lips against Galen's until Galen's own head felt as if it might detach from her body.

"You deserve the greatest proposal in history," Galen said, once she could catch her breath again.

"And don't forget a very, very large ring." Rowan winked and slapped Galen softly on the ass.

"You've become very spoiled, you know that?"

"Hey. I'm not going to marry you for your good looks."

"What about my intellect? Or my skills in bed?" Galen pouted, trailing behind Rowan, who was already heading for their bedroom.

"I'll have to think about that last one. But I might need a little more evidence." Before Galen could even get to her next thought, Rowan had stripped off the shirt she'd stolen from Galen, revealing nothing but her smooth, pale skin stretched over her naked body, and those very lacy, very black panties that barely covered a thing.

"You can have all the evidence you want." As she had to do so often, Galen forced herself to slow down, brushing her fingers up Rowan's bare torso and then through her hair. Even after all this time, she wanted Rowan with a hunger that felt like lifelong deprivation. It took everything she had not to devour all of her as soon as she was allowed. "As a matter of fact, you can have whatever ring you want. I'll buy you ten rings. Or maybe just one really, really big one."

Rowan curved her fingertips between the buttons of Galen's shirt and pulled it open the rest of the way, softly biting Galen's bottom lip, then her earlobe, and finally the nape of her neck, until Galen was dizzy with need. "How about I just get you? Forever."

"You have me," Galen whispered. "Forever."

The sun was long down by the time Galen gathered enough strength to nudge Rowan awake. Rowan didn't get many chances to sleep, which always racked Galen with guilt when she had to wake her.

"You should eat something, baby," Galen said. "It's after eight."

Rowan stirred and smiled, her eyes still puffy and her lids half closed. "I'm okay. I promise."

"Mhmm. And what did you have today?" Galen pulled Rowan's head onto her chest and stroked her hair.

"Some saltines. Two ice-cream bars. And…a bunch of mini Snickers bars?"

Galen laughed. "One cannot survive on carbs alone, my dear."

"I've done all right so far!"

Rowan wasn't far off, given that her youth and a particularly boisterous metabolism allowed her to eat like a toddler and still look like a Greek goddess. Still, Galen couldn't help but want to take care of her. "Let me make you something. How about an omelet? Extra cheese?"

Rowan's face lit up and she pecked Galen's cheek. "I'd love that. Thank you."

"Anything for you."

"What's gotten into you today? You're usually a hopeless romantic, but this is a little something extra…I can't remember the last time we had evening sex and omelets in bed. Not that I'm complaining."

Galen got out of bed and covered herself with her discarded undershirt she found near the door. "Talking to Pierce today about Cassidy just reminded me how lucky I am."

Rowan feigned displeasure "Talking about Cassidy has you like this?"

"Stop it." Galen walked back over to the bed and flung herself on top of Rowan until she was straddling her, Rowan's hands pinned behind her head. "Talking about the beginning, about finding that one, *the* one…I still feel that way about you, Ro."

"You promise?" Rowan's eyes twinkled with the hint of vulnerability Galen loved so much.

"Pinkie promise."

"I love you."

"I love you. More than you could possibly know."

Galen released Rowan's wrists and kissed her forehead. "Let me get to those omelets then."

"And when you come back, I want to hear all about the last of Pierce's love stories."

Chapter Ten

It had been the longest two days of Cassidy's life. Each minute of the forty-eight-plus hours seemed to drag by in excruciating seconds, as if she were staring at a clock whose hands just wouldn't move. For a few brief moments she could avoid thinking about Pierce. But these were usually in the ED, and usually when she held a patient's life in her hands and didn't have room in her brain for much else. Still, the instant the crisis settled, Pierce was back in her head, threatening her focus, and mostly, her sanity. After a couple of days, just the memory of kissing Pierce shouldn't feel so much like slipping into warm water. But it did. As she fumbled through her closet trying to decide on what to wear, she ached and writhed in the same pleasant way she had every time she imagined her lips against Pierce's again.

Cassidy didn't plan to sleep with Pierce that night. In fact, she was adamantly against it. In her younger life, before she came out, Cassidy had used sex with men as a form of protection, never about her wants or needs. Usually, it consisted of some gross boy with traces of a mustache wearing too much Axe body spray shoving his hand into her pants behind the bathroom stall at a school dance. Not anymore. She would never engage in sex for anything again except for connection, and pleasure, and intimacy. And all those things involved trust. That was why she had learned to wait to share those things with a woman and why she intended to wait with Pierce.

But when Pierce rang her doorbell ten minutes later, standing outside in the late spring sunset, wearing a pair of dark jeans over black motorcycle boots and a T-shirt that stretched over her broad shoulders and chest, Cassidy thought maybe waiting wouldn't be as easy as she'd imagined.

"Hi." She still felt insanely nervous every time Pierce was within a fifteen-foot radius. This wasn't altogether unusual, given Cassidy's tendency for shyness, but this was an entirely new level of rattled. Her hands shook in the pockets of her jacket, and her heart, which knew to stay steady even in the face of death, was skipping through her chest like a stone. It was the best kind of fear—perhaps a new norm for her.

"Hey." Pierce smiled her big, infectious smile that brought out two charming dimples on either side of her cheeks, and her green eyes grew just enough for Cassidy to notice. She took Cassidy in her arms, tentatively, as if she weren't sure whether the embrace would be welcome. This was all still so new, Cassidy reminded herself. This was the beginning, the part where no one knows exactly where they stand or what to do. Where no one wants to overstep the boundaries or push the other one away. Where no one wants to get hurt. But she was certainly glad Pierce had taken that risk. Because her embrace was all Cassidy had been thinking about for days.

And it felt even better than Cassidy had remembered. Pierce's arms, bare in the unseasonably warm weather, were soft and strong, and they gripped Cassidy with a sense of purpose. The air around them went dry, and a tingle of a thrill ran from where their bodies met all the way down between her legs. Reluctantly, one of them, Cassidy wasn't sure which, finally pulled away, but they remained connected by their fingertips, which they still kept gently pressed together. For a minute, Cassidy thought Pierce might kiss her again. Pierce's intense gaze stayed locked on hers, much like it had that very first night after Mike O'Leary's. Instead, Pierce looked shyly away and took a step back. This might become a battle of introverts, one always leaving the other to make the next move. However, if their last kiss was any indication, Pierce was anything but passive behind the bedroom door.

Even after two (two-and-a-half?) dates, not to mention months of working together, Cassidy worried she and Pierce would run out of things to say. She worried about the typical awkwardness that accompanied the majority of early dating experiences. As someone generally terrified of most social interactions, this was expected. Typical, even. But not with Pierce. Any fear she might have had about their connection floundering, or even being something slightly less than the fantasy she'd built in her head, tumbled down around her as soon as Pierce was in her sight.

"Come upstairs." Cassidy took Pierce by the hand with an unexpected confidence and led her up the creaking wooden stairs to her apartment. The baseball game was already showing on the oversized flat-screen TV on the wall of Cassidy's living room.

Pierce took a seat on the sofa, the cushions softening around her like white sand. "I hope you don't mind being at your place again. I really like it here. Brighton is so…"

"Full of students?" Cassidy pulled two Sam Adams from the fridge and popped off the tops.

"Yes!" Pierce laughed. "Honestly, I'm bitter about the fact I have to live there on a PA's salary. Boston is so ridiculously overpriced."

Cassidy brought the drinks to her and sat down, making sure she was close enough to Pierce to allow for some degree of contact. "Try doing it on a resident's salary. But it is the greatest city in the country, as far as I'm concerned."

"I've always loved it. It's always felt like home."

"Same." Cassidy's mind flashed to summers spent at Boston Children's Hospital—the smell of antiseptic, the sounds of monitors blaring to the background of some children's performer singing Disney songs in one of the common rooms, the heat of the city when she was allowed to take walks outside in the hospital garden. It was strange how such a horrible time, a time when she and everyone in her life honestly believed she would die, could be laced with such sweetness. She'd been well-cared for there. And even when the stress grew too much for her parents, Boston somehow began to feel safe to her.

"Have you spent a lot of time here? You know, before now?"

Cassidy smiled politely. She wasn't going into her past with Pierce. Not yet, at least. The last thing she wanted was to be seen as fragile—a ticking time bomb. "Some, but not as much as you, I'd imagine." Cassidy suddenly foraged for ways to change the subject. "So how come you left Atlanta?"

Pierce laughed with just a hint of a sneer and scratched her head. "I'd tell you, but I don't think you're supposed to talk about your exes on a third date."

"We're lesbians. The same rules don't apply. Go on. Tell me. You know, if you're comfortable, I mean."

"You're sure?"

"Absolutely. I like you, Pierce." Somehow that felt like the understatement of her life. "I want to know you, icky-girlfriend past included."

Pierce grinned and shifted closer to Cassidy until their thighs were touching. She slung one arm around the back of the sofa, just behind Cassidy's head, and Cassidy let herself drift toward her.

"It was a bad relationship. I gave, and she took. But she was never really in it, you know? Always one foot out the door."

"Ah. yes. I've had one or two of those myself."

Pierce scoffed. "I find that hard to believe."

"What? Why?"

"Who in their right mind wouldn't be absolutely obsessed with you?"

Cassidy felt her skin transform from its usual spring pale to a fiery red. "I could say the same thing about you."

"Well, Katie was one of them."

It was typical of women to carry some degree of relationship baggage with them into the next. But Cassidy took a long moment to search Pierce's face, seeing just how much this baggage still held claim on her. "Are you...over it?"

Pierce inhaled thoughtfully, paused, and then nodded with resolution. "Yes. I'll be honest, Cass. I haven't thought about anyone, or anything else, since we met."

Pierce locked her gaze onto Cassidy's. One hand moved to Cassidy's knee, and the other arm, still balancing on the back of the couch, curved around Cassidy, her remaining hand now gripping Cassidy's shoulder.

"Yeah. Me either." Cassidy wasn't even sure she'd said the words out loud, as they came through only in a hoarse whisper. Pierce tilted Cassidy's chin between her thumb and index finger, bringing their lips just a breath apart, and Cassidy closed her eyes, waiting. Their mouths met as if by some kind of biological or chemical destiny. Something stronger than either of them could ever be was pulling them incessantly together. The explosion came, this time seemingly more brilliant than the last. Cassidy ran her hand through Pierce's short, thick hair, grabbing pieces of it as Pierce's tongue skimmed hers.

"I really, really love kissing you," Pierce said between gasps of air.

"I really, really do too."

Cassidy placed her palm on Pierce's cheek and leaned near again, this time taking exactly what she needed, at a slow, deliberate pace that drove Pierce to grasp Cassidy's hips and pull her closer, until her legs were wrapped around Pierce's waist. Cassidy wasn't going to sleep with Pierce that night. As much as she wanted to, she needed to save that level of intimacy for a later date. But that was easier said than done when the heat coming off Pierce's jeans was radiating through to her own center. Pierce's fingers traced just inside the band of Cassidy's pants, resulting in no hope for this particular pair of panties she was wearing. Jesus. She couldn't remember ever wanting anyone so much.

Pierce continued to kiss her, confidently but with a sense of caution, as if constantly looking for consent. Cassidy liked this approach. She liked feeling in control. Pierce's hands now dared to venture up under Cassidy's flowing blouse, gently sketching patterns on the skin of her back until the ache between her legs grew insufferable. Pierce's touch moved slowly around to Cassidy's breasts, where she ran just one finger under the cup of Cassidy's bra and brushed one of her hard nipples. A jolt so strong it threatened to throw her from the sofa rushed through Cassidy. No way would she be able to wait for Pierce. And absolutely everything about that urgency felt right to her.

Succumbing to the burning in her skin, the throbbing in her chest, the lightness of her head, Cassidy pulled her blouse up and over her head, tossing it to the floor.

"Is this okay?" Pierce's eyes held a sweetness Cassidy hadn't seen yet, only confirming for Cassidy that this was very much okay.

"Yes. Is it okay with you?"

"More than okay."

No one had ever asked Cassidy that question before. Of all the boys she'd reluctantly given into in her earlier days, or even the few girls as she got older, none of them had asked for permission to touch her. And she had no idea consent could be so incredibly sexy.

By the time Pierce shifted her body weight onto Cassidy's, gently pinning her on the cushions, Cassidy was desperate for her. Pierce drove her thigh between Cassidy's legs, and Cassidy heard herself release a low moan. She deftly unhooked Cassidy's bra in one smooth flick of her fingers, then propped herself up to remove her own T-shirt. Cassidy took a minute to absorb the image in front of her, Pierce's toned, taut body every bit as perfect as Cassidy had imagined over and over again. This is the sexiest woman I've ever seen, Cassidy thought. And I'm in big fucking trouble.

Now skin to skin, Pierce's bare chest pressed against hers, the need was excruciating. Everything about Pierce felt so good. A fine layer of sweat built between them as they glided against one another. Pierce's hand slowly moved to the button on Cassidy's fly and carefully pushed it through the loop, then moved farther down, slowly rubbing outside Cassidy's pants with a budding tempo that made Cassidy buck her hips, begging for more, begging for everything. When Pierce seemed to decide she was ready, she dipped the hand inside Cassidy's waistband, once again slowing her pace to a blinding tease until Cassidy was sure she would cum in the next ten seconds. As if reading her thoughts, Pierce slid first one finger inside her, then a second, as Cassidy thrust against her hand, grasping Pierce's wrist as she released in waves of white heat that flowed one after another, finally collapsing in a heap of limp limbs and sweat and muscles fully depleted. Pierce smiled and rested her head on Cassidy's chest, which was still heaving.

"Wow." Cassidy was still waiting for her vision to fully return.

"You are insanely sexy," Pierce said, propping her chin up in her hand and looking down at Cassidy, who followed with a hearty laugh.

"Oh, I think that would be you."

"How am I so into you this soon?"

Cassidy's heart squeezed in her chest and her stomach tightened. "I think it's fair to say my feelings are way out of proportion here."

"Ha. Sounds like an ICD-10 code." Pierce laughed. "Billing code 10-5J9, feelings out of proportion."

Cassidy erupted after her. "One of the small perks of dating someone in health care—they find billing and coding jokes endearing."

"Or we just have the same lame sense of humor."

"Either way, it works. Look, I'm starving. Any interest in getting pizza delivered? Because no way in hell am I leaving this apartment for the rest of the night. We have to do that at least another five or six times."

Pierce leaned down and kissed Cassidy softly, her face reflecting pure contentment. "Pizza sounds amazing."

A few minutes later, Cassidy appeared from the bedroom where she'd gone to change.

"What?" Pierce was staring at her, a sly grin on her perfect mouth that Cassidy was still so enamored with. Cassidy sat on the arm of the sofa wearing a weather-beaten Stanford Med T-shirt over a black satin thong.

"You." Pierce shook her head, still grinning. "You are every single bit my dream girl right now, do you know that?"

Cassidy smiled back. "That may be the best thing I've ever heard."

❖

It had been a long time since Cassidy had experienced one of her nightmares, and she awoke in a cold sweat, beyond embarrassed that it had to happen next to Pierce. She glanced over at Pierce, who was still sleeping peacefully against Cassidy's shoulder, her mouth just slight agape. Thank God.

The dream was typical. Cassidy found herself in a doctor's office, usually one that looked like something out of the 1950s instead of the modern, sterile places she was used to. The doctor, who in this case was one of her old medical-school professors, told her the cancer was back. After nearly nine years in remission, the lymphoma had returned with a vengeance, and she would need to go through it all again—radiation, chemo, surgery. All of it. The fear was so tangible Cassidy still felt it when she opened her eyes. She took a deep breath and exhaled slowly, lying back down and curling up next to Pierce as close as she could without waking her. It was only a dream—a nightmare. She was healthy. And happier than she could ever remember being.

Chapter Eleven

The aftershock was unrivaled. Cassidy had never felt anything like it. Even in the wake of her nightmare, she woke up next to Pierce the next morning with a thrill, a stir in her she'd never really experienced before. She couldn't believe she was lying next to this woman.

"Hey." Pierce must have noticed Cassidy staring at her when she opened her eyes.

"Good morning."

Cassidy pulled her knees up and hugged them against her still-bare chest. It was after eleven a.m. She couldn't remember the last time she'd slept so long—or so well. They'd slept the way new lovers always do—limbs intertwined, heads on chests, each breath in sync with the other. Cassidy couldn't remember ever feeling so safe, so settled. And now, the aftershock. Pierce wasn't just a one-off or a daydream. She was real. This was happening.

"Do you need to rush off? Or do you want to grab some breakfast?"

"No, nope, I have nowhere to be." Cassidy decided she'd probably responded just a little too eagerly for her own liking.

"Great. There's a fantastic little diner I've been to a couple times. It's only a couple of blocks away. They make great waffles and..." Pierce stopped and glanced at her cell phone sitting on the bedside table. "Well, fuck me. I guess it's almost lunchtime, huh?"

Cassidy laughed, leaning into Pierce as Pierce's fingers gently stroked her back. "I guess so."

"So…sandwiches then?"

"Sandwiches sound great." Cassidy lifted her head and kissed Pierce's chin. Really, Pierce could have suggested breakfast, or lunch, or frozen TV dinners. Cassidy just needed more time in Pierce's arms, with her voice, in her orbit.

"You know," Pierce propped herself up on one arm, grinning down at Cassidy, "last night was…wow."

"I tend to agree. 'Wow' seems to be becoming a theme here already."

"It sure does." Pierce brought her lips to Cassidy's, the same bolt of heat from the night before setting through her like wildfire. As her mind emptied of everything that wasn't wanting Pierce, she rolled Pierce over onto her back, straddling Pierce's narrow hips and planting her hands on Pierce's chest. She slowly moved her own hips over Pierce's in small, torturous circles, until the muscles in her thighs tightened and pulsed, demanding she move faster until relief came. Pierce moaned in a low, guttural tone that made it even harder for Cassidy to control her tempo. When she didn't think she could hold on much longer, she slipped her hand between Pierce's legs, taking back the moment by giving Pierce exactly what she wanted, by taking everything that was hers. Cassidy noted the tension in Pierce's hips as she writhed closer to her, her breath quickening and the sweat budding over her neck and chest. It wasn't long before Pierce let out one last moan that sounded like it came from somewhere far in her depths, then went limp.

"On second thought." Pierce was panting still. "We could always have something delivered."

The day had flown by far too quickly. Pierce had noticed this about spending time with Cassidy. Days felt like hours, hours felt like minutes, and minutes felt impossible. Each day simply didn't have hours to be with her. How could that already be such an issue? They hardly knew each other. And yet, as they sat on Cassidy's couch, the late-May sun already setting behind the buildings stretched out in front of Cassidy's living room window, Pierce already dreaded leaving her. They'd had nearly two full days together. They'd walked around the city, had coffee in the park, dinner on the roof of the nearby restaurants. But mostly, they'd stayed in bed. The sex. God damn it, the sex was out of this world. Every little thing Cassidy did was the new sexiest thing Pierce had ever seen. Even watching her get out of the shower and towel off her hair was life-changing. But that all came in second to lying next to her, stroking the soft skin of her stomach or kissing her neck, and falling asleep only to wake up next to that smile. It would be so damn easy to get used to it all.

It was crazy. But Pierce had to do something to stay in Cassidy's presence for just a little while longer. "Have you heard they just did a series of *The Hot Zone* on HBO?"

She was desperate.

"You mean, like, that book by Richard Preston? I loved that one!" Pierce wasn't sure if Cassidy was actually that excited about Ebola or if she was just trying to keep the night going too.

"Me too! It premieres in about an hour. What if we…you know, maybe watched it? Together?" Pierce immediately felt foolish. She must have sounded pathetic, begging Cassidy to spend just another second or two with her. "You know, if it's not too much time with me…"

Cassidy's face lit up so brightly it almost cast shadows on the white walls behind them. "It's not too much time, Pierce. In fact, I can't seem to get enough time with you…"

Pierce smiled and put her arm around Cassidy's shoulder, pulling her closer. "I have this friend from Atlanta. Her name is Jayla. She's great, but the girl literally defines 'U-Hauling.' This girlfriend she has now came over on their first date and just kind of never left." Pierce chuckled and shook her head. "I always thought she was nuts. But you know, now I kind of see how that could happen."

Cassidy laughed with her, and Pierce found herself quickly relieved she hadn't come across as too crazy. "Yeah. I can kind of see that too."

❖

Of course Pierce hadn't left Cassidy's that night. Even after an entire six-episode binge of humanity-destroying viruses, their endless conversation and, of course, a little more sex (okay, a lot more sex) kept them awake until all hours. Cassidy hadn't needed to ask Pierce to stay over again this time. Instead, they both fell asleep blissfully in front of the open window which poured in slow gusts of warm spring air, blanketing Pierce in a sense of longing for things still to come and a steadiness she'd never before known.

If they were being honest, Pierce did ultimately leave because both she and Cassidy had to be at work. Cassidy was rotating through the ICU for the month, which meant Pierce wouldn't have the nearly hourly high of knowing Cassidy was right around the corner from her at any given point in time. It was disheartening, although they were both still in the same hospital. The ICU rotation was notorious for sleepless nights, twenty-four-hour days, and the near meltdown of most, if not all, emergency-medicine residents. Cassidy had tried to be optimistic about this situation, seemingly to keep Pierce around, but it was clear to Pierce that she wouldn't have a lot of time left for her during the upcoming weeks. She was fine with this prospect. She'd gone through PA school. And although it certainly wasn't the same as residency, she understood the demands of medicine in a way that those outside the world couldn't. Still, it didn't take away the gnawing pit that expanded in her gut when she realized it may be an indeterminate amount of time before she could see Cassidy again.

When she woke up the next morning, Cassidy's soft, warm shape still in the bed beside her, the pit was gone. Cassidy, who'd been standing in her closet attempting to piece together a clean set of scrubs, turned to her and smiled.

"You're awfully cute in the morning, you know that?" Cassidy, still in her usual tiny panties and oversized T-shirt that Pierce had learned to love so quickly, emptied her hands and jumped back into bed, curling into Pierce and nuzzling her head under Pierce's chin.

"Don't go to work."

Cassidy groaned. "I don't want to. Can't I just stay in this bed with you all day? Or how about until we die?"

"Mmm." Pierce kissed the top of her head, breathing in hints of flowers and lavender and musk from Cassidy's still-wild hair. "I will if you will."

"I'm going to miss not seeing your face every time I walk by an exam room."

"I'm only six floors down. But I know what you mean..."

"My next day off is..." Cassidy paused, her face hardening. "Twelve days from now. But will you please spend it with me?"

Pierce's eyes watered inexplicably, and she blinked hard trying to stop her tears. She was so momentarily touched that Cassidy had no free time and still wanted to spend it all with her. All of Pierce's hesitation in their first hours together at Mike O'Leary's or in Cassidy's apartment about Cassidy's want to commit to something had more than vanished. This was what she had been waiting for—someone who thought she was worth putting the time in. Someone Pierce thought was more than worth driving five-hundred miles at midnight or flying cross-country for. From the first instant their lips met, Pierce knew. Cassidy Sullivan was everything she'd ever dreamed of and so many things she could never have even imagined. But the really miraculous part was that Cassidy seemed to be feeling the same way.

"I'm yours." And Pierce had probably never meant any two words more in her entire life.

"Just promise me you'll try to pop up to the Unit and see me once in a while?" Pierce understood fully the complex sadness to Cassidy's voice, laced with hope and excitement and the thrill of that little voice in Pierce's head that was louder than ever—*this could be it.*

Pierce wasn't scheduled to work until later that night, and no way in hell was she going to get anymore sleep. Not when Cassidy's touch was still radiating off her, the brush of her mouth on Pierce's skin still so raw, so real, it was like it was still happening. The speedball was in full effect, and Pierce figured she might have a heart attack if this kept up. Well worth it, she told herself.

"What are you doing right now?" It was the middle of Galen's day, but Pierce hoped she could convince her to leave work and distract her.

"Working. You know I'm always working."

Pierce could hear Galen's espresso machine hissing in the background. "You don't have any cases today though. It's Monday. Conference day. So put down your charts, send your residents to clinic, and come out with me."

Silence on the other end of the line. Then, Galen exhaled thoughtfully. "And do what?"

"I want to buy a BMW."

Galen spewed laughter. "A BMW? Don't you think this hero-worship thing has gone on long enough?"

"Please. You aren't the only person on earth to drive a Bimmer, you know."

"Borrow my clothes. Find a girlfriend who looks eerily like mine. Work in my hospital. Now you want to drive my car?" But Pierce could hear the flattery in Galen's voice.

"Okay, so I like your car. And you have some pretty sweet Tom Ford jackets that look way better on me than you. Oh, and Cassidy looks nothing like Rowan." Maybe, if you squinted at a distance of about a hundred yards, at dusk, there was a little resemblance. But only a little. "Are you going to come with me or not? I found one I like at a dealer nearby, and honestly, I don't know shit about cars."

"Fine. I'll help. But only so you don't get ripped off."

"Thank you." Pierce smiled to herself.

"But just one question. Why a new car? This feels pretty impulsive."

Truth be told, it was impulsive. That was how Pierce made most of her decisions. In the past, that was how she'd managed her romantic relationships, job prospects, and just about every other major life decision. But she'd learned to slow down and think about those. She'd worked her whole career for the smaller things, the splurges that she knew deep down she could afford and would bring her a sense of success and pleasure. Pierce woke up that morning and decided she would trade her piece of garbage 2009 Subaru for a car that symbolized how she felt about the turns her life was taking. Something fun and sexy. Something that said "I've made it." And, though she'd never admit this fact to Galen, they both knew she idolized her cousin in an embarrassingly juvenile way.

"It kind of is. But fuck it. I have a good job. I make good money. I should drive a car that says I'm a successful career woman who lives in the big city. Not one that says 'I still have my parents' insurance.'"

"You know what I always say…"

"You can't take it with you?"

"You can't take it with you. I'll pick you up in an hour. Wear something that says 'don't try to pull a fast one on me, you bitch.'" Galen hung up the phone and Pierce laughed out loud, not feeling at all foolish for the sound echoing off the walls of her empty apartment. And she sent that same message out into the universe— don't try to pull a fast one on me, you bitch. Not when everything was finally perfect. Not now.

"She's a beauty," Galen said. She patted the hood of the car with her palm, took a lap around, and whistled.

"God, you are such a dad."

"Rowan's biological clock ticks with tiny baby shoes and infants in grocery stores. Mine comes out with bad puns and BBQ grills."

"You guys think you'll have a kid?" Pierce immediately pictured Cassidy, pushing a stroller, walking next to Pierce with a toddler strapped to her back, through a late-fall farmer's market. Jesus Christ, what was wrong with her?

"I do. But not anytime soon. Ro has to finish residency, and then she wants to do a fellowship in surgical oncology. So it'll be a long road."

"How did you get through it? You know, both of you being residents and all?"

Galen opened the door of the new-to-Pierce BMW and ran her hand gently over the buttery, black leather. "Get in. I want to take this girl out for a spin."

"What? I just got it! You think I'm going to let you drive it? I've seen your lead foot. Hell, no."

"Tough luck. That was the price of admission for getting me out here. Now get in. You're taking me out for ice cream." Galen pressed the button that started the ignition, and the car roared to life. "JP Licks? Or Coldstone?"

"Either one," Pierce said, climbing into the passenger seat and rolling down the window. "Just don't make me go to that vegan place Rowan likes."

"Hey, it's not that bad. But we're getting the real stuff today, my friend."

Galen parked the car a few miles away, on a busy metered street near the Boston University campus. It was early in the afternoon, but the sun still sat low in the sky, a subtle reminder that although the air was unseasonably hot for May, an entire summer stretched ahead of them. What could that upcoming summer look like? Lying on a beach next to Cassidy, under an umbrella, the ocean breeze tossing Cassidy's hair like a model's in a magazine photo. Late-night ice cream runs like this one. Falling asleep under the open window of Cassidy's bedroom, as they had the night before. It all felt too surreal, like a fairy tale Pierce never thought anyone actually lived. But there it was.

"You asked me about how Rowan and I managed when we were both going through residency," Galen said. She licked her ice-cream cone, a look that Pierce could only interpret as introspective painting her face, as they sat side by side on the one deserted bench on Comm Ave.

Pierce nodded.

"Why? Are you asking because of Cassidy?"

"She's in the MICU right now. You know what that's like. I won't see her for over a week." Twelve days, Pierce thought. Twelve days.

"Rowan and I had it a little easier, since we were in the same program. But a lot of times our shifts didn't line up. We'd go days without seeing each other, entire weeks on end when she was on days and I was on nights and we were lucky to pass each other in the hallway."

Pierce felt her brow dip and her mouth tighten into a thin line. "How did you make it work?"

"You just find the time when you can. Sometimes it's as small as a coffee drop-off and two minutes of face-to-face time. But you'd be surprised just how much that can do to get you through."

"Do you think it'd be weird? You know...if I surprised her and brought her coffee or something? Do you think it's too early?"

Pierce fished out the last spoonful of cookie dough from her cup and crushed the cup in her fist.

"Do you think she'd find it weird?"

Pierce pondered the question. "No. Not at all." After their tilt-a-whirl beginning, Pierce was certain Cassidy was exactly where she was.

"Then there's your answer." Galen clapped her on the shoulder.

"Thanks, G."

Galen nodded, and they were silent for a long time.

"It really is a nice car," Galen finally said.

Pierce chuckled. "It sure is...It sure is."

Chapter Twelve

The medical intensive care unit (largely known as the MICU) was every bit as horrendous as had been rumored. Cassidy was only four hours into her second eighteen-hour shift and had already intubated three patients, put in five central lines, and been yelled at by at least a half-dozen nurses for not putting a diet order in for Mr. Brodski fast enough or not prioritizing Mrs. Greenberg's anal itching. No matter how quickly she moved, Cassidy couldn't seem to be in enough places at once. And she couldn't shake feeling like she was slowly drowning in the deep end of a swimming pool, which also happened to be on fire, where she knew how to tread water just long enough to grow fatigued and eventually succumb to her own overexertion.

"Dr. Sullivan, Mr. Pond in bed five's heart rate is 60. Do you still want me to give the Lopressor?"

"Dr. Sullivan, I really need that Tylenol order for Mr. Newcomb."

"Dr. Sullivan, the new admission is bucking his tube. You need to give him more propofol."

The line of nurses who needed something from Cassidy was seemingly out the door, each request more daunting than the next. By the time Ginger, one of the less-heinous nurses in the MICU, asked her to see Mr. Brodski immediately for his complaint of new onset penile discharge, she only wanted to see Pierce again. Her bed had become her escape. Namely, her bed with Pierce. When the tubes and lines and crying family members and annoying nurses became too much, she retreated to the recent nights, with Pierce in her bed, by her side, her arms firmly around Cassidy like nothing could touch her. She took a deep breath and smiled, a sense of peace slowly entering the chaos, and went back to work. Somewhere in the middle of replacing Mr. Pond's nasogastric tube, a task the nurses usually did but reserved occasionally for new residents still working their way off the shit list, Cassidy heard a ding from her scrub pocket.

It was some time before she was able to check it. Probably a consultant finally responding about Mr. Brodski's new renal failure. Or maybe her mother texting to tell her the deer in their backyard had come back for the season. The message was from Pierce. And although it was about thirty minutes old, Cassidy nearly left the ground in her efforts to leave the unit. Pierce had said she was outside in the family waiting area. Cassidy hoped with every little bit of strength she had left that Pierce was still there.

"Ginger, I'll be right back," she called across the nurses' station. "Caroline is in the dictation room if you need anything."

The round, carrot-headed nurse, who Cassidy thought was aptly named, offered a brief smile and returned to her computer. Cassidy scanned her ID badge and pressed the large access button on the wall, sending the double doors creaking open so excruciatingly slowly she thought she might actually have to push them. Once out in the lobby, she looked to her left, then to her right. A middle-aged couple in complementary Vineyard Vines polos sat holding each other grimly. Cassidy recognized them as the daughter and son-in-law of Mr. Brodski, who was likely going to die of his metastatic pancreatic cancer in the next day or so. It was easy to disconnect from patients when they were just bodies on a stretcher, machines breathing for them, drugs keeping them alive. It wasn't personal, only a natural (or, sometimes not) transition to death. But the living got to Cassidy. Those who would be left behind.

She shook her head, letting the empathy that was all too strong at times fall away. She looked to her right again, at another person tucked away in the corner. Staring at Pierce was like breathing fresh air after being rescued from that burning swimming pool. It was survival.

"God, you are a sight for sore fucking eyes," Cassidy said. She placed her hands on Pierce's strong chest and collapsed, letting her head rest under Pierce's chin as she had just two long mornings ago.

"I'm sorry to keep showing up like this unannounced, but I thought you could use some coffee." Pierce brushed away a strand of Cassidy's hair that had fallen out of its bun, then reached behind her and picked up one of the coffees that had been teetering on a nearby chair.

"You have no idea how good it is to see you. I've been...I can't believe I'm about to say this...I've been missing you like crazy, Pierce."

Pierce grinned with her underlying confidence that stayed just far enough away from ego, and Cassidy actually swooned. "I miss you too. I haven't been thinking about much else for two days. Really, coffee is just a cover."

"It's a great cover." Cassidy took the cup and inhaled deeply. "The good stuff too."

"Pavement. I figured MICU calls for something stronger than that watered-down trash downstairs. Cream, no sugar, right?"

It was probably just the exhaustion, but tears welled up behind Cassidy's eyes and threatened to spill out in an embarrassing shower. "That's right." For the first time in her life, Cassidy felt like she didn't have to be so strong. For the first time, she felt taken care of.

"Oh, I almost forgot." Pierce reached behind her to one of the nearby waiting room chairs and picked up a white, waxed-paper bag with a few grease stains seeping through.

"What's this?"

"A glazed doughnut from Union Square."

Pierce handed Cassidy the bag, and the tears once again appeared, but this time it was like trying to kink a firehose. She threw her arms around Pierce's neck, partially out of sheer fatigue and gratitude, and partially out of a desperation for Pierce not to see her embarrassing display of weakness.

"Oh, God, this is so humiliating. I don't know what's wrong with me." She couldn't cover up her daft show of emotion. Not when Pierce's shirt was already soaked where Cassidy's face had been.

"What? Stop that." Pierce pulled away, lifting Cassidy's chin gently in her hand until their eyes were forced together.

"I'm a doctor, for fuck sake. I shouldn't be so soft. Please don't think I'm crazy. I swear, I'm not crazy."

Pierce laughed and kissed her softly, sending Cassidy's embarrassment cascading away in a waterfall of momentary peace. "You are not crazy. Not even close. And you are not soft, Cass."

Cassidy's stomach flipped once, then twice, at the sound of the nickname. "You don't think so?"

"Not even a little bit. You can be strong and still vulnerable, you know. That's what makes you a great doctor. That's what I love so much about you..."

Cassidy noticed the pink flush in Pierce's cheeks as her gaze shifted to the floor. "Thank you. For the coffee. For the doughnut. For letting me see your face and giving me the strength to get through the rest of this shift. Thank you for being so amazing."

"You are very welcome, Dr. Sullivan."

"I better get back in there. I can almost hear the nurses cursing me through the walls."

"Ten days, right?"

Ten days sounded goddamn impossible. "Ten days."

Pierce squeezed Cassidy's hand one last time and turned to leave. The image was beautifully agonizing. And in that moment, Cassidy would do whatever it took to be in Pierce's arms again for even one more minute.

"Pierce."

She'd almost made it to the waiting-room doors, though Pierce's pace suggested she was less than ready to go. "Yeah?"

"What are you doing tonight?"

"I was going to grill some steak tips and watch a documentary about Whitey Bulger...But my plans are pretty flexible."

Cassidy couldn't believe she was about to suggest this. Pierce was wrong; she was absolutely insane. "I love steak tips..."

"Is that right?" The corner of Pierce's mouth curled into a charming grin.

"I don't get out until around midnight, but if you wanted to come over…"

The other corner now joined, and Pierce's face lit up into a stunning smile, revealing all her straight, perfect teeth with just the hint of a gap in the middle that made Cassidy melt every damn time.

"I'd love that. If you're sure it isn't too late."

"I'm beyond sure."

"Then I'll save you some steak." Pierce was still smiling as she turned to leave the ICU.

It was barely ten a.m., and Pierce had the entire day to pass before she could see Cassidy. She couldn't stop thinking about the look on Cassidy's face when she asked Pierce to come over—sweet and unguarded, the expression of someone who cared and knew they were putting their heart out there. It was inconceivable, but somehow, Cassidy's heart seemed to be following the exact path of Pierce's. The same horrifying adjoining thought crept into her head, but this time it was louder, more poisonous than usual. *This can't last. This never lasts.*

She tried to whittle away at some of the hours by reading the latest Steven King. And when she couldn't focus anymore, which came about five pages in, she shut the book and went for a walk. It was a perfect May Boston afternoon. Pierce lapped the bike path around the Charles River twice, her headphones echoing some indy singer's latest release about new love. She mentally noted to add the song to her Spotify playlist she'd created that contained nothing but music that reminded her of Cassidy. Then she made another mental note to send the song to Cassidy. Not the whole playlist. That would be a bit much. But at least the song. She must have walked for hours before hunger got the best of her, and she stopped at a local dive and picked up a slice of pizza. Judging by the faintly dimming sky, it had to be at least six p.m.—late enough to go home and make Cassidy some of the best leftovers she'd ever had. At least that would be one more thing to distract her. But when Pierce glanced at her watch, she was dismayed to see it was only a quarter past four. Damn New England, with its stupidly short spring days.

With the slice of pizza gone, Pierce walked next door to a Café Nero, one of Boston's many coffee chains, and ordered an iced coffee. Caffeine was probably the last thing she needed, but she didn't care. When she walked back outside and saw an empty cab idling on the sidewalk nearby, an idea hit her.

Pierce opened the cab's back door. "Boston City Hospital, please."

The cabbie, a stout man with a thick, curly beard and a cowboy hat, nodded once and put the car in drive. Most people used ride-share services to get around the city now. But the cab was already waiting. And, aside from the astronomical price, Pierce liked that most of the cabbies had little to no interest in conversing with their patrons.

It was nearly five when she pulled up to the hospital, which was just about perfect. Galen would be finishing her day by now, and Pierce stood a good shot at wrangling her into killing time with her. Especially if Rowan was on call for the night. She thought about calling, but her odds were better if she just showed up at Galen's office door like she usually did. Pierce smiled to herself as the elevator ascended to the eighth floor. Galen had very quickly gone from stranger, to recently estranged cousin, to family. And that was everything to Pierce in a new city, where she could so easily have been alone. She could almost feel the pieces falling perfectly into place around her. Too perfectly.

"Almost done?" Pierce didn't bother to knock when she saw Galen's door open.

"What are you doing here on your day off? Again." Galen had mastered the façade of perturbed older sibling who secretly didn't mind their younger half hanging around.

"I went to see Cassidy in the unit this morning, like you said." Pierce sat on the edge of Galen's excessively sized desk, careful not to displace the piles of books and papers meticulously organized by some system Pierce would never comprehend.

"Hold on. I didn't say to do that."

"Um, yes. You did."

"Did it go all right?"

"Better than all right."

Galen's pinched face relaxed. "Good. Then I did say to do that. See? You should listen to me more often."

"Whatever. Anyway, I brought her coffee. I even stopped and got her a doughnut from Union Square on the way."

Galen nodded. "Nice touch."

Pierce thought so too. "She loved it. In fact, she actually cried when she saw me. Like, good crying though. Not who's-this-crazy-stalker-and-do-I-need-a-restraining-order crying."

"I mean, I'd cry if someone brought me a doughnut during my residency. So it went well. Then what are you doing here, Pierce?"

"Honestly? She asked me to come over tonight. After she gets home. Of course I said I would. But I'm driving myself nuts trying to find ways to kill time. I must have walked halfway across the city just for something to do to get me closer to midnight."

"And now you're looking for someone to distract you." Galen shrugged and unbuttoned the second button on her shirt, kicking her feet up onto the desk.

"Please. I'm desperate."

Galen laughed. "Lucky for you, Ro's working late, and I was just about to head out."

"Thank you. Thank you, thank you, thank you." Pierce toppled off the desk and hugged Galen so hard she nearly choked.

"Easy, kid." Galen sputtered dramatically. "There's one catch."

"Catch?"

"I'm on my way to workout. You want to hang, you have to come with me. Then we can go get some food or something."

Pierce swallowed hard. She knew Galen worked out like she did everything—with a force and intensity that often led to near-vomiting. Where Pierce was more about brisk walks and the occasional spin class, Galen spent hours a week doing CrossFit or some kind of martial arts. Maybe a near-death experience would be a good way to keep Pierce occupied though?

"Okay. Deal. Just go easy on me, okay?"

Galen laughed, but Pierce couldn't help but notice her refusal to answer her plea.

❖

The gym Galen used was even more intimidating than Pierce had imagined. She was surrounded by guys with their shirt sleeves cut off, their biceps erupting like small, sweaty mountains. They grunted and slammed their dumbbells on the ground and pranced around like they were the only ones who deserved to step foot in such a place. Pierce remembered instantly why she preferred the solitude of a gentle jog.

"Get on this rowing machine next to me," Galen said.

Pierce hesitated but then looked at Galen, whose arms were clearly no stranger to a pullup or two. Maybe a little bulking up wouldn't hurt.

After a progression of rowing, swinging heavy kettlebells, squatting, and something called "devil's presses," which Pierce thought surely came directly from hell itself, her heart was beating so quickly she realized she could only focus on how to catch her next breath. Maybe this would be a good way to push Cassidy to the back of her mind.

"Nice work. That was a decent warmup." Galen wiped a bead of sweat off her upper lip, still breathing heavily but looking far more comfortable than Pierce was sure she looked.

"Did you…say…warmup?"

Galen laughed. "Yeah. That was, like, ten minutes. Did you think you were done already?"

"I take it back," Pierce said, finally able to speak in full sentences again. "You aren't a dad. You're a bro. A giant, douche bro."

"You want guns like this, or don't you?" Galen winked and flexed. Pierce rolled her eyes, but for the millionth time, the thought did occur to her that Cassidy was nothing if not too good for Pierce. Dr. McSmokeshow, Pierce reminded herself. Her heart still hadn't steadied itself yet when she flashed to the image of Cassidy, her perfect body covered in nothing, perched unapologetically next to her.

"Fuck me. Fine, let's do it."

In between a sandwich of burpees and pushing some heavy cart which Pierce learned was called a "sled," Galen probed a little further into Pierce's new love life.

"What's bugging you about this, Pierce?"

"About what?"

"You and Cassidy. I can sense it. Something's up. Every time you talk about her, you have this sadness in your eyes."

Galen was more intuitive than Pierce gave her credit for. She wanted to answer but wasn't sure she had enough wind left in her lungs.

"You're scared of getting hurt again, aren't you?" Luckily, Galen, whose breathing had completely normalized already, had answered the question for Pierce.

"How did you know?"

"We've talked about a dozen times already. Come over here. Let's take five." Galen walked over to a giant truck tire lying in the corner, just waiting for some lunk to come and toss it around. She took a seat on the edge, Pierce following suit.

"Yeah. I'm scared. No. I'm terrified. The more time I spend with her the more I…I don't know how this is even possible, but I'm falling for her already. It's only been two weeks. But I can't deny it. It's just right there. Plain as day. And the more I fall for her, the more afraid I become."

"Katie really did a number on you, didn't she?" Galen put a sweaty arm around Pierce's shoulder.

"She really did. I can't go through that again. I wouldn't survive it."

"I told you this already, Pierce. You can't hold Cassidy responsible for Katie's mistakes. You can either trust her, or you can walk away. But you can't keep her around constantly worrying she's going to crush you. And you would survive it. I know it doesn't feel like it, but you would. I swear to you. Give yourself a little credit."

"I just don't see what someone like Cass could possibly want with someone like me."

Galen squeezed her tighter, into a pseudo-bear hug. "She has every reason to want someone like you. But we'll work on the self-esteem stuff. Maybe a few more burpees will take care of it?"

Pierce shoved her away. "You stink. You know that?"

"Like, literally? Or was that figurative?"

Pierce grabbed her nose. "Both! Come on. Let's finish this. You need a shower. Badly."

Chapter Thirteen

If it were possible, the day drew on even longer with the prospect of seeing Pierce later. It was longer, yes, but also happier. Much happier. Even Ginger's incessant requests to tend to Mrs. Jones's bad toenail fungus, which Mrs. Jones would not stop fixating on even in the setting of her failing liver and kidneys, wasn't enough to dampen Cassidy's high. She'd thought about offering Pierce her spare keys to let herself in while Cassidy was still at work. But that would be far too aggressive. It was frustrating that none of the usual rules seemed to apply with Pierce. It was completely impossible. But Cassidy was already falling for her.

Sometime around ten thirty p.m., the overnight medical intern straggled in, less than enthusiastic about taking sign-out from Cassidy. And after following up on a couple of CT scans, finishing a lumbar puncture, and cheerily telling the oncoming intern no, she would not be willing to stay late to help with a new admission that night, Cassidy logged off her computer and headed to the locker room to collect her things. In a moment of panic, she realized she was showing up to see Pierce in an eighteen-hour-old pair of scrubs, no makeup, and a top bun that no longer sat on top. Something told her, though, that if it had been long enough for Cassidy to feel the way she was about Pierce, it was long enough for her to see her unbridled, as her authentic post-shift self.

Usually Cassidy would take the T home after work. It never went anywhere in a great hurry, but at least it was cheap. That night, she picked up her phone and hailed an Uber. Not one of those shared rides either. Cassidy went right for the fastest possible route home. If she'd had a helicopter option, she probably would have chosen it. Once comfortably in the backseat, she texted Pierce that she'd be there shortly.

Ten minutes after Cassidy arrived home, Pierce buzzed her door, enough time for her to at least change into some sweats and wash her face. But after eighteen hours, even ten minutes felt excruciating.

Pierce stood in front of her wearing a pair of tight jeans and a tattered baseball cap, and Cassidy's mind immediately forged a picture of Pierce teetering an infant on her knee on a Sunday morning, cartoons in the background, while Cassidy flipped pancakes in the kitchen. *Get a grip, Cass.*

"Hello again," Pierce said. She smiled suggestively, and Cassidy thanked the universe, and science, that mind reading was not a thing.

"Hi." Cassidy held the door open for Pierce and gestured for her to come in. "What do you have there?"

Pierce held up the Tupperware containers she was balancing precariously. "Oh, you mean these here?"

"Yes, I do."

"Only the best steak tips you've ever had. With some corn on the cob and a farmer's salad. And I brought some extra. I imagine you don't eat much in the unit."

Cassidy's chest swelled. "That is maybe the nicest thing anyone's ever done for me."

"You aren't going to cry again, are you?" Pierce unloaded the leftovers onto the kitchen table.

"Shut up. And while you're at it, get over here, will you?"

Cassidy grabbed Pierce's hand and pulled her in until they were pressed together. They stood in exquisite silence, Cassidy savoring the feeling of Pierce's arms snugly around her waist. When the tension was just right, Cassidy put her hand around the back of Pierce's neck and kissed her, the anticipation of touching her again melting into reality.

"What's wrong?" Cassidy felt Pierce flinch, and when she pulled away, startled, Pierce was grimacing in pain.

"Galen made me work out with her today. It was just short of sadism, I think."

Cassidy kept her hand on Pierce's neck but began gently kneading the tight, spasming muscle. "Poor baby. Come on. Let's go into my room. I'll rub it for you."

"Are you kidding?" Pierce protested but leaned closer and groaned. "You're the one who just worked eighteen hours. I should be rubbing your neck."

"You just made me dinner for a week. It's the least I can do."

"Speaking of dinner," Pierce said, her eyes still closed, "you hungry?"

Cassidy was. She hadn't eaten anything but a hospital-issue peanut butter and jelly in twelve hours. But she wanted Pierce more. She tugged on the lapels of Pierce's jacket and kissed her again, this time eliciting an even deeper groan from Pierce.

"I am. But it can wait. I've been thinking about you all day."

Pierce smiled and ran her fingers through Cassidy's loose hair, winding strands around her fingers and tugging softly. "I had to get rhabdo at Galen's hands just to keep my mind off you."

Cassidy laughed. "I'm flattered. Although I hope your renal function is hanging in there."

"If not, I know a great ER doc…" Pierce grinned, pulling Cassidy into the unlit bedroom.

In spite of the late hour, Pierce seemed to want to take her time. She kissed down her neck, then back up to her ear, which always sent a quiver directly between Cassidy's legs, then, just when Cassidy was writhing underneath her, Pierce moved down to her stomach, lifting her T-shirt to her chin and running her tongue down to Cassidy's belly button. She dipped her tongue inside, and Cassidy gripped Pierce's shoulders hard, wanting to bring her closer— wanting to merge their every cell into one. Her mouth drifting lower, Pierce reached her hand up and tugged at Cassidy's nipple, which was so hard it actually hurt. It was the best possible pain—the torture of needing someone so badly you thought you could actually die. Pierce was hands-down the best sex of Cassidy's life. It was as if Cassidy had never even had sex before now. And whenever Cassidy thought it couldn't possibly get any better, Pierce somehow seemed to outdo herself.

"You are unbelievable." Cassidy was still breathing erratically, her body splayed out on top of the down comforter.

"Please. You are." Pierce was still propped up over her, smiling bashfully.

"You are the Tom Brady of sex. And I'm the Jimmy Garoppolo. I'm fine with that. Really. It's just the facts."

Pierce scoffed. "That's the most ridiculous thing I've ever heard."

"I'm serious." Cassidy tried not to let herself think about just how Pierce had become so skilled in bed.

"You are no one's backup. Especially not mine."

Cassidy hoped that were true, both in the bedroom and out. "Good." She kissed Pierce's head, overwhelmed by the connection, the very definition of intimacy she was feeling in that moment. "Now, how about that steak? I'm starving."

"You're on."

Cassidy watched as Pierce skipped around the kitchen, sometime after two a.m., wearing only a pair of sparse black briefs. "I could get used to this, you know."

"What's that?" Pierce tossed the reheating steak in a skillet. "Me cooking dinner for you at some absurd hour of the morning in my underwear?"

Cassidy laughed and came up behind Pierce, placing her hands on Pierce's hips. "You. At my place. All of this."

Pierce turned to face her, their eyes locked in a magnetic heat. Her arms circled Cassidy's waist, her hands brushing against her ass. "I'm afraid I've already gotten used to it."

The weather in Boston in mid-June is always anyone's guess. One day brings sunny skies and temperatures high enough to sit on the beach, and the next brings torrential rains and lows so low they seem to threaten snow. When Pierce woke up that particular day, the sun was high and hot, already beating through Cassidy's bedroom where the AC sat on the floor, still waiting to be put in the window. It was only seven a.m., and the air was already thick and musky, heavy with what Pierce could only worry was impending chaos. The first hot day of the summer always brought all of the crazies to the ER—the homeless who couldn't take the elements any longer and sought shelter, the troublemakers who for some reason became particularly stab-happy when the humidity topped eighty percent, and of course, the drug abusers who would normally have been left to sleep off their high in the nearby park, but instead were found by a well-meaning bystander who happened to be out for a walk. Whatever the cocktail of riffraff, it was sure to mean a busy day for Pierce.

"What are you doing up so early?" Pierce asked as Cassidy stirred next to her. "Go back to bed." She kissed her softly on the forehead, smoothing her bed-swept hair with her fingers.

"I can't." Cassidy groaned. "I'm back in the ED today."

Pierce couldn't believe it had been an entire month since Cassidy had started her ICU rotation. An entire month since they'd first spent the night in this very bed. Since then, it had been a near constant. Any night that Pierce wasn't working late, or Cassidy wasn't on an overnight shift, Pierce was there. They shared an unspoken knowledge that they wanted to spend as much time together as possible, even if that only meant a few minutes of consciousness at night before passing out in the other's arms. Every day had been better than the next. Pierce was living a fairy tale she thought surely had the makings of a romantic urban legend. And this morning, she would get to go to work with Cassidy too.

"I can't believe you're done with the MICU already."

"I can. That was the longest month of my life. I don't know how I could have gotten through it without you, you know that?" Cassidy nuzzled her head under Pierce's arm and tucked herself in.

"I didn't do much. I just brought you a few midnight coffees and cooked you some dinner."

"Now that's horribly inaccurate. You also cleaned my apartment for me when I was gone. And remember that time when you made me breakfast at three a.m. because I desperately wanted pancakes?"

Pierce laughed. "I do remember that, yes."

"But it was much more than that." Cassidy placed her palm on Pierce's stomach and stroked gently. "For every bad shift, every bitchy nurse, every patient I lost...you were there. You can't know how much it helped to have you to listen at the end of the day."

"I was lucky to get to do it." Pierce smiled. She couldn't help but think she liked the person Cassidy was making her. She wasn't proud of all her roles in past relationships, but she was proud of this one: her own strength, her newfound selflessness, and, more than anything, her ability to love so deeply.

Of course, Cassidy didn't know Pierce was in love. Or maybe she did. But Pierce certainly hadn't said so. And Cassidy hadn't either. At times, many times actually, when they'd finished making love, or fallen asleep to the sound of the sirens, or even just stood in the kitchen laughing and making dinner, where Pierce felt it so strongly it threatened to rise up out of her and spill out in one embarrassing admission. Three words. Just three stupid, overused words she'd said before, and maybe only halfheartedly. They'd never felt quite so big before. And she couldn't get herself to let them slip out for fear Cassidy might not be in as deep.

Pierce once again considered how rare it was to find that kind of reciprocity. What were the odds she could love someone as much as they loved her back? Or more so, the reverse? That certainly hadn't been the case with Katie. And, as she thought about it, it wasn't the case with any of the girls she'd been with in the past. Someone always seemed to love the other more. And Pierce was certain beyond a doubt that she was that person with Cassidy.

"So are you glad to be back in the ED?" Pierce asked, pulling herself back out of her own head.

"Beyond. But it's even better knowing you'll be there."

"Speaking of that...Are we going to be, you know, open about this? About us?"

Cassidy paused and narrowed her eyes, seemingly pondering the question. Pierce hadn't given much thought to whether they should let their coworkers know about their relationship. They'd been too wrapped up in each other to care. But now that Cassidy was back in the department, they had to decide.

"Fuck it. There's no rule, is there?"

"I don't think so. Look at Galen and Rowan. Galen is pretty much Rowan's boss right now. It was even worse when she was her chief. So yeah. Fuck it. Let them all know."

Cassidy giggled. "All right then. Besides, you're too good of a secret to keep. I want the entire world to know you're mine."

Pierce rolled up onto one elbow and kissed her. "If anyone has anything to brag about here, it's me. Now, if you'll excuse me, I'm going to get dressed so I can rush into work and tell everyone I'm dating Dr. McSmokeshow."

She jumped up out of the bed just in time to miss the pillow Cassidy had tossed at Pierce's head. "I'll see you in the ER then."

"I'll see you in the ER, Dr. Sullivan."

By the time Cassidy pulled into the parking garage at the hospital, it was already oppressively hot out. The air conditioning in her '09' Ford Explorer hadn't worked in years, and she was too broke to think about fixing it. Especially when she'd had the luxury of being chauffeured around in Pierce's Bimmer for the last month or so. That day, their shifts were a couple of hours apart, and Pierce was already somewhere beyond the ER doors. In spite of the sweat collecting under her scrubs, the thought sent Cassidy nearly sprinting to the entrance of the building.

It was nice not to have to search for excuses to find Pierce at work. Without pretense, Cassidy simply sought her out, spotting her at a nearby workstation and approaching without giving a damn about the impending teasing that would come from her coworkers.

"Hi." Cassidy leaned down to kiss Pierce's cheek, momentarily forgetting her surroundings, and then thought better of it. Although they had no plans to hide their relationship at work, they weren't going to flaunt it either, especially not in the middle of the floor.

"Well, hello again." Pierce's face lit up brighter than the unseasonable June sun ever could, and Cassidy's stomach did some still unfamiliar acrobatics.

Cassidy didn't know what working with Pierce would be like. Sure, they'd been working together for months, but not side by side. Not since they'd become...them. A million worries had flittered through her brain at the prospect. Would it be too distracting? Would she still be able to be a good doctor knowing Pierce was just around the corner? Would they step on each other's toes at all and annoy each other? Would it be awkward or challenging or unpleasant? Or would it just mean getting to spend more time with this woman she couldn't seem to get enough of?

So far, it had been nothing but the latter. Cassidy stood in room 5, interviewing a fifty-six-year-old woman who was coming in with chest pain and shortness of breath. She rode the high of knowing Pierce was hers, acting as gasoline to the spark she already carried for her work. Cassidy was on her game like never before, nailing diagnoses, making patients smile, and dazzling her superiors. And, in spite of the heat, the morning had been quiet. In almost the immediate second Cassidy had this thought, she was surrounded by blackness.

Chapter Fourteen

That was strange, Cassidy thought. But in another ten seconds, the backup generators seemed to kick in, and everything more or less seemed to resume as usual. She continued her discussion with her patient, asking more details about her pain and her medical history, as if nothing had happened. It probably wasn't all that unusual to lose power in a heat wave like this. Hospitals were well equipped for this kind of thing.

As she walked out of the room, though, it became clear that everything was not resuming as usual. The computers, which were the crutch that left the ER crippled without them, had rebooted but wouldn't go back online. The ambient hum of machines was absent. And, if she hadn't noticed the flurry of nurses running around trying to figure out what was happening, something was eerily peaceful about the whole scene.

"What's going on?" Cassidy found Pierce around the corner, scribbling notes on a piece of scrap paper.

"I don't know. The power went down. Now the generators are on, but we have no EMR. Everyone's losing their shit."

The chair of the department, a sharp-featured Scandinavian man named Tom Newton, emerged from the office he usually hid in, looking frazzled and nervous. "Okay, everyone. Let's gather up over here."

Staff had already all essentially congregated to the center of the nurses' station, talking anxiously in muted tones.

"I just got word that CT is down. So is MRI. X-ray is okay for the moment, but the cooling system has been completely knocked out, which means every machine in this hospital is currently overheating."

It seemed to strike Cassidy at the same time as the rest of the staff just how big of a deal this was. A hospital without power was essentially a structure to house bodies in. Without imaging studies, without lab work, they were functionless, left to retreat to the time when all a doctor had was a stethoscope and well-refined exam skills to diagnose a patient. And even if you could make the proper diagnosis, treatment was nearly impossible without access to medications, which computer passwords and fingerprint IDs guarded. Cassidy suddenly felt blind, fumbling. She took a mental inventory of her patients: the man in room 14 had an ankle injury. His X-rays were already done, and he just needed a splint put on. The woman in 5 still needed lab work—an EKG and a chest X-ray—but she was stable. The woman in 7 had pancreatitis. Her labs were back, but her blood pressure had been skimming the boundaries of dangerous, and if she went any further, Cassidy was in big trouble.

As the hours passed, the power didn't return. The local public-works department was reportedly working furiously, but it could be several more hours before anything was back up and running again. The electronic medical records were still down, leaving every order to be handwritten and every prescription to be called in to the local pharmacies. That was, until the phones went down too. The patients who needed to be were all shipped out to local ERs who could accommodate them. But the real problem was the heat.

Cassidy walked by room 12, where Pierce was suturing the leg of a teenager who'd fallen off his dirt bike. The *V* of Pierce's scrub top was dark with sweat, and her bangs fell limply over her forehead. She turned to Cassidy and smiled, but she looked as if she'd been running a marathon in late July. Everyone did. Doctors had stripped off their white coats, and nurses were dabbing their necks with cold cloths. Rumor had it that the babies in the NICU were all turning into little preemie burritos, and the poor elderly patients on the top floor were essentially lying in an attic, shriveling to raisins. The crazy had set in. Cassidy had known it was coming when she woke up that morning. The heat always made people crazy. Of course, she'd never dreamed it would be the staff of the hospital.

Hours had gone by, although without the ambient hum of the AC, the torrid sounds of chaos that usually encompassed the ER, and the steady rumble of patients and staff moving from one area of the hospital to the other, they had no metronome to mark the passage of time. The day was oddly peaceful. But the temperature continued to rise, and the very young and very old were approaching real danger. Those far above Cassidy and Pierce's paygrade decided to evacuate the hospital, to transfer the patients still left to whatever nearby facility could accommodate them. And the staff of Boston City would carry out the evacuation.

"Hey." Pierce emerged from around the corner. She'd discarded her usual white coat and was fanning herself furiously with a package of sterile drapes.

"Hey. What a day, huh?"

"Seriously. I'm just happy to lay eyes on you." Pierce smiled and glanced around them coyly, sending Cassidy's stomach lurching with want. Although it was ten thousand degrees, and they were surrounded by disgruntled patients and hyperthermic coworkers, the hint of sweat around Pierce's forehead guided Cassidy's mind back to the night before, Pierce's firm, steady body gliding across hers in the early summer heat wave. A shudder ripped through her.

"Me too." She reached for Pierce's hand, gently clasping their fingers. It wasn't nearly enough, but it would have to do.

"I just got word I have to stay and evacuate. I'll probably be here all night."

"Same." Somehow, the prospect of being locked up with Pierce all night, even in the hospital while shuttling patients down multiple flights of stairs, thrilled her.

"Really? They're making the residents stay too?"

"All hands on deck." This wasn't exactly true. Cassidy's supervisor had said that since the residents weren't technically contracted employees, they could go home. But knowing full well Pierce would not have that luxury, Cassidy had volunteered her services. Still, it would be far too embarrassing to ever admit that act to Pierce.

"I guess we're stuck here together then." Pierce tossed her a sly wink and let their eyes lock just long enough for Cassidy to know Pierce was thinking exactly what she was.

"Yo. Parker."

Pierce immediately dropped Cassidy's hand at the sound of Margot approaching.

"What's up?" She took several steps back from Cassidy and fiddled nervously with the tie on her scrubs.

"I need some help in 10. This ninety-year-old guy fell, and we have to send him out to Beth Israel, but he has a massive lac on his head. The thing's a mess. Basically scalped himself. I'm tied up next door doing an LP on someone we can't run because the lab is down. Giant cluster fuck is what it is."

"So you need me to suture."

Margot made her index finger and thumb into the shape of a gun and pointed at Pierce with a nod. Pierce duplicated the gesture, and Margot strutted off.

"What was that?" Cassidy felt a near-immediate surge of something unpleasant she could only equate with jealousy.

"What was what?"

"You and Margot. That little handshake? She was flirting with you, Pierce."

Pierce's cheeks turned a deep crimson, and she let out an overly manufactured string of laughter. "What? That's crazy."

"It is not! You can't tell me you don't notice how she looks at you. Those big, chocolate eyes and bright-red lips that she can't help but just pout your way. I mean, come on."

A grin manifested on Pierce's lips, and she moved back closer to Cassidy, placing a hand on her shoulder. "Dr. Sullivan. I didn't know you had a jealous streak."

"Oh, please. I'm not jealous." But Cassidy was. She knew it, and it deeply unsettled her. Cassidy was not familiar with jealousy. In all of her past relationships, she'd never felt threatened or even insecure. And she'd certainly never dived off the deep end like this with accusations and crazy talk. But everything was different with Pierce. The stakes were higher. The loss would be so much greater. The love was so much deeper already.

"It's okay. I find it very endearing. Maybe even a little sexy." Cassidy pulled away and tossed her head dramatically in the air. "Yeah. I bet you do."

"Aw, come on Cass. Margot doesn't want me. And besides, even if she did, I have less than zero interest in her."

"Look at her. She's gorgeous. You know, in an Addams Family-Hot Topic kind of way."

Pierce laughed, this time sincerely and with what sounded like a hint of empathy. "I don't see it. She's not my type. You know I have a thing for tiny blond doctors..."

"You think you're very charming, don't you?" Cassidy couldn't help but soften just a little.

"Occasionally, yes. You're all I want. You're all I see. There's literally no one else in the world."

Cassidy rolled her eyes, but her internal monologue screamed at her to tell Pierce just how in love with her she really was. She was terrified that if she opened her mouth, it would come out. So she opted for silence.

"I've got to go suture. I'll find you after?"

Cassidy nodded, allowing the corner of her mouth to rise just a little.

Two a.m. in the hospital is usually the witching hour, that calm before the storm. The phrase "it's always darkest before the dawn" often comes to mind, in the most literal sense. Patients are sleeping. Staff are scant, and the ones that remain are usually talking quietly over their computers, sipping on cold coffee from the night before. Sometimes the soft buzz of an electric floor cleaner can be heard in the distance, but otherwise, the hour is usually hushed. Not tonight, though. Every floor of Boston City was lit up, a multitude of staff members lining the stairwells as patients were passed down step by step on backboards and in chairs. The ones on ventilators and life-saving drugs went down the single working elevator, but this took time as well. Outside the hospital doors, a parade of ambulances waited to take patients to area hospitals. It was now 87 degrees in the ER and probably much, much hotter on the higher floors. Pierce, Cassidy, and their colleagues were exhausted, dehydrated, and more than ready to go home.

By four a.m., the last ambulance carrying the last patient flipped on its lights and left the parking lot. The hospital was empty, save for the staff who'd stayed behind to help.

"Kind of eerie, isn't it? Like one of those post-apocalyptic movies or something." Pierce found Cassidy sitting in the nurses' station, holding a Diet Coke limply in one hand, dark circles under her eyes. Cassidy's flair of jealousy earlier had surprised her. Especially over Margot, of all people. With her hair that changed color daily, her nose ring, her overly peppy demeanor, Margot was the antithesis of Pierce's type. It was absurd to think Pierce could be interested in her. Actually, it was absurd to think Pierce would ever be interested in another woman ever again. She did feel badly about it though. The unsettling hurt in Cassidy's eyes stabbed Pierce directly in the heart like a thousand tiny needles. She wanted to take that pain away from her, as quickly as possible.

"I don't know. I think it's peaceful. My mom's a teacher, and on the last week of summer before school started, she used to take me with her to help set up her classroom. The halls were empty. Everything was clean and waiting and ready. It reminds me a little bit of that, actually."

"You always find the good in things. I love that about you." Pierce found herself stuttering a little with the word, as if it might give way to what she really felt for Cassidy. The urge to confess she was totally in love was building like a pressure cooker, threatening to explode any second. She had to meticulously think through everything she said for fear those words would find an escape route and slip out before she was ready—or worse, before Cassidy was ready.

"Listen. I'm sorry I went all *Single White Female* on you earlier. I promise I'm not an inherently jealous person."

"And I'm sorry if I gave you any reason to feel insecure, Cass. I'm telling you, nothing is going on between Margot and me. I want this with you. Indefinitely."

Fuck. The word was just short of "forever." Essentially a fucking synonym. Pierce might as well have proposed right then and there for all the crazy she was letting out. She couldn't backtrack. She just had to play it off and hope Cassidy hadn't noticed.

"Indefinitely." Cassidy's face brightened even over the shadows under her tired eyes. So she had heard Pierce. And she didn't seem to mind. In fact, she seemed…happy.

"Let's go for a walk." Pierce took Cassidy's hand and led her out of the ER and down the hall to the elevator. They took it to the sixth floor, which on a normal day was the inpatient neurology unit. But that morning, it was silent. Clean. Empty. Custodial staff had gone through and straightened up the debris left from the evacuation. Beds were made with crisp hospital corners. Computers were off. Only the dim lights from the generators remained.

"What are we doing here?" Cassidy asked.

"I wanted to see if you were right."

"Right about what?"

"If this is peaceful or creepy." Pierce looked around. "There is something kind of nice about it."

"Like the week before school."

"Exactly."

They stood in silence for a while, taking in the quiet, reveling in the stillness after a night of madness. Moved by the nothingness that somehow felt like everything all at once, Pierce put her hand on Cassidy's waist and stepped closer to her, gently pressing her lips against Cassidy's. Cassidy grasped the back of Pierce's head, pulling her in farther, and Pierce's torso warmed from her neck all the way down between her legs, where the heat built into a blazing need. No one else was in sight. Cassidy stepped back just far enough, taking Pierce by the hand and guiding her into the deserted patient room directly behind them. Pierce felt the flashover through her entire body as Cassidy placed a palm on Pierce's chest and pushed her onto the empty bed. She climbed on top of her, straddling Pierce's narrow hips, her hands still balancing on Pierce's chest.

"I've been wanting you all night," Pierce mumbled.

"Good." Cassidy grinned and pulled her scrub top over her head so painfully slow Pierce grimaced. Underneath was a red bra adorned with lace, revealing just enough of a crest of cleavage to leave Pierce writhing beneath her. Cassidy always seemed to be wearing sexy underwear. She said she liked how it made her feel, knowing it was under her scrubs every day. Pierce nearly bit her own finger off out of frustration when she heard this and remembered it often when she slept alone at night.

It was still sweltering on the sixth floor, but it had become impossible to differentiate this from the heat building between their bodies. Still pinned under Cassidy's small frame, Pierce reached and stroked the skin under Cassidy's neck, down to the small peak of breast just begging to be released from the confines of her bra. Cassidy moaned and reached behind her, unclasping it and tossing it to the corner. Watching Cassidy undress had pushed Pierce over the edge of the cliff, and she ground her waist into Cassidy's, hoping for some sort of relief. Cassidy took one of her own nipples between her two fingers and pinched, throwing her head back, her long hair moving across her shoulders. She slid her hands under Pierce's shirt, untucking it from her pants, and feathered her fingers down Pierce's belly.

"I need you," Cassidy said, climbing off Pierce in one smooth motion and tugging at her own pants, until she was completely naked. Pierce rose to kiss her, commanding Cassidy's mouth with her own and shifting her much-larger body on Cassidy's.

"No." Cassidy put both hands on Pierce's shoulders, but Pierce didn't have time to be perplexed. Cassidy pushed her back down onto her back and resumed her position, where she began to ride Pierce, her hips bucking to meet Pierce's. "I want to be on top."

Pierce felt the blood drain out of her face and probably to other places in her body that needed it more, and a loud, involuntary groan rose from somewhere visceral.

"Whatever you want."

Cassidy put both hands on Pierce's stomach this time and braced herself, bucking harder and faster until Pierce was sure she was about to cum. They hadn't known each other long. But they already knew each other well. And Pierce recognized that look—the way Cassidy's eyes rolled back in her head, the pitch of her breathing, the rhythm of her hips. And then, the explosion, a fit of release, a few choice expletives from her girl-next-door mouth. And finally, the collapse. Cassidy's body went limp like a marionette and collapsed in a beautiful, lifeless heap onto Pierce's chest, where she promptly fell peacefully, soundly asleep.

Chapter Fifteen

Sometimes it was almost too easy for Cassidy to forget about the past. She was, after all, just a normal, healthy twenty-seven-year-old. She was a physician, in her dream specialty, living in the best city in the world. And she'd fallen in love with a sexy, brilliant PA who was more than Cassidy could have ever dreamt even existed. On most days, life was good. Very good, even.

On others, she was reminded it was also too short.

The next patient on the "to be seen" list was a fourteen-year-old girl named Carly Mattson. Her chief complaint was "fever." But on further investigation into her medical records, Cassidy learned Carly had a history of acute lymphoblastic leukemia. Usually, a quick glance at the EMR for meds, allergies, and current medical problems was all Cassidy took the time for. But that day, Cassidy pored over every note she could find on Carly before she even went to see her. Carly was diagnosed with ALL at age ten. After a couple of rounds of chemo, she was deemed cancer free. Six months ago, she came down with what her parents thought was a simple virus. But blood tests revealed a spike in her white-blood-cell count, and the cancer had returned from its dark hiding place. She was currently on her third round of an experimental chemo regimen Cassidy had never heard of. Most of her treatment was through a children's hospital in Philadelphia, where her cutting-edge oncologist resided. But when Carly's temperature reached 104 that afternoon, her parents panicked and rushed her to the closest ER—Cassidy's ER.

Cassidy took a deep breath, trying to brace herself for the emotional cataclysm that would follow every minute of this case. She considered trying to hand it off to someone else. But that would mean offering some kind of explanation she wasn't ready to give.

"Hello, Carly. I'm Dr. Sullivan, the ER doctor here." Cassidy spoke before looking directly at the young girl sitting in the bed at the back of the exam room. When she did, what Cassidy saw was a pale, fragile child, whose eyes were sunken with fever and whose mouth was pasted dry. Almost immediately, it was Cassidy in that bed. Seventeen-years old, fighting for her life. Carly's parents, almost as pale and fragile, flanked her bed. Tears were left straggling in her father's eyes, and Cassidy could tell from the way the parents looked at each other that they'd been fighting. Cassidy took another deep breath, grateful for the paper mask covering her mouth to hide the terror and uncertainty on her own face.

"Hi." Carly's voice was strained and weak—the voice of someone in the process of giving up.

Cassidy fought to bring herself back to the moment, trying to remind herself she was not in this hospital bed. Carly was. And she needed someone. She glanced at the bedside monitor, taking a mental inventory of her vital signs. Carly's heart rate was far too fast. Her oxygen levels were dipping lower than Cassidy liked. And her temperature had reached nearly 105, in spite of a hefty dose of Tylenol.

"Tell me what happened today."

"I just haven't felt very good. Yesterday I had a sore throat and a headache. Then I got the chills, and my temp was over 103. I have a cough now, and my lungs hurt." Carly paused, seeming to have expended all of her energy. "And I'm scared."

"She's going through chemo right now." Carly's mother, whose name Cassidy didn't bother to get, jumped in nervously. "Her oncologist is Dr. Walter Hofstra at CHOP. It's an experimental treatment. Some combination of 5FU and Nivolumab, or something... Some kind of immune modulator...oh, I can't remember...I'm so sorry."

"Mrs. Mattson. It's all right. I can get all the specifics from CHOP. That's very helpful. You just focus on being here for Carly right now."

"What's her white count?" Mr. Mattson said.

"Stop, Tom. Let the doctor speak."

"I'm just trying to find out what's going on," he snapped back. "She's my daughter too."

Apparently Cassidy had been correct about the fighting.

"Guys, that's enough. I'm fine. Honestly." A freezing-cold chill shot down Cassidy's spine. It was like being in a nightmare where you find yourself trying to run from something horrible, but your legs just won't move.

"We don't have the labs back yet. But I promise as soon as we do, I'll let you know." Cassidy returned her attention to Carly. "Is it okay if I take a listen?"

Carly nodded, and Cassidy placed her stethoscope to Carly's back. In the middle of the first breath, Carly erupted into a fit of violent coughing, her heart rate on the monitor racing faster. Cassidy didn't know what was making Carly so sick. But whatever it was, wasn't going to be good.

"Fuck." Cassidy was so fixated on her computer screen she didn't notice Pierce had come up behind her.

"What's wrong?"

She turned to Pierce's comforting face, and for a moment, the horror that had accompanied the day ebbed just a little. "Nothing."

"Come on. That didn't sound like nothing. What are you looking at?" Pierce leaned over Cassidy's shoulder and squinted. "Shit. That's like the lowest white count I've ever seen."

"0.2. She probably has five working white blood cells right now." Cassidy's forehead fell into her hands.

"Neutropenic fever?"

"Yeah. She's fourteen. ALL. On some weird experimental chemo. Fever of almost 105."

"Jesus." Pierce put her hand on Cassidy's back. The warmth emanating off Pierce's skin did little to thaw the freeze that had settled into her bones. "Let me know if you need anything, okay?"

Cassidy wanted to tell Pierce she did need something. She needed to tell her she was that little girl not so long ago, to say that she'd almost died, and that she worried every day that the cancer might just be lying dormant, waiting for everything in her life to be utterly perfect before shattering it into dust. But she couldn't. If Pierce had that information, she'd worry. She'd treat her differently. And if the monster did return...Pierce didn't deserve that.

The next time Cassidy returned to Carly's room, she was in full protective equipment, from her gloves to her gown to her hair. It wasn't to protect Cassidy. It was to protect Carly, whose immune system had essentially been obliterated by the life-saving chemo drugs.

"We don't know what's causing the infection," Cassidy said. "But her..." She quickly corrected herself, turning and addressing Carly directly. "Your white blood cell count is very, very low. Which means—"

"I know what it means. I'm neutropenic. I have nothing to fight this thing with," Carly said sharply.

"Yes..."

"What is the white count?" Mr. Mattson asked.

"0.2."

"Jesus..." Mr. Mattson's eyes widened, but his wife remained silent, shaking her head. "This can't be happening. She was doing so well with this new treatment."

"The most important thing right now is to get these antibiotics going while we figure out what the source is. But I need to know where you'd like Carly treated. Obviously, Philadelphia is a long way away. We could potentially arrange for transfer there, but it won't be quick or easy. And with her vital signs and labs looking the way they do, it could be dangerous as well. I'd feel much better if she stayed here at Boston City," Cassidy said.

"But Dr. Hofstra is at CHOP," Mrs. Mattson protested.

"I know." Cassidy moved to her side and put a reassuring hand on her shoulder. She found that touching patients could be the difference between good medical care and a soul being comforted. Sometimes, it took only a simple gesture to make someone feel like they weren't in this alone. "And I promise you, I've been in touch with Dr. Hofstra all day. He knows all about Carly and what's going on. He also feels it's best if she stays here for now. We have some great pediatric oncologists, and when she's stable, if need be, we can send her to CHOP."

"I don't know about that," Mr. Mattson shot back.

"Maybe she's right, Tom."

"She needs to be with Dr. Hofstra. They know her there. They're the best. And what if she needs a bone-marrow transplant? Do we really want that done here?"

"Dad. You don't know what's going to happen. Can you both please just stop fighting for a little while?"

The Mattsons looked at each other with what appeared to be a beat of tenderness and then turned back to their daughter. Cassidy had watched this very scene play out in her own life several years ago, and it had ended with a nasty divorce and endless resentment. That was, if Carly even survived this illness.

"Let's just work on getting her admitted here. One step at a time," Cassidy said.

"I don't want to go all the way to Philly," Carly said, her voice stronger than it had been all day. "My friends won't be able to visit me, and besides, I like Cassidy."

Cassidy warmed for the first time in hours. "I like you too."

"If I stay here, will you come visit me?"

"Absolutely."

The Mattsons exchanged glances again, then nodded simultaneously. "She'll stay. As long as Dr. Hofstra is involved."

"He will be." Cassidy offered a cordial smile and started to leave.

"And Doctor?" Mrs. Mattson said softly. "Thank you."

If Pierce didn't know better, and really, she didn't, she could have sworn Cassidy was avoiding her. After their brief exchange at Cassidy's computer earlier in the day, Pierce had hardly seen her. They passed in the halls and shared a smile when they did, but Cassidy didn't seem to be seeking Pierce out like she usually did. Maybe she was just busy. Or maybe Pierce was being paranoid. Or, most catastrophically, maybe Cassidy's feelings for her were fading. She had realized quite early on that the heat between two people that boiled so hot and spread so quickly could also burn out. And she lived with a relatively periodic fear that Cassidy would do just that. Pierce was supposed to come over after her shift that night. Whatever was going on, they could talk about it.

"Hey." It was nearly ten p.m. when Cassidy finally approached Pierce. But her tone was tentative and morose, her words unusually curt.

"Hey. How's your day been?"

"Oh, you know. Fine. Listen, about tonight. I think I just need a night to myself. Is that okay?"

Pierce's heart ricocheted to the floor like a faulty elevator. This was everything she had come to fear. Cassidy had burned herself out and was no longer interested.

"Is everything okay?"

"Sure. Everything's fine. Just tired."

Pierce's stomach pitched. She was becoming physically ill. The thought of losing Cassidy was far more caustic than anything she could have ever imagined. In an instant, her entire world had been corrupted. Cassidy had become the glue that held together everything in her life. Her work. Galen. Even the places she went for coffee and the bike path she walked along the Charles. Cassidy had permeated everything. And now it was all going to fall apart.

"Okay. Well, see you tomorrow, I guess?"

"Yes." Cassidy turned around without so much as a brush of her hand against Pierce's or even a smile, and Pierce's heart continued to break in succession.

"Cass, wait." She couldn't let her go like this. Not without knowing if it was really over between them. "Is it…us? I mean, did I do something?"

Cassidy's brow furrowed, and her voice dropped into a low tenor. "Not everything is about you, Pierce."

❖

It wasn't enough that Cassidy had to relive her childhood trauma. She also had to push the love of her life as far away as possible. She lay in her queen-sized bed, alone. The bed had never been so big without Pierce beside her. The apartment was cold, or maybe she was just still frozen from the day. Cassidy hadn't meant to push Pierce away. But she knew exactly why she had. She was not the one who was sick—Carly was. And as sad as that was, it wasn't going to ruin the best relationship she'd ever had. Cassidy needed to make things right with Pierce. But she just wasn't ready to tell her why yet.

The clock on Cassidy's cell phone read close to one a.m., but she had a feeling Pierce wouldn't be sleeping either. She'd been unfair. She'd hurt Pierce. And she had to fix it before it was too late.

"Cass? Are you okay?" Cassidy could hear the worry in Pierce's voice interlaced with a hint of excitement. Pierce's mind had gone to its worst, darkest corners. She would have done the same thing if Pierce had treated her the way she had earlier.

"Yes. I'm okay. Can you…come over?"

"Now?"

"If that's all right. Or I can go over there. I just need to see you."

"Of course. I'll be right there."

It was hardly twenty minutes before Pierce was ringing the buzzer outside Cassidy's door. She stood silently in a worn, gray hoodie and basketball shorts, her cowlicks protruding in ways that made Cassidy's heart tug with a feeling she could only articulate as home. She threw her arms around Pierce's strong shoulders and gripped hard, burying her face in Pierce's neck, taking in the sweet, musky scent of her skin. Pierce was her safe place.

"What's going on?" Pierce asked, still holding Cassidy's hips.

"I'm sorry, Pierce."

"For what?"

"Today. For pushing you away. I promise, I can explain."
Cassidy took Pierce's hand and led her into the bedroom. She

climbed under the covers she'd been cocooned under all night, and Pierce followed. Her body fit seamlessly with Pierce's, an endless expanse of soft skin and warmth that all at once set everything right in the world. Cassidy kept her head firmly on Pierce's chest, one arm draped across Pierce's stomach as Pierce stroked the hair falling across Cassidy's forehead.

"It wasn't you. Or us," Cassidy said. "Remember that patient from earlier? The young girl with the ALL?"

"Yeah?"

"I just..." Cassidy wasn't sure just how much she was planning to disclose. "It really got to me. I don't know why. I'm sorry I was cold."

It wasn't the entire truth, but it wasn't exactly a lie, either. Was it?

"That's okay. It happens to all of us at one point or another. But I have to say, you had me really freaked out."

Cassidy sighed and lifted her head until her eyes met Pierce's. "I know. And I'm so sorry. Trust me. I know what it's like to feel insecure. Especially about this."

Pierce scoffed. "You? I highly doubt that."

"I'm serious. I have mini-crises about it just about daily. Most of the time I have to call my sister in Nevada just to reassure me I'm completely out of touch."

"Really? You worry about, you know, me?" She couldn't miss the delight in Pierce's tone.

"Are you kidding? All the damn time, Pierce. You're incredibly sexy, and smart, and funny, and caring..." If ever there was a moment for Cassidy to leak those three fragile words, it would be now. They were so far to the tip of her tongue she thought they might just fall out.

Pierce kissed her chin, temporarily quieting the turmoil in her mind but accelerating the storm in her heart.

"Whenever you feel like that just remember one thing..." She watched the lump in Pierce's throat rise and fall as she swallowed hard. "It took me only one month to fall absolutely, head over heels in love with you."

Cassidy's vision dimmed to near black. The sounds of the street below, the whirl of the ceiling fan, the clunk of the radiator—it all stopped, a frozen moment in time she would remember for as long as she lived.

"I love you too." Overwhelmed. Terrified. Overjoyed. The release washed over her like a thousand calming waves, as every muscle in her body let go at once. Those three words she'd dreaded, anticipated, tried so hard to hold back were every bit more powerful than she could have imagined, each syllable carrying with it a promise for tomorrow. Taking Pierce's face in her hands, she kissed her with every single one of those promises, until her fears, her apprehension, her past melted into one perfect future.

Chapter Sixteen

Pierce would never have described herself as "outdoorsy." She did enjoy the occasional hike and could start a campfire after a few tries, and really that was only because her parents forced her to join the Girl Scouts for a year. Still, if given the choice, she'd take room service at the Four Seasons any day of the week. But when Galen proposed that she, Rowan, Pierce, and Cassidy take a weekend trip to the Burgess family cabin in northern New Hampshire, Pierce jumped on it. It was rare for all four of them to have an entire weekend off together. And the image of curling up to Cassidy on some private dock was all the coaxing Pierce needed.

Being the only one of four with a sensible car that could actually fit them all, Cassidy pulled up in her fifteen-year-old Subaru Forester outside of Pierce's apartment a little after eight a.m. The mid-July heat suddenly felt seasonably appropriate. Even at the early hour of the morning, the sun was already blazing, and a dreamy haze had settled in the sky. Pierce smiled, threw open the back door, and chucked her duffel bag onto the seat.

"You know, I must say, this distance has been unbearable," Pierce said, sliding in next to Cassidy.

"You joke. But even one night was far more than I'd like."

Pierce leaned over the center console and kissed her, the heat from the open window beating down on her back. "Speaking of that, why don't I drive? You must be exhausted."

She examined Cassidy's face closely for signs of wear from the overnight shift she'd just been relieved of.

"I'm okay. I just had an enormous coffee. And besides. Gerty is a little touchy. Not everyone can handle her sticky brakes and overzealous gas pedal."

Pierce laughed. "I'm sure I could manage. Just let me know if you get too tired. It's a bit of a drive up there. And whatever you do, don't let Galen drive. She thinks she's a Formula One racer most of the time. We'd be lucky to make it there in several pieces, never mind just one."

"Noted."

The Boston traffic was light with city dwellers out of town for the weekend and the hungover twenty-somethings still in bed. Pierce kept her fingers lightly wound in Cassidy's for the entire fifteen minutes it took to reach Galen and Rowan's place.

Much to Pierce's surprise, the two sat on a bench outside of their building, large cups of takeaway coffee in hand. Their bags flanked them, and upon seeing Pierce and Cassidy pull up, Galen tapped her watch dramatically.

"Surgeons." Pierce mocked them.

Galen lifted both of their pieces of luggage in one easy swoop and placed them next to Pierce's.

"Hey, thanks for the lift," Galen said, climbing into the tattered backseat.

"Sorry it's not exactly the lap of luxury," Cassidy said. "But Gerty will get us there, won't you, Gert?" She tapped the steering wheel affectionately.

"I'm just glad one of us has a car actually suitable for camping."

"I wanted to talk to you about this camping business, G," Pierce cut in from the passenger seat.

"What about it?"

"We aren't really, like, camping, are we?" Pierce could see Galen and Rowan exchange amused glances through the rearview mirror.

"Pierce. It's a five-bedroom cabin on Lake Winnipesauke. There's a freakin' sauna in the bathroom. And yes, to a Burgess, that's camping. But you're more than welcome to pitch a tent in the yard if you like."

Cassidy raised one hand from the wheel. "If she does that, I'm sleeping with you guys in the house."

"Hell, no. I'm relieved this is a full-on glamping experience," Pierce said. "I'm far too pretty to get dirty."

"You and me both, kid. You and me both." Galen leaned forward to offer her fist to Pierce, who immediately met it with her own.

"What if we just left these two off somewhere and had the place to ourselves, Cass?" Rowan said.

"I like that idea even better."

"Hey! You can't do that," Galen retorted. "I have the key. Besides, I know where my dad hides all the good booze."

"Twenty-five-year-old McCallen?" Pierce asked.

"Think older. I only drink scotch that's been around longer than I have."

Pierce smiled. Her roots were far humbler than her cousin's, but she couldn't deny they shared a serious love for the finer things.

Two hours later, Gerty came to a stop outside a stunning cabin heavily shaded by the boughs of luscious trees and shrubs. The house was set far back from the narrow gravel road that led them there. Acres of fertile grass spread out around them, leading down to the still, expansive lake that sat majestically in the background. At the farthest point of the horizon sat the Presidential Mountain Range, a smoky blue-gray in the mid-day summer heat. Pierce was immediately struck with a sense of calm that was pure juxtaposition to the city, and every bit of tension and worry she'd been carrying surrounding her ever-expanding attachment to Cassidy dissipated into a comforting gratitude for everything her new life in Boston had brought her so far.

For an entire day, Cassidy hadn't thought about her past or what might come of the future. She couldn't remember the last time that had happened. Maybe never? It was strange that she was a little more tired than usual. But the last couple of weeks had been long, and she was an ER resident. Just part of the gig, she told herself.

But as she sat with Rowan at the end of the dock, their toes skimming the dark, cool water, the tiniest corner of her brain nagged at her. Maybe she should make a doctor's appointment? Just get some blood work to be sure? No. She was just tired.

"Okay, it's finally just us," Rowan said, jarring Cassidy out of her own head. "Time to spill."

"Spill?" Cassidy laughed.

"Yes! I want all your deepest, gushiest thoughts and feelings about Pierce. Spare no details."

Grateful for a distraction, and for the opportunity to talk about Pierce, Cassidy angled her body toward Rowan, tucking one bare foot underneath her. It was unsettlingly dark without the ever-present city lights, but she could still make out Rowan's eager face.

"What do you want to know?"

"It's been a few months now. Are you guys...serious?"

Cassidy had thought so. Had Pierce said differently? "I'd say we are...But I can't speak for Pierce." Her heart dropped just a little.

"Oh, I know what Pierce thinks. She hasn't shut up about you since you met. I'm surprised she hasn't proposed yet." Rowan laughed. "I wanted to see if you returned that sentiment. I haven't known her long, but Pierce is Galen's family. And she's already become like family to me. I really want to see her happy."

"Well, listen, if it's any reassurance from my end..." Cassidy glanced around in the darkness, making sure Galen and Pierce were still back on land getting the fire started. "I'm absolutely nuts about her."

Cassidy could make out Rowan's pleased smile in the shadows. "Good."

"Maybe even more nuts than I've ever been about anyone, actually."

"As in...you're in love with her?"

"As in...big time."

Rowan wrapped her arm around Cassidy's shoulder and pulled her in tightly, a delighted giggle escaping into the quiet night. "Girl!" Rowan appeared too excited to say anything else.

"I think both Pierce and I want what you and Galen have."

Rowan released her but kept her hand on Cassidy's knee. "What you two have is even better. Because it's yours."

"I certainly wouldn't trade it."

"What were your past relationships like? You know, if you don't mind my asking."

A swell of panic rose in Cassidy. The past was her least favorite topic of conversation. But she sensed something safe about Rowan, something to be trusted.

"I didn't come out until I was older. Really not until my early twenties. And to be honest with you, I was sort of…preoccupied in my youth."

"What do you mean? Like, with school and things?"

"That, and other stuff. I spent a lot of time in and out of the hospital when I was a teenager." Cassidy exhaled in immediate disbelief that she'd just disclosed one of the most sensitive parts of her to someone she hardly knew. But with that exhale came a sense of relief, like someone had finally poked a pinhole in her deepest secret, letting it ease out of her, releasing the pressure she didn't realize had been suffocating her.

"Oh my God, Cass. Were you sick?"

"Non-Hodgkins. Twice, actually. Sonofabitch almost killed me."

"Holy shit…But you're okay? I mean, it's all gone, right?"

That was the question Cassidy seemed to ask herself nearly every day. "Yeah. I mean, as far as I know."

"I'm so sorry. I can't imagine what that must have done for your childhood."

Cassidy stared off into the blackness. "It split my parents up. They couldn't take it, always wondering if I was going to make it or not. They started blaming each other, and the resentment just festered until one day my dad left. Went and shacked up with the principal of the school he worked at."

"Jesus." Rowan shook her head.

"Yeah. But I'm fine now. I hardly give it a second thought."

Rowan nodded silently and followed her gaze out into the horizon.

"That was a lie," Cassidy said. "I don't know why I just lied to you. I'm not used to talking about this."

"You don't have to if you don't want to. Really."

"I know." But Cassidy did want to talk about it. For the first time in years, it felt good to share her past, her fears, with someone. Rowan wasn't just a stranger. She was a friend. And she felt like more than that even. She felt like family. "There's something about you, Ro. You're really easy to talk to."

"Look, Cass. I know this is all new, with Pierce, and with coming into our little circle here, but I see you as my friend already. A good friend. And Pierce is Galen's family, which sort of makes her my family by proxy. And that sort of makes you my family too…If that's okay, I mean."

Warmth flooded Cassidy's insides, and a threat of tears assaulted her eyes. "That's okay with me."

"Good. Now come here." Rowan grabbed Cassidy by both shoulders and crushed her against her chest, and Cassidy was overwhelmed by a sense that she had found her people. Her tribe.

"I lied when I said it doesn't affect me," Cassidy said, her head still propped on Rowan's shoulder, the wool of Rowan's sweater scratching Cassidy's cheek.

"How do you mean?"

"It's kept me from getting close to people. This is going to sound really dumb, but a few weeks ago, I had this patient. She was a young girl with ALL. Neutropenic fever. She reminded me so much of me at that age. And her parents…Jesus, it was like I was re-watching the worst moments of my life. I didn't talk to Pierce the entire night after that. I completely pushed her away. I even snapped at her when she asked and told her it wasn't always about her. I just kept thinking, if I love her, how could I risk putting her through that again?"

"You can't think like that. You don't know whether the cancer will ever come back. In fact, it probably won't. You can't just push people away on the small chance they might love you and lose you."

"I know."

"Did you tell Pierce?"

Cassidy didn't answer. She looked down at her lap, studying the gray outlines of her hands.

"You didn't, did you," Rowan answered for her.

"No. She can't know. She'd just worry all the time."

Cassidy shook her head. "I can't tell you what to do. But I think you should tell her. She adores you. She's already planning her whole damn life around you. She'd be crushed if she discovered you were keeping this from her."

"I've thought of that once or twice."

"You should give Pierce more credit, you know. She'd already go to the ends of the earth for you. If anything ever happened to you, she'd be there the entire way."

That was exactly what Cassidy was afraid of.

"I'll tell her at some point, okay? I'm just…I'm not ready yet."

Rowan pursed her lips in apparent disapproval. "Don't sit on it too long. Life's shorter than we think."

"Preaching to the choir, my friend. Preaching to the damn choir."

Four bottles of Stella Artois in the hole, what appeared to be a modestly drunk Cassidy followed Pierce up the stairs to their room.

Pierce gawked. "This is bigger than my whole apartment." The guest room was tastefully decorated with nautically themed wall hangings that looked more expensive than Pierce's car, the bed covered in cream and blue striped pillows that swam on a cloudlike duvet. Pierce never felt bitter about the fact the Burgess side of the family had done so much better for themselves than the Parkers. But she was impressed and not above reaping some of the benefits of her newfound closeness with Galen.

"You know, as much as I love spending time with Galen and Ro, I still like nothing better in this world than being alone with you." Pierce shut the door behind them and folded her arms around Cassidy's waist, their bodies so close hardly a part of them wasn't against the other. She couldn't get close enough to her, at least not enough to mirror the osmosis their souls had seemed to manage.

"I was just thinking the exact same thing." Cassidy gently grasped the back of Pierce's head and kissed her softly, her lips moving in teasingly slow patterns rivaled only by the painfully calculated movement of her tongue against Pierce's. Pierce's chest warmed, the sensation moving through her torso in either direction. It had always taken only one kiss for Cassidy to send her blood hurtling through her body like a rip tide, her heart fighting to keep tempo with the electricity pulsating across her skin. Pierce had never been kissed the way Cassidy kissed her—with a passion, a promise, a steadiness she hadn't known was possible.

"Pierce. I want to tell you something." Cassidy had broken away abruptly, her face worried and free of the light, drunken humor of the evening. Pierce's heart, still quivering, shifted almost audibly to panic mode.

"No good conversation ever started with those words." Pierce laughed nervously as Cassidy fidgeted around her. She remained silent for a time. Whatever she wanted to say, she was clearly afraid to say it.

"I just wanted to say…I love you."

Pierce's heart slammed back to a near-normal pace, and she smiled. "Is that it?"

"Isn't that enough?"

"More. You just looked like you had something more ominous to say. You know you can tell me anything, right?"

Cassidy nodded and smiled politely, but Pierce wasn't convinced. A part of Cassidy was still a black box, a piece of her locked up tightly with the key hidden somewhere deep.

CHAPTER SEVENTEEN

Rowan had likely been right about Cassidy needing to tell Pierce about the cancer. *The cancer.* Cassidy made it sound like some heinous monster, lurking in the closet, waiting until she went to sleep at night to come out and torment her. And in a way, that's what it was. Not an inanimate thing, but a living, breathing being, waiting to prey on everything good in her life. But, as it usually goes with monsters, the lights come up and daylight makes everything look a little less frightening. And the monster is forgotten about. At least, until the night comes again.

So Cassidy did not tell Pierce. Weeks went by. The summer blossomed. And she was happier than she'd ever been. Why ruin all that with something as detrimental as the past?

It was difficult for Pierce at times not to dwell on just how horrid the previous summer had been for her. Katie, who Pierce really hadn't even given a second thought to since meeting Cassidy, had broken up with her, and Pierce was floundering through a pool of endless first dates that led nowhere. Now, in less than a year, she found herself in a new city, with a new family, and the most stunning, brilliant woman in the passenger seat of her BMW.

"What are you grinning about over there?" Cassidy laughed and squeezed Pierce's bicep.

"Just thinking about you. Wondering how I got so lucky."

The windows were down, hot August air blowing in a futile breeze. Cassidy had put Vance Joy on the radio—their song. Pierce glanced over at Cassidy, her arms sticking up through the sunroof, her long, loose hair flowing freely across her face. She laughed again, this time with a lightness, an ease that set Pierce's own heart on fire.

It was difficult for Pierce not to dwell on the past. Not when she now had everything she'd ever wanted.

The day was so hot, there was nothing to do but fall asleep. And that's exactly what Pierce and Cassidy did as soon as they returned to Cassidy's apartment. They only awoke an hour later because a heavy rain had settled in over the city, a futile attempt to cool the scorching pavement below.

Pierce knew Cassidy was awake too. She'd seen her eyes flutter open sleepily. But she let the grogginess dissipate, gently kissing a line down the salty skin of Cassidy's bare shoulder. Cassidy moaned contentedly but still didn't speak. The rain pelted the windows, and the temperature had seemed to drop precipitously, even in the stuffy second-floor apartment. A pleasant gray consumed the sky, not dark, exactly, but enough to paint the busy Boston neighborhood with a sense of quiet. Pierce wrapped one arm around Cassidy's middle, weaving their fingers together, and gently nipped just below her ear.

"Be careful..." Cassidy finally mumbled into her pillow.

"And why is that?"

"If you keep doing that, you're going to have to follow through." She rolled onto her back to face Pierce, her eyes glassy with need, her lips curled into a cunning smile.

Pierce put her hands on either side of Cassidy's face and kissed her hard, her hands migrating further south until the tips of her fingers grazed the band of Cassidy's panties.

"You know I always do."

Sex was always enjoyable for Pierce. Necessary, even. But sex with Cassidy was something else entirely. Never had she experienced something so raw, so easy. It was like their bodies knew each other immediately, each touch exactly what the other needed. They had little need for talk, although Pierce quite enjoyed that as well. Cassidy set her skin on fire. Her hands knew the map better than Pierce herself did. And Pierce's body always quit long before her mind and desire did. Still, as much as she loved the way Cassidy touched her, she loved nothing more than learning Cassidy's body. The way her muscles clenched and released, the pleas for more, the feeling of her fingernails in Pierce's back...It was everything.

Cassidy wasn't sure whether it was the heat, the perpetual exhaustion from a life of shift work, or the security of being in Pierce's arms, but she had somehow managed to fall asleep again. This time, upon waking, the sun was low in the sky, and the streets of the Fenway neighborhood had been resurrected by the welcome breeze that had followed the rainstorm. The poor insulation of her windows allowed the more-than-ambient sounds of eager college students left behind for the summer, seeking out their next bar hop, and excited tourists on their way to see the Red Sox game to seep through. Spending many years in various small towns, Cassidy always found it strangely comforting, knowing someone nearby was always awake, like falling asleep with the TV on as a child. Pierce must have fallen asleep again too, because when Cassidy glanced over at her, she was snoring softly, her lips just parted in the most adorable way Cassidy had ever seen. As if on cue, Pierce released a quiet groan and smiled, turning over to face Cassidy and nestling her head under Cassidy's arm.

"I can't believe we went to sleep again," Pierce said, her voice thick and gravelly.

"I can. I think we're both carrying about six months of cumulative sleep debt. And that heat. Seems like the rain cooled things off a bit."

"We could even venture out to find some food in a little."

Cassidy tightened her grip around Pierce, and Pierce buried her head closer. "I don't know. You're going to have to do a lot of coaxing to get me out of this bed."

Pierce propped herself on one elbow and grinned. "I could get on board with that."

She leaned down and kissed Cassidy, her free hand roaming through her hair that splayed wildly across the pillow. As they so often seemed to, Pierce's hands had plans of their own, and one shifted down lower until it was softly caressing Cassidy's breast, her fingers pinching and flicking Cassidy's nipple with a sharpness that contrasted to the teasing brushstrokes of the skin of Pierce's palm. A jolt immediately rocked Cassidy, ending between her legs with a wet heat that rivaled that of the outdoors. She was so engrossed with Pierce's touch, it took Cassidy a moment to notice Pierce had stopped, focusing instead on what appeared to be a small area in the lower part of Cassidy's left underarm.

"Cass. What's this?"

"What do you mean?"

"There's a lump here. It feels like a big node to me."

Cassidy's heart skittered through her chest, and a tiny fist reached in and began to squeeze. It was subtle at first. But then the intensity built until her lungs were being crushed and a tunnel of gray built around her vision. This couldn't be happening. No. This was just another nightmare. She'd wake up in a minute, next to Pierce. Safe.

"I don't know." Cassidy closed her eyes and took several deep breaths, willing herself to wake up. But she didn't.

"How long has it been there?"

She had to keep it together. For all Pierce was aware, this was just a harmless lymph node. A virus, maybe. "Honestly, I didn't notice it."

"Does it hurt?"

"Not really, no." It didn't hurt. It didn't hurt at all. Which was exactly how *the cancer* had started the first time—a large, painless lump in her groin area Cassidy had found while taking a shower one morning.

All at once, the world ended for Cassidy. The picture in her head she'd just barely let herself conceive, one of her and Pierce, and maybe an overall-clad toddler, running the beach in late summer, dissolved into a cruel dust. And any hope of continuing to run from the monster was replaced by faded snapshots of hospital stays, chemo, and a ragged Pierce giving up her entire life for something she couldn't stop either.

Cassidy feigned the most nonchalant smile she could muster from her terrified depths. "I'll make an appointment to get it checked, okay? I'm sure it's no big deal."

The anticipation nearly consumed Cassidy, but she managed to wait until the next morning when Pierce left for work to call Dr. Lucas Hedges at Boston Children's Hospital. She felt silly calling a pediatric oncologist, now that she was in her mid-twenties. But she didn't know what else to do. The minute Pierce was out the door, Cassidy grabbed her phone and began searching for the number. Once she found it, though, it took nearly fifteen minutes to get up the courage to dial. If she made an appointment, if she acknowledged she had a lymph node, this became real. If she ignored it, maybe it would just…disappear. But her logical, medically trained brain told her if she ignored it, and it was the monster raising its hateful head, it wouldn't disappear. She would just get sicker. And then maybe it really would be too late.

It was Pierce who pushed her to eventually let the call go through. Not Pierce herself, exactly, but the thought of her. If she was sick again, she wanted to get better so she could build a life with Pierce. So they could die together, as two cranky, exhausted ninety-five-year-olds in their nursing home, bickering about which pitcher the Red Sox should start.

She also felt safe. When she had first learned she had cancer, she'd counted on her parents to protect her. Like most kids, she'd figured she didn't have any problems Mom and Dad couldn't fix. They'd never let anything bad happen to her. Now that she was an adult, she knew better. Her parents were just fragile, flawed humans like everyone else. They couldn't cure her non-Hodgkins, and they certainly couldn't keep it from coming back. And neither could Pierce. Yet, somehow, the thought of going through it all again with Pierce by her side brought back that same sense of security. Pierce wouldn't let anything hurt her.

"Yes, hi. Can I make an appointment with Dr. Hedges?" Cassidy was momentarily jarred by the voice on the other end of the line announcing that she'd reached the Pediatric Oncology Practice of Greater Boston.

"Certainly. And what's the appointment regarding?"

"I'm a...I used to be a patient of Dr. Hedges. I found a lump..."

"Okay." The receptionist's voice didn't hold the amount of concern for her Cassidy thought was warranted. "What's your name, dear?"

"Cassidy Sullivan."

"Let me just pull you up here. One minute." After an excruciating silence came some audible tapping. Would her records even be accessible since she had been a patient so long ago? They were probably archived in some dusty cardboard box somewhere in the bowels of the medical-records department.

"Here we are. September 2, 1989?"

"Yes. That's me." Cassidy had almost forgotten her birthday was coming up in a couple of weeks. Every birthday she'd celebrated in recent memory had been a declaration of one more year without *the cancer*. Maybe her twenty-seventh wouldn't be quite so fortunate.

"Great. I have an opening on September 14th. Ten a.m.?"

"That's three weeks away. I can't wait that long," Cassidy snapped.

"Let me just see if there's anything else, okay?"

"Thank you."

"It looks like he had a cancellation tomorrow. Eight a.m. Can you make it in?" The woman's voice remained soft and kind.

"Yes! Thank you. I really, really appreciate it."

"You're welcome, dear."

"Just one thing...Is it, you know, weird?"

The woman laughed politely. "That you're an adult? Not at all. We have many patients that the doctors follow well into adulthood."

For the most fleeting of moments, the kind secretary on the other end of the phone, and Dr. Lucas Hedges, lifted the weight of Cassidy's worry from her shoulders. Until Cassidy remembered she still had a lymph node. And the monster was still nearby.

❖

The Pediatric Oncology Center of Greater Boston was almost exactly as Cassidy remembered it. The walls were still the same overly cheerful yellow, and countless photos of kids who'd won their battles with cancer smothered a mammoth bulletin board, boasting just how good Dr. Hedges and his team were at beating the odds. As a child, Cassidy used to stare at the board endlessly, dreaming of her picture being up there someday. Two other people were waiting to check in at the reception desk, and Cassidy couldn't help but search for her photo. Sure enough, so many years later, it was there—a dirty-blond, braces-clad, acne-ridden teenage Cassidy, smiling like she'd just been told she was going to Disney World. She remembered that day, her last visit to this office. The day the great Lucas Hedges had told her she was "cancer free." *Now look at me, Lucas, you motherfucker.*

"Can I help you?" Cassidy immediately recognized the voice coming from the woman behind the reception desk from their pleasant exchange the previous morning.

"Yes. I'm here for my appointment with Dr. Hedges. Cassidy Sullivan."

"Very good. I'll just need you to fill these out. It's been a while since we've seen you." The woman's heartening smile was exactly what Cassidy had imagined through the phone.

"Sure." Cassidy took the clipboard that was handed to her.

"Welcome back, dear."

It was a rather odd thing to say, "welcome back." As if anyone would ever want to step foot in a place like this ever again, cheerful yellow walls and all.

It took only ninety seconds for Cassidy to update her latest contact info, her medical problems (none, as far as she hoped), allergies, and medications. She sat on a polka-dot beanbag chair at the edge of the room. A flat-screen TV in the corner, which she acknowledged was new since her time as a patient there, played a cartoon featuring a family of pigs who wore dress clothes and ate at the dinner table. On a beanbag adjacent to her sat a fidgety adolescent boy, his scalp bald and his skin void of the usual flush of a child's cheeks. He pounded furiously on an iPad, his mother periodically reminding him it was the only iPad he had, and he needed to be careful with it. Outdated issues of *Highlights Magazine* sat neatly on the table in the center of the room, just like they had years ago. Cassidy thought they'd stopped making *Highlights* years ago, which only added to the strange déjà vu of the scene that sent a cold chill shooting down her neck. She should have called her parents. At least her mother. Or she should have told Pierce. Anything would have been better than being alone in that waiting room in that moment.

"Cassidy?" A nurse in lavender scrubs with cartoon puppies on them entered and looked directly at Cassidy. She wasn't hard to miss, being the only patient in the room born before the Obama administration.

"Right here." She stood quickly, the rush of blood to her feet leaving her woozy and unsteady.

"Come this way. We'll just get your height and weight."

"Everyone's favorite." Cassidy forced a laugh, wondering when humor had become a defense mechanism for her. Probably when she started working in emergency medicine, and it had to be.

The nurse in the lavender scrubs seemed to have a difficult time finding a paper gown large enough to fit a fully grown human, and Cassidy suddenly doubted just how many "adult patients" Dr. Hedges really had. And then, she was alone again. The door to the exam room was shut. Her bare legs dangled off the edge of the still absurdly high exam table. The gown crinkled and crackled with every movement, scratching her skin as it went. Isopropyl alcohol permeated the air—a scent Cassidy encountered on a near-daily basis, but one that smelled entirely different that day. She'd gotten so good at being a patient, when she was younger. Always smiling, optimistic. Never a tear shed or a scrap of fear shown. At least, that was how it looked to everyone else. Cassidy was the best pediatric patient she knew. And now, all she could manage to be was afraid.

Strangely, Cassidy recognized the tender knock on the exam room door as Dr. Hedges'. Or maybe the familiarity just came from the nightmares that ruined her sleep near weekly.

"Come in." Cassidy's throat swelled. She wasn't sure if it was the overzealous air conditioning or just the panic rising in her, but she tremored ever so slightly.

"Well, I'll be damned. Cassidy Sullivan. Or should I say, Doctor? It's been too long." Dr. Hedges was exactly as Cassidy had remembered him—tall, with striking white hair curled over his lush white brow. He had aged just a touch, but the deep blue of his eyes still conveyed the same sense of compassion and reassurance Cassidy always liked about him.

"I mean, I wouldn't say *too* long, personally, but...And hey, how did you know?"

"I keep tabs on all my patients. At least the special ones. That, and your parents sent me your medical-school-graduation announcement." He smiled at Cassidy, and she felt more at ease than she had in nearly forty-two hours. Dr. Hedges had all those pictures on his wall for a reason. He really was that good. And if anyone could save her, three times, it would be him.

Chapter Eighteen

"So. Emergency medicine, huh? I always knew you were a little bit crazy, kid." Dr. Hedges took a seat on the stool across from Cassidy. She was surprised to find she enjoyed the pleasantries, finding them a welcome distraction from what felt like impending doom.

"We can't all save the world like you." She smiled.

"I only do my part. Now tell me, Cassidy. As great as it is to see you again, I have a feeling you didn't come in just to talk about the Red Sox's horrendous pitching staff. What's bugging you?"

"It's nothing really. I just…I found a lump the other day, or actually, my girlfriend did, and I thought I should have it checked."

Dr. Hedges' thick, white brow deepened, and he scratched his scraggly beard. "Hmm. A lump. I see. Whereabouts?"

"Left axilla. I honestly had no idea it was there. It's completely painless. About the size of a dime."

"I see. Any fevers? Night sweats? Weight loss?" Dr. Hedges stood and moved toward the wall, spritzing his hands with alcohol.

"No. Nothing. Just a little tired. But I mean, I'm a resident."

"Just go ahead and lie back on the table here, and let's have a look, shall we?" He lifted half the paper gown, exposing Cassidy's left breast, and began to feel around her underarm, his hands stereotypically cold and large.

"I'm sure it's nothing."

Dr. Hedges didn't answer, instead just pursed his lips into a thin, concerned line and nodded gravely. For several more agonizing seconds he continued to palpate the tissue around the area, always returning to the problematic lymph node. Cassidy's stomach lurched. She was hoping he would say it felt benign, normal even. But his face was telling Cassidy something else entirely.

"Mhmm. Yes." Finally, he removed his hand, stood up straight, and returned to the hand-sanitizer dispenser on the wall. "I'm sure it's nothing as well. But, given your history…"

Cancer. He means your cancer…

"…we should get a biopsy just to be sure."

"Right. That sounds like a good idea." Cassidy knew this was the likely next step, but she still didn't like hearing it.

"I'll put you on the schedule for next week. How does Wednesday work?"

Cassidy sat in a dreamy haze, the dissociation unlike anything she'd ever experienced. But she knew better now. This was no lucid dream. She was not going to wake up in Pierce's arms in a few minutes, her life devoid of sickness. This was happening.

"Dr. Hedges?" Cassidy was shocked by the feebleness of her own voice.

He looked up from the computer where he was taking notes. The knot of his tie was loose, his shirt sleeves rolled haphazardly. He wore no white coat. Now that she was a grown-up, Cassidy thought he looked more small-town pediatrician who made house calls than world-class oncologist. She wanted to jump up and hug him, cry onto his white oxford until she felt comforted. Dr. Hedges was the only person in the world who knew she was there. That made him, sadly, the only person Cassidy had.

"Yes?"

"It's going to be okay. Isn't it?"

Dr. Hedges offered her an appeasing smile, and Cassidy was bowled over by yet another memory—one of this same doctor, offering that same smile, as he told Cassidy and her parents the chemo had not worked.

"Let's just wait and see what the biopsy shows."

❖

The small sense of relief Cassidy had experienced in Dr. Hedges's office had vanished by the time she left the parking lot. Pierce had sent several texts, but Cassidy left them unanswered. She'd have to respond eventually, but until she figured out what to tell her, it was easier to keep her distance.

Cassidy took the turn onto Memorial Drive and squeezed the accelerator just a little too hard, her elderly car lurching forward with more pep than Cassidy had anticipated. Her mind was on Pierce still, her body feeling physically torn between wanting her forever by her side to fight this demon and wanting to keep her safe from it. She pressed her blinker to exit the off-ramp toward Fenway and hit redial on the last number she'd called.

"Hey! Are you all right?" Pierce's voice cloaked her in a soothing comfort, pulling her in like a warm bath.

"I'm fine. I miss you though." Cassidy smiled.

"I miss you too. I was worried for a minute. Thought maybe you moved to New Delhi and didn't tell me or something."

Worse, Cassidy told herself. "Nothing like that. I just got caught up with some things and didn't have my phone. I'm okay. I promise." She fucking hated lying to Pierce.

"Good. Listen. I have to work late tonight. Greg needed me to swap shifts with him. But I can be over sometime after midnight?"

"I uh...actually have plans tonight. I'm hanging out with Rowan. But you should come over after."

"Rowan? Really?"

Cassidy hadn't known she was spending the evening with Rowan until that moment. And, of course, Rowan didn't know it yet either. But it felt like the best idea she'd had all day.

"Yeah. We thought we could use a girls' night."

"Does that mean, like, painting each other's nails and doing face masks and whatever?"

Cassidy laughed as she pushed the shifter into park on one of the nearby side streets. The car halted with a sharp jolt.

"More like pillow fights in our underwear."

"In that case, can I come?"

"Not a chance. But you should come over after you're done with work. I still really want to see you…"

It was going to be hard to keep her distance from Pierce—far harder than Cassidy had anticipated.

"Of course. And for the record, I love that you and Ro are spending time together. It's like we're all one little gay family."

She could hear the delight in Pierce's voice. The anxiety inside her deepened into a dark sadness. She didn't want to lose that little family. But she didn't want to steal any of Pierce's joy either. Maybe, if she just slowly faded away, the loss wouldn't be so unbearable.

The second phone call Cassidy made was to Rowan.

"Rowan, it's Cassidy. Hey, so what are you doing tonight?" No point in being coy when Pierce already thought they had plans.

"I mean, nothing much? Galen and I were going to watch some garbage on Netflix probably. Why?"

"Can we do something? You know, as in, just the two of us?"

Cassidy held her breath as she waited for a response. She hoped the conversation she and Rowan had shared at the end of the dock several weeks back was enough of a gateway to make the invitation less awkward. The truth of it was, she needed a friend, someone she could trust who wasn't quite as close to her as Pierce. And Rowan felt like just that person.

"Hell yes, we can!" Rowan's enthusiasm lifted Cassidy's melancholy just enough. "Galen's home, but I can kick her out. She can go play Fortnite in the office or something. I'll get her a pizza from Georgio's and a bottle of whiskey, and she'll leave us alone for the night."

"Are you sure?" Cassidy didn't love the idea of Rowan rearranging her plans for her, but Rowan's excitement swayed her.

"Absolutely. Please, come over. Bring the rosé. I'll take care of the rest."

❖

Two bottles of rosé in hand, Cassidy arrived at Galen and Rowan's apartment shortly after six p.m.

"If we're planning on drinking all that, it's a good thing I made plenty of snacks." Rowan opened the door before Cassidy even had a chance to knock.

"Actually, I made the snacks." Galen appeared from down the hall, a video-game controller gripped between her fingers.

"She did," Rowan said.

"How did you know I was here? I didn't even ring the bell."

"Oh. That's Galen too. She's convinced someone's going to come try to kidnap me while she's at work one night. Installed this crazy-ass security camera so she can watch from her phone while she's gone." Rowan swatted Galen gently in her abdomen, smiling.

"I'm not sure if I find that really sweet, or extra creepy," Cassidy said, placing the bottles of wine on the counter and kicking off her boots.

"I haven't decided yet either," Rowan said. "Okay, G. I'm sending you back to your office. We have girl things to do."

"But...I'm a girl!" Galen crossed her arms defiantly.

"Sorry. Just the two of us tonight, love. Besides, how often do I tell you to go play video games? There's a fresh bottle of Glenlivet on the bar cart. Go have fun."

Galen took Rowan by the shoulders and kissed her on the forehead. "I love you."

"I love you more."

Watching them left Cassidy with an excruciating longing for Pierce. For a moment, she wanted to leave. She wanted to run to Pierce and tell her everything. She wanted to share this fear with her, let it be a catalyst to bring them closer together. But the fortress Cassidy had deftly built around herself for years stood stronger than her need to be near Pierce, and her resolve once again returned.

"Sorry about that. She'll be occupied for the rest of the night." Rowan took two wineglasses out of the cabinet and walked into the living room.

"You didn't need to kick her out." Cassidy laughed.

"I know. But I got the impression you were looking for some one-on-one time. As in, maybe you have something to get off your chest?"

Cassidy wasn't surprised to find her plea for a play date had set off red flags. It wasn't as if she and Rowan ever spent any time together without Pierce and Galen. At least not until tonight.

"That obvious, huh?"

"It's cool. I won't make you spill right away. We'll get some of this wine going first." Rowan thrust a glass at Cassidy, who gladly accepted.

❖

It was difficult to talk through the ever-hardening face mask covering Cassidy's mouth.

"I can't believe we're actually doing this," she said, the mask cracking around the edges of her lips as she did.

Rowan laughed. "Stop. Don't make me laugh."

"What's wrong? Don't I look sexy?" Cassidy framed her face with her hands and arched her neck.

"You look ridiculous."

"Oh? And what about you?"

"I look fabulous." Rowan picked her phone up off the floor and held it out in front of them. Cassidy pressed her face against Rowan's and smiled as big as she could through the crinkling, hard clay, and Rowan snapped a chain of photos. Upon reviewing them, they erupted in an explosion of laughter, tears streaking the chalky gray on their cheeks.

"Okay, you're right. I look ridiculous." The laughter escalated until Cassidy's belly ached, and ever briefly, she forgot why she was really here.

Cassidy's face must have fallen, her laugh vanishing into the night.

"Time to tell me what's going on, Cass." Rowan disappeared into the kitchen and returned with the second bottle of wine, refilling both of their glasses nearly to the rim.

"Remember all that stuff I told you a few weeks ago? About my…past?" Cassidy took several large sips, letting the sweet bite of the drink fade into a steady, soothing burn.

"Of course I do."

"I found a lymph node." Cassidy swallowed again, the burn now nothing but a dull heat.

"What? When?"

"The other night."

"Cass…" Rowan's posture straightened, and she nodded resolutely. "I'm sure it's nothing. People get nodes all the time. Just a virus is all."

"Right. That's what I said." Cassidy ran a hand through her hair and pressed her eyes shut. Time for honesty, she told herself. "That's what I've been trying to convince myself of too."

"Did you get it checked yet?"

"I went to my oncologist earlier today."

"And? What did he say?"

"Not much. I have a biopsy scheduled for next week. But you know that face we make? The one we make when we're pretty sure we're going to have to give a patient bad news?"

Rowan nodded. "You mean the one I give patients when I'm pretty sure their tumor is going to be malignant but can't tell them yet?"

Cassidy looked at the floor, her stomach pitching.

"Oh…God, I'm sorry. That was a stupid thing to say." Rowan touched Cassidy's shoulder, her expression remorseful.

"It's okay. Really. That was exactly the look he gave me."

Rowan's hand remained on Cassidy, and she placed her other one on Cassidy's thigh. They remained silent for the moment, the somberness of the words permeating the evening's previous delight.

"I don't mean to be such a downer. I just needed someone to talk to. Someone to take my mind off this."

"Please! You aren't a downer. And you know I'm here for you. No matter what happens. We all are. Galen, me…Pierce."

Cassidy's heart tugged hard again. "Thank you. You have no idea what that means to me."

Rowan hugged her as Cassidy battled a few tears that were managing to break through her faultless barrier.

"What did Pierce say when you told her?"

Cassidy remained silent. She had no answer. At least not a good one.

"Jesus. You didn't tell her?"

"I…I was going to…"

Rowan shook her head, her lips pursed together into a hard line. "Oh, Cass. You have to. You can't keep this from her."

"I can't put her through this."

"She loves you!"

"Exactly," Cassidy whispered.

"I don't understand. Why would you ever want to go through something like this alone?"

Cassidy didn't want to go through it alone. She wanted nothing more than to have her one great love by her side to fight the monster that hunted her. "I'm not alone. I have you. And Galen. And I'll have my mom, once I tell her."

"Pierce can handle this. She needs to know."

"No. She needs to move on. She needs to find someone who isn't sick. Someone who will be around for a long time." Cassidy hadn't been brave enough to even think the words until now, and hearing them out loud sent the rogue tears waiting at the corners of her eyes spilling out with a vengeance.

"Don't you love Pierce too?"

Cassidy smiled but the tears continued. "More than I've ever loved anything, which is why I have to let her go. Before I destroy her."

"Losing you will destroy her."

"Heartbreak from being dumped is nothing compared to watching the person you love be slowly eaten away by cancer."

Rowan shook her head again, her eyes narrow and her irises dark. "So that's your grand plan? Just break up with her?"

Cassidy hadn't really decided until just now. The idea devastated her, but it was better than any alternative.

"It's the only way."

"That's the stupidest thing I've ever heard. You don't even know this is anything yet!" Rowan was doing a fine job playing the devil's advocate.

"Even if it isn't this time, it will be eventually."

"God, you're frustrating! You can't possibly know that." Rowan clapped her hand on the wooden coffee table, resulting in a thunderous echo that reverberated throughout the oversized room.

"You're right. I don't know for sure. But I saw what my being sick did to my parents. They fell apart watching me nearly die. And they were my parents. My blood. They had to stick by me, and each other, and they couldn't even manage that."

Rowan inhaled deeply, the fists she'd held clenched on her knees slowly releasing, and Cassidy thought maybe she should try yoga too.

"You know, Galen and I almost didn't happen."

Cassidy was relieved to move the conversation away from herself. "How come?"

"I was with this guy, Brian. For a really long time. He was pretty much all I ever knew. He was kind. He was safe, and comfortable. He wasn't going to hurt me. And then, I met Galen, all passion and fire and enigma. She made me feel things I'd never even dreamed of. She breathed life into me. But she was a liability. An enormous one. So I chose safe. I chose Brian. I knew he wasn't going anywhere. And if he did? I'd survive. Not Galen, though. That was a loss I'd never get over."

"But obviously you changed your mind."

"My heart changed it for me. My mind told me to protect myself at all costs. And to protect Brian. But my heart…that was all Galen's, from day one. It was a risk. It's still a risk. Love means vulnerability. It's a gamble I take every day. One you're taking with Pierce. And one Pierce is taking with you. If you tell her the cost, she'll take it without question."

The crying was nearly uncontrollable at this point. But it felt good. It felt like release.

"I know she would, which is why I can't tell her. I can't let her go through this, because she'll want to. And she has no idea what that means."

"You need to give Pierce more credit. She's strong. She's loyal. She'd lie down and die for you if someone asked."

"But she doesn't know what's ahead. She has no idea what it's like to watch someone you love in a hospital bed, getting doses of cell-shattering chemo. What it's like to hold someone's hair back as they vomit the entire contents of their stomach day after day. When they lose their hair. When they fall into a deep, nasty depression because it's not fair that they have to go through this again. She doesn't know what it's like to hear a doctor say 'the treatment isn't working,' and 'there's nothing more we can do.' She doesn't know what it's like to worry like that. To hurt like that. And I will never let her."

Rowan threw her hands up in the air, the exasperation returning. "Fine. Then run. Break her heart. Break your own. But just know that by doing this, you're already lying down to die. You're already giving up."

Chapter Nineteen

Hiding from Pierce wasn't an option. The two of them had spent nearly every day together since their first kiss. Simply fading away wouldn't be possible. But Cassidy still longed for the slow departure of love—the easy good-bye. Not that any good-bye with Pierce could ever possibly be easy. Every time she thought about it, she felt sick. A gnawing, turning sickness in the very deepest pit of her stomach told her everything she was planning to do was wrong. Maybe it was. But it was also right. The two, after all, aren't always mutually exclusive.

The night was already awful. Once she'd made the point to Rowan and, more importantly, to herself, she couldn't go back. She couldn't just pretend everything was fine when she saw Pierce, although she'd certainly considered it. It felt dishonest not to tell her right away, now that her mind was made up. Then again, the whole thing was dishonest, wasn't it? Cassidy was going to try to convince the woman she loved more than anything on this earth that she didn't.

She had no other choice. She couldn't love Pierce without destroying her. Rowan had called Cassidy nothing but a "cowardice martyr." And she was probably right. Cassidy wasn't doing this quite as much to protect Pierce, as she was to protect herself. She'd already watched people she loved fall apart because of her. And it had been the single most painful experience of her life—worse than nearly dying. She couldn't imagine what watching Pierce leave would feel like.

Whoever she was doing it for, Cassidy was just glad she wasn't going to give herself enough time to change her mind. If she waited too long, even one second too long, let herself look far into Pierce's strong face or touch her sturdy shoulders, she'd never have the courage to go. The hold Pierce had on her was too strong. It would be a miracle if Cassidy even survived this at her own hand.

The sound of keys in the lock triggered a single deep breath that did nothing to cleanse Cassidy of the heartache she was already suffering.

As the door swung open, she allowed herself one last, long look at Pierce. She stood in front of Cassidy, a smile so pure and unknowing it nearly brought Cassidy to the floor. Her youthful green eyes were clear. Her shoulders were straight and square. Pieces of stray hair had fallen to frame her perfect face. In a movie-like montage, Cassidy saw flashes of that face every morning in bed. She saw that smile looking down on her with the city lights spread out behind them. She saw summer drives and coffee shops, and then, she saw the future they were supposed to have. One with fenced-in suburban yards and Sunday farmers' markets, and maybe even the toddler in overalls Cassidy had never dared wish for. And the anger rushed her with such ferocity, she found herself unsteady. She would never have those things now. The future had been ripped away from her like last week's bulletin on the wall—gone. Irrelevant.

"Hey." Pierce was still smiling, and Cassidy realized she probably hadn't been staring for nearly the eternity it felt like.

"Pierce. We need to talk."

She knew that no more ominous sentence in the history of any relationship existed. But it didn't matter. The subject was ominous. It was ugly. Cassidy just wanted to get it over with so she could cry. Alone.

"Okay…"

It wasn't hard to see the color draining from Pierce's ruddy cheeks. She paced jerkily near the sofa where Cassidy had sat, defeated. To Cassidy, the battle had already been lost. Pierce just didn't know it yet.

"Sit down."

Pierce sat silently, keeping several feet of space between them. Maybe Pierce didn't know exactly what was coming, but she knew it wasn't good.

"Cass, just tell me." The lids of Pierce's eyes were already brimming with tears. It seemed impossible that anything was left of Cassidy's heart to break.

"This won't be easy to say. So I'm just going to say it. I haven't been happy lately." A taste of bile followed closely behind the words.

"What? What do you mean?" Pierce now bounced one foot rapidly against the hardwood floor. She had been hurt before, in a not nearly distant-enough past. Anxiety must have begun coursing through her at the thought of another good-bye, another ending. Pierce would be blindsided again too. But this was the choice, the only way.

"I really care about you." Cassidy managed a patronizing hand on Pierce's jittering knee, keeping her face cold and indifferent. "I just don't think this is going to work. I can't really explain it. It's just…something's missing."

Pierce wasn't going with softness and apprehension. She was going with a nuclear explosion. Cassidy had to blow her entire world up. And to do that, she had to sink as low as she possibly could. Pierce had told Cassidy exactly how Katie had phrased their ending. She knew how the ambiguity, the very idea that she just somehow wasn't enough, would crawl under Pierce's heart and lay roots, leaving her no other option but to give up on Cassidy.

"How can you say that?" The tears now spilled unabashedly out and onto Pierce's jeans. This must have been what Rowan meant when she said watching Galen crying was like watching a great city fall. Pierce's usual strength and unending fortitude, Cassidy's safe place, had crumbled to the ground, now a defenseless child needing consolation.

"I'm sorry. I really am." Cassidy had only a few more minutes before her own tears broke past the barrier of her lashes, like protestors threatening to weaken her pathetic stance.

"Are you saying that I'm not…" Pierce's throat rose and fell visibly, her lap now damp, her breathing ragged. She finally uttered the fateful words. "I'm not the one?"

Cassidy squeezed her eyes closed, fighting off the tears that now beat at the gates of her defenses, slowly hammering their way through. When she opened them again, her composure had returned, her heart steadier, the haze in her vision now clear. "Yes. I'm so sorry, Pierce. I really am."

Cassidy leaned near to kiss Pierce's cheek, but Pierce jerked away, standing quickly. Cassidy wasn't sure whether Pierce was going to yell, or storm out, or fall to the ground in a heap. But she did none of that.

She smiled a cordial smile, one that said she'd been expecting this all along, and turned around. Her coat still on, Pierce reached for the door handle, then back into her pocket, where she pulled out Cassidy's spare keys. She handed them to her, their skin brushing in a way that reminded Cassidy so much of their first night at dinner that she couldn't stop the tears any longer. They cascaded in sheets down her face, the pieces of her shattered heart surely expelling themselves from her body. It was all over. Now all she could do was hope Pierce would leave quickly, without a fight. Without any more tears.

"Goodbye, Cassidy."

The door shut behind her. No keys turned in the lock. Pierce Parker was gone.

CHAPTER TWENTY

A part of Pierce had always seen this coming. From the moment her lips first touched Cassidy's, she'd envisioned a very likely possibility that she would end up here, walking the streets of Boston in the middle of the night, thick, muggy air suffocating her with every gasp. And her gasping wouldn't stop because the crying was too heavy, the gravity of her sadness rolling downhill too quickly to catch it. It didn't matter anyway. The only people spotting the dimly lit street were the unaware vagabonds and the intoxicated college students too wrapped up in their own drama to care about the gush of tears pouring from Pierce's eyes.

She didn't know where to go. She didn't know what to do with the hurt that smothered her like an all-encompassing poison fog. But she did understand this sense of loss, the pain. The knowledge that everything you'd hoped for had just crumbled to ash in front of you without so much as a calm before the storm was not new to Pierce. She'd felt it with Katie. And she'd known it was coming with Cassidy. Sooner or later, she was bound to lose. But this loss was so much worse than anything she could have anticipated. The bigger the love, the harder the fall. And Pierce had fallen, was still falling, spiraling, lost, wishing she'd never known what it had been like to love Cassidy.

Somewhere around the 7-11 on Huntington Avenue, an overwhelming anxiety devoured the crying, one that prompted Pierce to remove her phone from her pocket and desperately swipe and click until she found Cassidy's number. She wanted to call her, to beg her to take back what she said and love her again. She wanted to turn the clock back three, four hours, maybe even less, to a time when she was Cassidy's, and Cassidy was hers, and this night was nothing but an irrational fear that haunted Pierce's occasional dreams. But she couldn't reverse time. And her power to make Cassidy love her was even weaker than that.

Pierce stared at her phone, the background photo still a picture of Cassidy, sunglasses-clad, smiling at her from the passenger seat of Pierce's car. She mentally noted to change the photo immediately. But she wouldn't delete it. She wouldn't delete any of them, because a part of Pierce still couldn't believe this was actually it. Instead of dialing Cassidy's number, Pierce clicked the phone off and placed it back in her jeans pocket. She was no longer the serial monogamist so afraid to be alone that the mere thought of it sent her running to the closest embrace. She was in love with one woman, and one only. And that was the only embrace Pierce wanted.

Something else was different about this heartbreak, though. Pierce refused to call. She refused to beg or try to talk someone into wanting her who didn't. She had done that with Katie and lost so much of herself in the process. The world was upside down and backward, tilted and shifted, reeling since the day she first touched Cassidy. Now that axis had shifted. Nothing was right. But Pierce was absolutely sure of one thing: she would never settle for anything less than being truly, deeply loved ever again.

1:19 a.m. 2:05 a.m. 3:32 a.m...The numbers on Cassidy's cell phone just kept moving, changing, but she was stuck in neutral, the wheels spinning, screaming Pierce's name. Taking control was supposed to make the hurt better. Wasn't it? The illusion of sleep reminded her of the night after their first kiss, the clock ticking by with a similar slowness. But the delicious air of promise and excitement was missing. Now only emptiness filled her, a shallow, visceral loneliness unlike anything Cassidy had ever experienced.

She turned onto her right side, tucking one hand under her pillow and closing her eyes for the billionth time. The streets were unnervingly quiet, and even the clunking radiator seemed to be hibernating for the night. Cassidy longed for some noise, some stimulation, something to pull her mind out of the hole it was so hopelessly stuck in. This was going to be hard. The bigger the love, the harder the fall. And this love was enormous. Cassidy had anticipated this result. But the fall wasn't the problem.

It was the impact. The sound of bones crashing onto pavement and disintegrating into dust. The air being sucked from every inch of her lungs. The anguish of the slowing of her heart until it stopped. She couldn't have anticipated the impact. And Cassidy wasn't sure she'd survive.

❖

Days had passed. Or it could have been weeks. Or even hours. Pierce wasn't really sure. Time had become irrelevant, marked mostly by waves of pain followed by small valleys of anger and tiny hills of hope. She was familiar with this pattern as well, the pattern of a broken heart. And after spending the first thirty-two hours in bed, blinds drawn, ignoring anything outside her bedroom, Pierce forced herself to get up, eat more than just a box of Cinnamon Toast Crunch, and take a shower. She was a damned adult. An appropriate amount of time was allowed for wallowing, and then, life had to go on, at least superficially. Fortunately, she had a couple of days off from work before having to return to the ED. But the inevitable had finally caught up with her. She would have to cross paths with Cassidy.

Pierce spent the last several of her thirty-two hours in bed deciding how to deal with this. She had two options: ignore Cassidy at all cost, or act as if nothing had ever happened. Pierce didn't like either option. Both felt childish and insincere. But she had one more. She could improvise, feel it out. Of course, if seeing Cassidy sparked a homicidal rage or a level-five meltdown in front of her coworkers, she might have to rethink things. But she would deal with that as it came. She wouldn't run from Cassidy. This was her hospital too. And Pierce didn't want to be perceived as vulnerable or fragile. She wanted Cassidy to think she would be okay, even when Pierce herself wasn't so sure.

Pierce hadn't realized she'd acquired such proficiency in navigating a broken heart. But by the time Tuesday morning rolled around and it was time to face the world—and Cassidy, again—she was as ready as she'd ever be. Pierce spent a little extra time combing her hair and made sure the bags under her eyes weren't quite as prominent as they had been, and as she dressed, she recognized the sizable part of her that was excited to see Cassidy. Pierce's insight was one of her greatest attributes and also sometimes one of her most detrimental. She wished she could just ignore the fact that she was hoping Cassidy would change her mind. In the corners of her mind, she was silently daydreaming about the moment Cassidy would lay eyes on her again, only to realize immediately she'd made a monumental mistake and express her undying love again. As much as Pierce scolded herself for allowing such unrealistic fantasies to permeate reason, she realized this was just part of the process. So she allowed herself that sliver of hope, all the while reminding herself over and over again that she would not plead for anyone's love ever.

Cassidy had done little more than force down a few crackers and several pots of black coffee over the last several days. But she awoke that morning with a nauseating heat bubbling up from the depths of her stomach, until what insignificant amount of food that was left in her threatened to expel itself. She'd been lucky enough to avoid Pierce at work since that night. She missed her with such a sickening fortitude that her soul actually ached. Not a moment passed that she didn't fixate on every little thing about her and long to touch her skin and feather her hair one last time. Seeing Pierce again would only intensify that craving, maybe even push her completely over the edge into the abyss, where she stood no chance of return.

The bristles of Cassidy's toothbrush threatened to provoke a gag waiting readily in her throat as she thought about seeing Pierce again. Her heart clenched, its usual slow cadence now unrecognizably quick. She spit the toothpaste into the sink, managing not to bring up anymore bile with it, and splashed some water on her face. The cold temporarily jolted her to alertness, distracting her from the unrelenting nausea and paralyzing anxiety. It was now or never. And never was not an option. Cassidy was a doctor. She had a job to do, and a broken heart was a sad excuse to be anything less than her best. This was not the self she'd worked so hard to build over her adult life—the self who put hard feelings aside for the betterment of her future and others around her. Besides, she'd broken her own heart, done this to herself, and she could have no regrets.

As she made her way through the ambulance doors, Cassidy could only pray for a busy day, not only offering her a valid excuse to avoid Pierce, but enough blood and illness to divert her from her own pathetic struggles. Her petty problems were nothing compared to the sick and dying splayed throughout the hallways, and Cassidy always found that reality helped her regain her perspective. Fortunately, the department was already brimming with people in need, even at eleven a.m. Each bed in the hallway was already full, and the waiting room occupied at least a dozen waiting to be seen. The fluorescent overhead lights burned shards of white into Cassidy's vision, helping ground her back in the present. She could do this. She just had to keep herself buried in other people's tragedies.

The bile had almost settled back down into the pit of her stomach, where it belonged, when Cassidy turned the corner to the locker room, nearly barreling into Pierce.

"Oh. Sorry…" Pierce, who was clearly headed somewhere in a hurry, raised her head, seeming to just now realize it was Cassidy who'd very nearly taken her out. The color had sifted out of Pierce's face, and she was now as white as the fluorescents above, her green eyes wide and stunned.

"I'm sorry…I…hi…" The terror-inducing nausea that had been plaguing Cassidy for days had disappeared, and she was left with only a deep, permeating sadness. She had been pushed, no, thrown completely over the abyss. And there was no coming back.

"Hi…" Pierce managed a weak smile, but her own pain was so visible on her earnest face that Cassidy's reserves crumbled further, until all her strength was depleted, leaving her deflated and hopeless. Cassidy wanted to wrap her arms around Pierce and be absorbed into her strength and grace she'd already come to depend on.

"How are you…you know, doing?" It was the stupidest question she'd ever asked. But she didn't know what else to say.

"Good. You know, great. I'm doing really great." Pierce's face appeared to strain painfully as she forced her smile bigger.

"Good. I'm really glad." Cassidy reached out a friendly hand and touched Pierce's arm. She had meant it to be a gesture of comfort, an olive branch. But instead it sent Cassidy's heart farther tumbling, crashing, through some infinite wormhole where the pain just kept multiplying and the impact never came. It spun and spun through space, no gravity to stop it, its axis a continually shifting course surrounded by nothing but black.

Cassidy met Rowan outside her apartment building not long after sunrise the next morning. As excruciating as acting like her life was going on without Pierce had been, at least it distracted her from the reminder of the day ahead of her. The biopsy would soon be over, and Cassidy would have answers. She'd spent the last several weeks assuming that the cancer would be back. But the night before she had seriously considered the possibility that it might not be. Hope was a dangerous thing. But if that tiny flitter of hope proved right, and she was okay, would she try to win Pierce back? Cassidy hadn't even pondered this question until twelve hours earlier, though she'd quickly told herself that wasn't fair to Pierce. Cassidy had already crushed her, and the catastrophe was inevitable. If the cancer didn't return today, it would sooner or later. And she couldn't invite Pierce back just to be a part of that.

"Thank you for coming with me." Cassidy had planned to go to the appointment alone. But the night before, lying in her bed staring at her ceiling, she just couldn't find the courage. Rowan was the only one who knew, her only real friend right now.

"I'm happy to be here for you. But don't think this means I'm not still pissed."

"That's fair. How is Pierce, anyway?" Cassidy wasn't sure she really wanted to know.

"I shouldn't tell you. Not after the way you tossed her out like last week's trash. But for the record, she's a mess."

"Oh...I'm sorry to hear that..." Cassidy stared at her feet as they walked down Boylston Street toward the hospital.

"You are not. Look. I know you think what you did was noble and selfless, but it wasn't. Trust me." Rowan's tone clearly reflected just how angry she still was.

"I did what was best for Pierce."

"I thought the same thing when I broke up with Galen, that I was cleaning up everyone else's mess, making myself miserable so they could be happy. I considered myself a damn martyr. But I just screwed everything up so much more. I was lying to Brian. I'd broken Galen's heart a million ways. And worst of all, I gave up the love of my life. I was miserable. All because I thought I was doing what I had to."

"I know what you're saying. But it's not the same thing."

"It sounds pretty similar to me. Can you tell me you aren't miserable without Pierce?"

Cassidy stuffed her hands into her pockets and stared far out to the horizon. "No. I can't. I'm devastated, Ro. I love her. Still. Probably always. And yeah, this is the worst fucking pain I've ever felt."

"So you agree. You're an idiot."

"No. Maybe. I don't know. I only know this stupid biopsy is about to change my life again, and I don't want Pierce anywhere near that."

❖

Cassidy spent most days of the week in a hospital, but the smell was different that day. The antiseptic and bleach and plastic weren't foreign to her, but even the scents of the hospital were different now that she was a patient. The same dread and apprehension Cassidy had felt as a child flooded back at the sounds of singing monitors and the wafting smell of cleanliness that somehow always signaled the close proximity of death. She spent nearly every day in the hospital. But this was like being dropped on a strange planet, one she'd seen before in vague nightmares but always awoke from. Until today.

"I'm here for my eight o'clock appointment. Cassidy Sullivan." Cassidy inhaled as deeply as her lungs allowed, trying not to fidget too much while she waited in front of the oversized reception desk. Rowan's hand landed on her back, and she absorbed the comforting warmth from Rowan's reassuring touch.

Cassidy remained silent as she flipped through an outdated issue of *People*, never actually stopping to read a word. Her knee bounced through the air, and she chewed mindlessly on her lower lip until it was raw and sore. Rowan stayed in the seat beside her, also silent but ever ready to hold Cassidy up if need be. A TV in the corner played CNN on silent. It was early, and the surgical waiting room was still largely empty. Cassidy stared at the closed door that led to the exam rooms and pre-op areas and, ultimately, the OR, where she would be escorted any moment. She was used to being on the other side of that door, ushering the helpless patients through to help cure whatever ailed them. Cassidy once again remembered just how vulnerable it felt to be the one in the waiting room.

"Hey. This is nothing. No big deal. You know that." Rowan squeezed Cassidy's thigh.

"I know."

"It's just local, right? They aren't even putting you under?"

"No. Just local." But the procedure itself hadn't left Cassidy feeling like she'd woken up in the middle of her worst recurring nightmare. It was the aftermath—what cells lay hidden in that stupid lump under her armpit.

"I'll be here as long as they let me." Rowan smiled. Cassidy was grateful for her friendship, but she also longed beyond words to have Pierce by her side.

"You know what really sucks? Even when this is all said and done, it'll take about a week to get the path report. That means when I walk out of here today, I still won't know if this is cancer."

Rowan sighed, her face echoing Cassidy's despair for the first time that morning. "I know."

They were out of time to wallow and worry. A nurse in Tweety scrubs came out from behind the magical door and called Cassidy's name. For a moment, she forgot she was in a children's hospital. But the hall leading to the exam rooms adorned with balloon wallpaper and Dora the Explorer stickers added an almost comical twist to her fear. It was strange. In all her dreams, Cassidy found herself back in this same hospital, surrounded by sick children and balloon wallpaper, as if time had yielded to the terror too. This was as real as any bad dream.

"Go ahead and change into this. We'll be ready for you down in the OR shortly." The nurse handed Cassidy an adult-sized gown, which surprised her. She wasn't sure what she was expecting—a tiny, pediatric johnny with Tweety Bird to match the nurse's scrubs that barely covered her breasts? She shook her head and chuckled at herself, forgetting that Rowan was still in the room with her. "Oh, and your friend needs to stay in the waiting room."

"Are you going to be okay?" Rowan asked.

"Sure." It was nothing more than an automated response, like a prerecorded message. *Cassidy can't answer you honestly right now, but this is what she's supposed to say.* The fear that had been simmering in her on a steady, low heat suddenly flashed over, bringing with it all the sadness and longing and regret she'd forced down. The bright white of the sterile room intensified to almost blinding, and the sounds of the world outside the room blunted to a dull hum. A surprising vat of tears Cassidy had not known were waiting spilled out like a desert rain, flooding the gown that still sat folded on her lap.

"Cass?"

"Rowan." Consumed by panic, Cassidy grabbed both Rowan's hands, squeezing them so tight the tips of her fingers blanched. "I need you to go find Pierce."

"What? Really?"

"Yes. I can't do this without her. I was an idiot to think I could." Cassidy was as surprised as Rowan appeared to be by the words leaving her mouth. But as she said them, a sense of reprieve embraced her, and she forgot why she'd been pushing so hard.

"I...okay. I'll call her right now."

"Thank you. And tell her...tell her I'm sorry...I'm so sorry."

Chapter Twenty-one

The door closed briskly behind Rowan. It was only a matter of minutes before the nurse came back to take Cassidy to the OR, but she didn't want to go without talking to Pierce, without making things right. Of all the time she'd spent analyzing how to cast Pierce aside to spare her heart, it took only a single second for Cassidy to decide she'd made a terrible mistake. Sometimes love isn't logical. And it's almost certainly never safe. Pierce was willing to take this risk on her, and she needed to take it on Pierce. Cassidy only hoped she wasn't too late.

Two minutes later, Rowan returned.

"Well? Is she coming?" Cassidy was still wiping tears away.

"She didn't answer, Cass. I'm sorry…"

"She must be at work or something. I need her to know I'm here. Please, Rowan. Do something."

The gentle, familiar knock of Dr. Lucas Hedges interrupted Cassidy's pleas.

"How's my favorite patient?" Dr. Hedges's usual calming presence did little to ease Cassidy's inner battle.

"I'm okay." Cassidy knew her bloodshot eyes and tear-streaked cheeks said otherwise. "Is it possible to wait just a little longer? Even fifteen minutes?"

"Sorry, kiddo. OR schedule's pretty tight today. You'll be fine though. This is no sweat."

Cassidy nodded solemnly, but the panic had consumed her.

"I'll see you in there." Dr. Hedges smiled and left the room.

"You have to find her." Cassidy's eyes welled again, and her breath came in short, petrified gasps until her fingers tingled and began to go numb. "Please." She breathed faster still. "Find her. I need Pierce here."

"Hey. Hey, look at me, okay?" Rowan took Cassidy's face in her hands and forced her blurry gaze onto Rowan. She'd never had a panic attack before, but this was one. In time she'd probably feel foolish, even downright stupid, for something so small eliciting such a weak response. But in the minute, logic had vanished. The world was closing in around her, and she wanted to crawl the walls, gouge her way out with her fingernails, not just of this room but of this life, of this moment in time. Cassidy understood the oft-described need to crawl out of her own skin. A claustrophobia unlike any she'd ever known had locked her in, the fear building and building with nowhere to escape.

Cassidy couldn't respond. She couldn't speak. Consciousness seemed to be slipping steadily away from her, although she knew that wasn't possible.

"You're hyperventilating. Just breathe with me. In..." Rowan took a long, slow breath, gesturing the movement of her diaphragm with her hands. "And out."

Cassidy focused on Rowan's strong face, breathing with her until her hands regained feeling and the room stopped swirling around her. "I'm okay." She took in one more deep breath. "I'm okay. But please, Ro. Try to find Pierce?"

The Tweety Bird nurse reentered the exam room. "Time to go."

Cassidy couldn't tell whether her curt tone was personal, but she was too distraught to care. Where was Pierce?

"I'll try, okay? I promise. I'll try my hardest. You're going to be fine." Rowan squeezed Cassidy's hand she was sure was as frigid as ice and walked out.

❖

Work had been a godsend for Pierce. That was, when Cassidy wasn't there. Thankfully, Pierce had to stomach only that one encounter so far. Otherwise, Cassidy had been oddly absent. Still, all it had taken was that one exchange, that one glance, to send Pierce into a tailspin. What tiny modicum of progress she'd made, which, admittedly wasn't much, had been blown to pieces when she looked at Cassidy again. And then, when Cassidy had reached out and touched her, Pierce wondered if she'd ever be okay again.

But she would be. She had to be. She had no other option. The morning in the ER had been fast-paced and high-stakes— exactly how Pierce liked her shifts. It wasn't even ten a.m. yet, and she'd already intubated a woman with heart failure, had a psych patient call her a "cunt," and a consulting cardiologist chastise her. Things had settled down only a little as Pierce worked on placing a central line on a young man in Room 4 with sepsis. Her sterile field was pristine, and she'd managed not to snag the line on any major structures on her way in. All in all, a success considering she didn't get to do the procedure very often. After securing the wires, Pierce pulled off one glove then the other, tossing them gracefully in the trash and swooping her hands up in an Alley-Oop. She left the room, tugging at her paper gown and mask. The halls were full, and the background clatter was as high as ever. But Pierce saw Galen standing at the reception desk immediately.

"What are you doing here?" Pierce recognized the apprehension on her face. It wasn't a look Galen wore often, or well.

"It's Cassidy. She's in the hospital."

Pierce closed the remaining few feet of space between them, pulling close to Galen's side. "What? Is she okay?"

"Yes. And no. She's going to have to explain it to you. But she needs you there. She's over at Children's Hospital."

Pierce was too confused, had far too many questions circulating through her brain to ask anything else.

"Can you get someone to cover for you?" Clearly, Pierce had been staring blankly at Galen.

"Uh…Yeah. Yeah, of course. Hang on."

Margot was documenting on a computer in the corner. "Margot. Can you cover for me? Something's happened to Cassidy. She's in the hospital. I'll be back as soon as I can. I promise."

"Is she okay?" Margot stood from her chair.

"I'm not sure."

"Yes! Go! I'll take care of everything here."

"Thank you." Pierce patted Margot on the shoulder and chased Galen, who was already sprinting toward the exit.

The Children's Hospital was directly next door to Boston City, a long, poorly lit tunnel connecting the two. Pierce's heart bounded as she struggled to keep pace with Galen. She still didn't know what was happening, and as much as Pierce had tried, Galen had disclosed little additional information since her arrival. All Pierce really knew was that Cassidy was in the hospital—the Children's Hospital, for whatever reason—and Rowan had frantically sent Galen down to get her when Pierce didn't answer her phone. Her mind outraced her footsteps, bringing a million different scenarios, none of which seemed quite right. An accident made the most sense. But why would she be at Children's Hospital and not Boston City? If she really was all right, why hadn't she called Pierce herself? The answers would come, but not soon enough for Pierce's liking.

After what felt like an endless sprint, Pierce and Galen finally arrived in the lobby.

"Will you please tell me what's going on?" Pierce pleaded with Galen as they stood, panting, waiting for the elevator doors to open.

"Cassidy will explain everything. All I can tell you is that she's okay. She just really needs you to be here."

Pierce groaned at Galen's once-again maddeningly vague response, but before she could protest more, the elevator stopped on the eighth floor. Pierce wasn't familiar with the Children's Hospital at all. She'd walked by it a million times but had never actually stepped foot in the place. Only the signs up above them reading PRE-OP AREA and OR SUITES offered any clarity.

"She's in the OR? Oh my God!" Pierce's prior reassurance suddenly fell to the ground in a heap, and panic flashed over in a sickening heat. "Someone better tell me what's going on right now, Galen."

Galen placed her hand on Pierce's shoulder as they walked down the corridor. "It's going to be fine. I promise."

The OR was every bit as frigid and alien as Cassidy remembered. It was strange. She'd stepped foot in the OR a hundred times before as a medical student. But this time, being the one wheeled through on the gurney, felt like the first. Or the second, actually. The first had occurred at age fourteen. Her first lymph-node biopsy. Her first fight with the devil. Cassidy was fully awake when the nurse stomped the brake on the bed. They'd offered her some Ativan to help her relax, but she'd refused. The procedure was simple. A tiny needle would inject local anesthetic around the site, and a scalpel would painlessly carve out the petulant mass.

It wasn't the biopsy that bothered Cassidy. She could do needles and incisions and the like all day, if need be. It was what came after the biopsy that terrorized her. It was what had launched her into a full-fledged panic attack, crying out for Pierce without the slightest hesitation. Pierce. God, she wished Pierce was here with her. Even knowing she was in the waiting room would have given her the last bit of hope she needed to get through this.

"Are you ready, Cassidy?" The general surgeon working with Dr. Hedges, whose name Cassidy didn't have time to process, was a serious man with a swath of salt-and-pepper hair on a handsome, chiseled face.

"Sure. Go ahead."

The lidocaine bit like a dozen tiny bee stings, but the pain was a welcome distraction from the feelings that were once again threatening to rise up and out through Cassidy's eyes. A single tear collected in the corner, sticking to her lashes for only a moment before falling helplessly to the ground.

❖

The entire surgery, which Cassidy couldn't even bring herself to call a surgery, was done in twenty minutes. Once she was bandaged and her blood pressure was rechecked one more time, Cassidy was wheeled out of the OR suite. She tried to refuse the wheelchair but was told it was hospital policy. Now that the entire ordeal was complete, Cassidy felt more foolish than ever. Except the ever-looming darkness was still very much here, and she wouldn't be truly free until the monster was dead and gone.

"By the way, I think you may have some visitors." It was the first hint of friendliness Tweety Bird scrubs had alluded to all day.

People? Cassidy figured Rowan would be waiting for her. But hadn't she just said "visitors"? As in more than one? Cassidy tried hard not to get her hopes up as they rounded the corner and passed through the door, which, she found, was far less ominous going through in that direction.

The waiting room had filled to near capacity since she'd been there, but she spotted one face immediately. Pierce sat, her mouth pinched and worried, flanked by Galen and Rowan. Cassidy's heart leapt completely through her chest, and for the first time in days she felt whole again. Whatever was up ahead, she could take it, as long as Pierce was by her side.

"Jesus, you guys. You look like I died or something. Talk about a bunch of sad sacks." Cassidy sprang out of the wheelchair, kicking it behind her so hard it almost pushed into Tweety Bird scrubs.

Pierce, who'd been apparently too busy studying the laces in her shoes, set her eyes on Cassidy for the first time, her face lighting up brighter than the late-summer sunsets that echoed off the mirrored faces of the skyline. She jumped from her seat, running to Cassidy, but stopping just before they touched.

"Are you okay?"

"I am now." Cassidy threw her arms around Pierce's neck, wincing at the searing pain as her underarm brushed Pierce's shoulder. Still, she felt better in that moment than she had in days.

"What's going on?" The perplexed squint in Pierce's eyes said Rowan hadn't filled her in on anything yet.

"How much do you know?"

"Literally, nothing." Pierce threw her hands up in the air. "This crazy person," she gestured to Galen, who was still sitting near Rowan, smiling, "came barreling down to the ED demanding I come with her because you were in the hospital. That's it."

"And you?" Cassidy looked at Galen. "How much do you know?"

"Me? Oh, I know everything. Rowan told me last week." Galen shrugged, and Cassidy shot Rowan a scowl.

"I'm sorry! I can't keep things from her." Rowan smiled apologetically.

"I get it. But Pierce...we have to talk..."

"Last time I heard that from you..." Pierce said with a slight sneer in her voice.

Rowan and Galen stood simultaneously, Galen awkwardly wiping her palms on her dress pants.

"We're, uh...going to go. Glad everything's okay, Cass. You guys, uh...good luck, you two." Galen clapped Pierce on the shoulder.

"Yeah." Rowan kissed Cassidy on the cheek, lingering just long enough to whisper, "Let her love you. She won't let you down."

With Rowan and Galen gone, Cassidy and Pierce were left standing only inches apart, the only two in the room yet surrounded by other patients and families oblivious to all the things Cassidy so badly wanted to say to Pierce but hadn't figured out how to.

"Maybe we should go somewhere else?" Pierce finally said.

They took the elevator silently down to the lobby, where Cassidy led Pierce out to a quiet courtyard on the east side of the hospital. She knew the hospital campus well. Too well, actually. And Pierce was about to find out why.

Cassidy sat on a nearby bench, the anesthetic beginning to wear off just enough to remind her she'd just had a piece of her removed. But that was nothing compared to the piece of her that had left with Pierce. Pierce stayed standing, her hands apprehensively on her hips, her mouth pursed in a straight line that screamed uncertainty.

"I have so much to explain to you." Cassidy didn't even know where to begin. She took Pierce's hand and gently guided her down beside her, angling her body so their eyes met.

"Are you sick, Cass? Why are you here? Why am I here?" Cassidy imagined Pierce had far more questions than answers at this point.

"No. Yes. I don't know." She sighed. "I was. When I was younger. I had cancer, Pierce. Non-Hodgkins." Cassidy wasn't sure how to delve into the subject of her parents' divorce and the subsequent destruction of her family and everything that came with her near-death. She had no tactful way, so she settled for blurting it all out in one long, gusty monologue. As she neared the end, Pierce's face suddenly registered understanding.

"Oh my God. The lymph node."

Cassidy nodded. "I lied to you. Not only by omitting all these parts of my past that still apparently contribute to my general state of fucked today, but by telling you I didn't love you."

"I don't understand." Pierce shook her head, as if it were brimming to the top with things she couldn't process, and she was trying to free it.

"I pushed you away *because* I love you. When you found that lymph node, I realized I could never let you deal with me being sick. I could never put you through that."

Pierce flushed with obvious anger. "Don't you think that should have been my choice to make?"

"Yes. It should have been." Cassidy took one of Pierce's trembling hands in her own. "And I'm so sorry I never gave you that chance. I love you, Pierce. You're it for me. The only one I've ever wanted and the only one I could ever want."

Cassidy fully expected Pierce to gather her in her arms and welcome her back in, ignoring the way Cassidy had discarded her only days earlier. That assumption was foolish, selfish even. Pierce did not take Cassidy in her arms. She could only seem to stare at her, her eyes narrowed and focused, not exactly angry, but not forgiving either. Pierce's hands were balled into tight fists against her knees, her silence louder than anything Cassidy had ever heard.

"A part of me understands why you did what you did. God knows I'm no stranger to the fear of getting hurt or hurting others. But you really fucked me up, Cass."

The cracks in Cassidy's heart opened again. It was possible, likely even, that Pierce wouldn't give her another chance—an outcome Cassidy hadn't allowed herself to consider until now.

"I know. And I'm so, so sorry. If I could go back in time, I would. And I know it's not much consolation, but I swear I've been even more lost than you. I need you, Pierce. I've never needed anyone before. It terrifies me. But I can't run from it anymore. Please. Let me need you."

She watched Pierce closely, her expression stern and pondering, her gaze fixed on her hands as she picked at the cuticle on her thumb. Cassidy waited. She wasn't much for religion, although she had found herself praying quite a bit lately. It wouldn't hurt to try one more time. She asked, begged even, God, or the universe, or whatever was out there to give her back the love she'd been so careless with.

"I love you," Pierce finally said. She raised her eyes to look at Cassidy for the first time since they'd sat down. Relief washed over her like a fine mist, cooling her days of anguish that had scorched her. "And I will be there for you. Always." Pierce paused dramatically, and Cassidy had a feeling there was more. "As a friend."

"A friend." Hope splintered around Cassidy once again, and the future, which had finally held some hint of light ahead, was once again as black as a country night.

"For now. The rest, I need to think about." Pierce wrapped her arm around Cassidy's shoulder and pulled her close. It was all Cassidy had been wanting for days, to be engulfed by Pierce's faultless strength and warmth and security. Pierce was Cassidy's home. And in her arms, she was safe.

CHAPTER TWENTY-TWO

The second Pierce saw Cassidy being wheeled through the waiting room doors, she was powerless. If Cassidy was asking for her again, she would come calling. Pierce was in love, the kind that defies reason and allows for forgiveness on a level she'd never consider otherwise. When Cassidy offered her explanation to Pierce, begged for Pierce to love her again, she knew she would ultimately never say no. But she needed time to absorb the parts of Cassidy she was just now learning and to release some of the wreckage Cassidy had left, however inadvertently.

"I had a feeling I'd find you here." Galen opened the door to her own apartment later that evening, Pierce sprawled out across her expensive Italian sofa.

"I needed someone to talk to."

"That's why I gave you keys. But for real, dude, can you at least take off your shoes? That couch was like ten grand." Galen tossed her leather shoulder bag in the corner and crossed to the couch, picking up Pierce's feet and repositioning them to the coffee table, where Galen's feet soon followed. Without saying anything else, Galen grabbed her phone and began scrolling, apparently uninterested in whatever was on Pierce's mind.

"You aren't being very helpful right now, you know." Pierce had her arms crossed over her chest, pouting.

"Shut up. I'm ordering Georgio's. I assume this is going to be an all-nighter?" Galen put her phone down on the arm of the sofa and grabbed Pierce into a bear hug that sucked all the air out of her chest, which comforted Pierce more than she'd been in days.

"Got any scotch?" Pierce mumbled into Galen's muscular shoulder, which was still smothering her.

"Do I have any scotch? Is that even a question?" Galen released her and a few minutes later returned with two tumblers brimming with Glenlivet on ice, resuming her place next to Pierce.

"I don't know what to do." Pierce sighed and picked up the scotch, letting the warmth coat her throat and flood down her esophagus to her stomach.

"Tell me what happened."

"She wants me back. She told me the whole breakup was a lie, that she'd always loved me. She was just trying to protect me."

"Yeah. I know." Galen unbuttoned the first two buttons of her shirt and reclined with her hands behind her head.

"You know?"

"Rowan told me. The night everything went down, she confided in Rowan she was going to do it. And she told her how much she loved you. I can understand why you're hesitant. And what she did was really stupid. But she's telling you the truth."

"Sure. Now she is. But how do I know she won't keep things from me in the future? Or run off when she thinks I need to be saved or whatever."

"Interesting…" Galen nodded thoughtfully.

"What's interesting?" Pierce snapped at her.

"I've had this same conversation before."

"You have?"

"I was you. A few years back. When Ro wanted me back, I couldn't imagine trusting her again. I felt like I would be betraying any sense of self-worth by letting her back in. I actually asked myself these same questions. What would stop her from doing it again? And the answer I kept coming back to over and over again was…nothing. Nothing was going to stop her. It would always be possible. And was I pushover for taking her back?"

Pierce thought about it. "Of course not. Look at you two now."

"Really, it didn't matter, Pierce, whether I thought it was right or wrong to forgive her. My heart wanted Rowan Duncan. I never had a choice. I knew from the second she left that if I had the chance to love her again, I would without a second thought."

Pierce didn't have a second thought either. She knew from the minute Cassidy told her she still loved her that she would never turn her away. And she took solace in learning that Galen, the most impenetrable person she knew, had found her Achilles heel as well.

"Do you believe her? Cassidy?"

"More important, do you?"

Pierce didn't hesitate. The answer had been swirling around her head all day. She felt it in a place so innate she couldn't even identify it. She trusted Cassidy. She believed her reasoning for breaking Pierce's heart, and she believed Cassidy had honestly thought she was doing what was right.

"Yes."

"Can you get past this?" Galen asked.

"How did you do it? You know, with Rowan?"

Galen smiled reflectively. "It's surprisingly easy to forgive someone when their heart's in the right place. When you love someone the way I love Rowan…the way you love Cassidy."

Pierce didn't respond, only plucked her cell phone from her pants pocket and hit speed dial.

"What are you doing?"

"I'm calling her," Pierce answered simply, as if it was the most obvious solution in the world. And it was.

Galen just bumped her fist against Pierce's thigh in approval and smiled while Pierce waited for the call to connect. It only took one ring before Cassidy answered.

"Pierce? Hi." Cassidy's voice was laced with an excitement that made Pierce's arms tingle.

"Can I see you?"

"Now? Yes. Of course. I mean, please. Do you want me to come over? Or I can meet you somewhere. Anywhere."

"Are you home right now?"

"Yes?"

"Good. Stay put. I'll be right over." Pierce disconnected the line, smiling proudly. She stood from the couch and was already at the front door before Galen had a chance to call out to her.

"Go get her, buddy. Go get her."

Still draped in the same ragged sweats she'd worn to the hospital that morning, her hair up in a hapless bun, Cassidy raced around her apartment trying to put herself together before Pierce could get there. It was ridiculous, as if putting on some fresh makeup and a change of clothes might convince Pierce to let her in again. But she could use whatever help she could get.

It must have been only seven or eight minutes before the buzzer to her apartment rang. She was expecting the jingle of Pierce's overstuffed key ring but then remembered Cassidy's spare sat on the kitchen counter still, after Pierce left the key that night. *Jesus, she got here quickly.* Cassidy figured she must have been coming from Galen and Rowan's. She hoped they'd swayed Pierce back to her, but she didn't deserve that.

After smoothing down some stray hairs, Cassidy exhaled a gust of hot air and buzzed Pierce in. She heard Pierce's clomping footsteps, which always seemed disproportionately louder than her short frame, and the familiar fist in her chest clenched, this time overshadowed only by an overwhelming excitement of what this visit must mean.

Pierce knocked tentatively, and Cassidy opened the door. She was standing in front of Cassidy, sturdy and sure, a tight white T-shirt spread across her strong chest and firm arms, accompanied by an even tighter pair of black jeans that always made Cassidy's legs unsteady. Cassidy had never wanted anything more in her life than she wanted this woman. Forever.

Without thinking, Cassidy threw herself at Pierce, clasping Pierce's neck and pushing up hard against Pierce. She stayed there, breathless, eyes closed, breathing in the sweet musk of Pierce's skin that had become so fundamental to her mere existence, the warmth of Pierce's strong body wrapped around her own.

"I'm so happy you're here," Cassidy finally said, never disconnecting herself from Pierce.

"Me too." Pierce slowly pulled them apart, but only enough so she could look into Cassidy's face. "I understand, Cass."

"You do?" The tears that had become all too frequent visited Cassidy once again, and this time she didn't care when a couple slipped out beyond her puffy lids. "I do. I mean, I don't like it. And I wish you'd just told me the truth. But I love you. God, do I love you...And I want to do this with you. Whatever's up ahead, whatever that biopsy shows, I want to be here."

Cassidy's feet nearly left the floor, and she was suddenly bulletproof, even the monster unable to touch her. "Are you saying you'll take me back? That you'll love me again?"

"I never stopped." Pierce took one hand and cupped Cassidy's cheek, the tears now unapologetically flowing down her face and bouncing off Pierce's skin. Pierce wiped several away, then leaned in slowly, not with trepidation but with security and purpose, and kissed her. A soft, pillow of warmth descended upon Cassidy, settling between her legs in a surprising arousal. She hadn't realized how starved she'd been for Pierce until now.

"I will never lie to you again. And I will never push you away."

"I know." Pierce held her around her hips, keeping them pressed tightly together. "I'm here. No matter what happens next, we'll do it together."

It was the single most comforting sentence anyone had ever spoken to Cassidy. Something about the safety and security of Pierce's words and the feel of them still joined, pressed so close Cassidy was sure Pierce could feel the heat coming off her jeans, sent Cassidy spiraling into a fit of desire.

Pierce clawed at her, cupping Cassidy's ass as she went back to kissing her, this time, harder, with an urgency that said she'd never have enough time with Cassidy, even if that time lasted forever. Pierce lifted her, placing her securely on the kitchen table, her hands moving now from her hips and landing in Cassidy's hair. Cassidy inhaled her, took in her every cell, her every atom. Cassidy freed

Pierce's shirt, pausing to run her fingers down Pierce's stomach to the band of her jeans. She kissed Pierce's bare chest as Pierce held her close, still stroking the strands of her wild hair.

"I want you always, Pierce." Her words were soft and breathy, but they released the anchoring weight of every fear that had been plaguing her. Cassidy was free. Pierce moved her hands to Cassidy's hips again and lifted her off the table. Cassidy's legs wrapped tightly around her, Pierce carried her into the bedroom as they fell into a heap on the unmade bed.

Whatever happened, whatever came next, Cassidy had Pierce. Everything else was just background noise.

CHAPTER TWENTY-THREE

I don't know, Pierce. Something just feels…off." Cassidy paced the living room, cell phone in one hand, the other anxiously pulling at a stray piece of hair.

"What are you saying?" Pierce's already racing heart picked up its pace, and she rose from the chair she was sitting in to go to Cassidy.

"He should have called by now. It's almost three p.m." Cassidy tapped the screen of her phone again, as if willing it to ring. Pierce came up behind her and wrapped her arms around her waist, forcing her to stand still, if not for just a moment. She could feel the muscles of Cassidy's body, wound up like a clock, release just a little into Pierce's embrace. Her eyes closed, and she leaned farther into Pierce's chest.

"He'll call. He said by three, right? I'm sure he just got caught up in something." Pierce stroked the smooth, soft skin of Cassidy's arm, but the fear wasn't lost on her. One call from Dr. Lucas Hedges at Children's Hospital could change everything. Pierce didn't know what the rest of their day, their week, or even the rest of their lives would look like. In fact, Pierce didn't know much of anything. But she was absolutely sure of one thing. And that was Cassidy.

A jarring, shrill tone came from Cassidy's phone, and they both jumped.

"It's him," Cassidy said, her voice as scorched as desert sand. Her chest rose and fell, and she held the phone up to her ear, her free hand grabbing Pierce's mercilessly. Her grip sent a grinding pain up Pierce's wrist, but she didn't mind. It grounded her, keeping her connected to Cassidy as if she might suddenly be pulled from the earth without warning.

"Hey." Pierce stared hard into Cassidy's eyes. "Whatever happens...I've got you."

"Hi, Dr. Hedges." Cassidy squeezed harder, and the room spun around Pierce. Her strength was waning. The thought of a world without Cassidy in it had been just too much for her to process. But the moment had come. And that thought was suddenly as tangible as any.

"Uh-huh." Cassidy nodded in understanding, and Pierce searched her face desperately for a sign, any sign, as to what was being said on the other end. Cassidy hadn't wanted to use the speaker phone. If the news was bad, she wanted to be the one to tell Pierce. Her face remained immobile though, almost plastic, and Pierce's anxiety grew like the cancer she was now sure was ravaging Cassidy's body. "Uh-huh," Cassidy said again.

Pierce raised her eyebrows at Cassidy, shaking her head and shrugging, silently begging for answers. She hoped she saw the smallest hint of a smile emerge from Cassidy's pale mouth. But hope felt like a dangerous thing in that moment.

"I see. Well, thank you for the call. I really appreciate it. Bye." Cassidy ended the call, her jaw still limp and eyes wide as she placed the phone down on the table.

"What? Cass, what is it?" Pierce's hands were on Cassidy's shoulders, nearly shaking her to attention, but Cassidy's gaze remained fixed on nowhere, her pupils engulfing most of her iris. It had been a week since the biopsy, and every minute had been more excruciating than the last for Pierce. She'd never handled uncertainty well. And now, Cassidy was making her wait even longer. An irrational anger rose up in her, and she shoved it back down. Cassidy had to do this on her own time. Pierce just hoped time wasn't running out.

They stood in silence, Pierce staring into Cassidy's face, which was still focused on something Pierce couldn't see. She registered the disbelief. Pierce just couldn't tell where it was coming from.

"It's…benign." And then, as quickly as she'd gone, Cassidy returned to the world, back to this moment, where Pierce was waiting with whatever scrap of patience she could find.

"What?" Pierce felt nothing. Not the crushing weight of anxiety that had been hovering for the last seven days. Not the relief and elation of the best news she might ever hear. She felt nothing. It was as if her heart was still stuck several seconds in the past, having yet to catch up with the improbable words coming from Cassidy's mouth.

"It's a lipoma, Pierce." Cassidy shook her head, still clearly dumbstruck.

"A lipoma?" As Pierce spoke, the reality of it all crashed into her so forcefully her legs swayed.

"Yes." A chain of joyful laughter like the August sunshine bubbled out of Cassidy until she was crying, holding her hands over her abdomen. "A damn lipoma."

When it finally came, the relief was immense. Pierce wasn't sure whether it was knowing or whether it was seeing Cassidy's tears of happiness and amusement and surely of possibility for a future they didn't know would come, but Pierce's own eyes flooded, and she wept recklessly, her laughter mirroring Cassidy's.

"All of this…this whole time?"

The laughter consumed them now until Cassidy collapsed to the floor, sprawling out onto her back in a snow angel. "The whole time."

"So…it's not cancer." Saying the words aloud cleansed Pierce like a baptism. "Wait." She lowered herself to the floor next to Cassidy, propping her head on her hand so she was looking down on her. "Are you saying you broke up with me…over a harmless fatty tumor?"

A silence fell over them. It was so quiet Pierce could hear Cassidy's heart echoing in her chest still. The same joyful laughter that Pierce thought was the most beautiful sound she'd ever heard and would ever hear again tumbled back through Cassidy's lips. The tears, which had stopped only long enough to allow the laughter to resume, followed suit, soaking the tile floor beneath them. Pierce collapsed into Cassidy's arms as they cried. She cried for the fear they were leaving behind, for the path fate chose not to take.

She cried for the love she never dreamt she'd find and, now, would get to keep. Forever.

THE END

About the Author

Emily Smith was born and raised in a small town in New Hampshire, where she started writing at an early age. Her grandmother was a children's author, and she comes from a family of English teachers.

When she isn't writing, which is rare, Emily works as a PA in the emergency department. She is a Boston resident and wouldn't have it any other way.

Books Available from Bold Strokes Books

Death Overdue by David S. Pederson. Did Heath turn to murder in an alcohol induced haze to solve the problem of his blackmailer, or was it someone else who brought about a death overdue? (978-1-63555-711-4)

Entangled by Melissa Brayden. Becca Crawford is the perfect person to head up the Jade Hotel, if only the captivating owner of the local vineyard would get on board with her plan and stop badmouthing the hotel to everyone in town. (978-1-63555-709-1)

First Do No Harm by Emily Smith. Pierce and Cassidy are about to discover that when it comes to love, sometimes you have to risk it all to have it all. (978-1-63555-699-5)

Kiss Me Every Day by Dena Blake. For Wynn Jamison, wishing for a do-over with Carly Evans was a long shot, actually getting one was a game changer. (978-1-63555-551-6)

Olivia by Genevieve McCluer. In this lesbian Shakespeare adaption with vampires, Olivia is a centuries old vampire who must fight a strange figure from her past if she wants a chance at happiness. (978-1-63555-701-5)

One Woman's Treasure by Jean Copeland. Daphne's search for discarded antiques and treasures leads to an embarrassing misunderstanding, and ultimately, the opportunity for the romance of a lifetime with Nina. (978-1-63555-652-0)

Silver Ravens by Jane Fletcher. Lori has lost her girlfriend, her home, and her job. Things don't improve when she's kidnapped and taken to fairyland. (978-1-63555-631-5)

Still Not Over You by Jenny Frame, Carsen Taite, Ali Vali. Old flames die hard in these tales of a second chance at love with the ex you're still not over. Stories by award winning authors Jenny Frame, Carsen Taite, and Ali Vali. (978-1-63555-516-5)

Storm Lines by Jessica L. Webb. Devon is a psychologist who likes rules. Marley is a cop who doesn't. They don't always agree, but both fight to protect a girl immersed in a street drug ring. (978-1-63555-626-1)

The Politics of Love by Jen Jensen. Is it possible to love across the political divide in a hostile world? Conservative Shelley Whitmore and liberal Rand Thomas are about to find out. (978-1-63555-693-3)

All the Paths to You by Morgan Lee Miller. High school sweethearts Quinn Hughes and Kennedy Reed reconnect five years after they break up and realize that their chemistry is all but over. (978-1-63555-662-9)

Arrested Pleasures by Nanisi Barrett D'Arnuck. When charged with a crime she didn't commit Katherine Lowe faces the question: Which is harder, going to prison or falling in love? (978-1-63555-684-1)

Bonded Love by Renee Roman. Carpenter Blaze Carter suffers an injury that shatters her dreams, and ER nurse Trinity Greene hopes to show her that sometimes hope is worth fighting for. (978-1-63555-530-1)

Convergence by Jane C. Esther. With life as they know it on the line, can Aerin McLeary and Olivia Ando's love survive an otherworldly threat to humankind? (978-1-63555-488-5)

Coyote Blues by Karen F. Williams. Riley Dawson, psychotherapist and shape-shifter, has her world turned upside down when Fiona Bell, her one true love, returns. (978-1-63555-558-5)

Drawn by Carsen Taite. Will the clues lead Detective Claire Hanlon to the killer terrorizing Dallas, or will she merely lose her heart to person of interest, urban artist Riley Flynn? (978-1-63555-644-5)

Every Summer Day by Lee Patton. Meant to celebrate every summer day, Luke's journal instead chronicles a love affair as fast-moving and possibly as fatal as his brother's brain tumor. (978-1-63555-706-0)

Lucky by Kris Bryant. Was Serena Evans's luck really about winning the lottery, or is she about to get even luckier in love? (978-1-63555-510-3)

The Last Days of Autumn by Donna K. Ford. Autumn and Caroline question the fairness of life, the cruelty of loss, and what it means to love as they navigate the complicated minefield of relationships, grief, and life-altering illness. (978-1-63555-672-8)

Three Alarm Response by Erin Dutton. In the midst of tragedy, can these first responders find love and healing? Three stories of courage, bravery, and passion. (978-1-63555-592-9)

Veterinary Partner by Nancy Wheelton. Callie and Lauren are determined to keep their hearts safe but find that taking a chance on love is the safest option of all. (978-1-63555-666-7)

Everyday People by Louis Barr. When film star Diana Danning hires private eye Clint Steele to find her son, Clint turns to his former West Point barracks mate, and ex-buddy with benefits, Mars Hauser to lend his cyber espionage and digital black ops skills to the case. (978-1-63555-698-8)

Forging a Desire Line by Mary P. Burns. When Charley's ex-wife, Tricia, is diagnosed with inoperable cancer, the private duty nurse Tricia hires turns out to be the handsome and aloof Joanna, who ignites something inside Charley she isn't ready to face. (978-1-63555-665-0)

Love on the Night Shift by Radclyffe. Between ruling the night shift in the ER at the Rivers and raising her teenage daughter, Blaise Richilieu has all the drama she needs in her life, until a dashing young attending appears on the scene and relentlessly pursues her. (978-1-63555-668-1)

Olivia's Awakening by Ronica Black. When the daring and dangerously gorgeous Eve Monroe is hired to get Olivia Savage into shape, a fierce passion ignites, causing both to question everything they've ever known about love. (978-1-63555-613-1)

The Duchess and the Dreamer by Jenny Frame. Clementine Fitzroy has lost her faith and love of life. Can dreamer Evan Fox make her believe in life and dream again? (978-1-63555-601-8)

The Road Home by Erin Zak. Hollywood actress Gwendolyn Carter is about to discover that losing someone you love sometimes means gaining someone to fall for. (978-1-63555-633-9)

Waiting for You by Elle Spencer. When passionate past-life lovers meet again in the present day, one remembers it vividly and the other isn't so sure. (978-1-63555-635-3)

While My Heart Beats by Erin McKenzie. Can a love born amidst the horrors of the Great War survive? (978-1-63555-589-9)

Face the Music by Ali Vali. Sweet music is the last thing that happens when Nashville music producer Mason Liner, and daughter of country royalty Victoria Roddy are thrown together in an effort to save country star Sophie Roddy's career. (978-1-63555-532-5)

Flavor of the Month by Georgia Beers. What happens when baker Charlie and chef Emma realize their differing paths have led them right back to each other? (978-1-63555-616-2)

Mending Fences by Angie Williams. Rancher Bobbie Del Rey and veterinarian Grace Hammond are about to discover if heartbreaks of the past can ever truly be mended. (978-1-63555-708-4)

Silk and Leather: Lesbian Erotica with an Edge edited by Victoria Villasenor. This collection of stories by award winning authors offers fantasies as soft as silk and tough as leather. The only question is: How far will you go to make your deepest desires come true? (978-1-63555-587-5)

The Last Place You Look by Aurora Rey. Dumped by her wife and looking for anything but love, Julia Pierce retreats to her hometown, only to rediscover high school friend Taylor Winslow, who's secretly crushed on her for years. (978-1-63555-574-5)

The Mortician's Daughter by Nan Higgins. A singer on the verge of stardom discovers she must give up her dreams to live a life in service to ghosts. (978-1-63555-594-3)

The Real Thing by Laney Webber. When passion flares between actress Virginia Green and masseuse Allison McDonald, can they be sure it's the real thing? (978-1-63555-478-6)

What the Heart Remembers Most by M. Ullrich. For college sweethearts Jax Levine and Gretchen Mills, could an accident be the second chance neither knew they wanted? (978-1-63555-401-4)

White Horse Point by Andrews & Austin. Mystery writer Taylor James finds herself falling for the mysterious woman on White Horse Point who lives alone, protecting a secret she can't share about a murderer who walks among them. (978-1-63555-695-7)

Femme Tales by Anne Shade. Six women find themselves in their own real-life fairy tales when true love finds them in the most unexpected ways. (978-1-63555-657-5)

Jellicle Girl by Stevie Mikayne. One dark summer night, Beth and Jackie go out to the canoe dock. Two years later, Beth is still carrying the weight of what happened to Jackie. (978-1-63555-691-9)

Le Berceau by Julius Eks. If only Ben could tear his heart in two, then he wouldn't have to choose between the love of his life and the most beautiful boy he has ever seen. (978-1-63555-688-9)

My Date with a Wendigo by Genevieve McCluer. Elizabeth Rosseau finds her long lost love and the secret community of fiends she's now a part of. (978-1-63555-679-7)

On the Run by Charlotte Greene. Even when they're cute blondes, it's stupid to pick up hitchhikers, especially when they've just broken out of prison, but doing so is about to change Gwen's life forever. (978-1-63555-682-7)

Perfect Timing by Dena Blake. The choice between love and family has never been so difficult, and Lynn's and Maggie's different visions of the future may end their romance before it's begun. (978-1-63555-466-3)

The Mail Order Bride by R Kent. When a mail order bride is thrust on Austin, he must choose between the bride he never wanted or the dream he lives for. (978-1-63555-678-0)

Through Love's Eyes by C.A. Popovich. When fate reunites Brittany Yardin and Amy Jansons, can they move beyond the pain of their past to find love? (978-1-63555-629-2)

To the Moon and Back by Melissa Brayden. Film actress Carly Daniel thinks that stage work is boring and unexciting, but when she accepts a lead role in a new play, stage manager Lauren Prescott tests both her heart and her ability to share the limelight. (978-1-63555-618-6)

Tokyo Love by Diana Jean. When Kathleen Schmitt is given the opportunity to be on the cutting edge of AI technology, she never thought a failed robotic love companion would bring her closer to her neighbor, Yuriko Velucci, and finding love in unexpected places. (978-1-63555-681-0)